TROUBLE IN PIOCHE

A SLIM CALHOUN, BULL MORRISON WESTERN

JOHNNY GUNN

WOLFPACK
PUBLISHING
— EST 2013 —

WOLFPACK
PUBLISHING
— EST 2013 —

Trouble in Pioche
A Slim Calhoun, Bull Morrison Western

Paperback Edition
© Copyright 2021 Johnny Gunn

Wolfpack Publishing
5130 S. Fort Apache Road 215-380
Las Vegas, NV 89148

wolfpackpublishing.com

Paperback ISBN 978-1-64734-753-6
eBook ISBN 978-1-64734-752-9

TROUBLE IN PIOCHE

CHAPTER 1

IT WAS ONE OF THOSE BEAUTIFUL LATE SPRING MORNINGS IN SOUTH-eastern Nevada, the beauty of which wasn't recognized by the two men standing on a hillside, looking down on the North Pass mine. North Pass had been failing for years but still maintained a full crew and helped fill the saloons in Pioche, Nevada. The town was known as one of the most wicked in Nevada and served as the Lincoln County seat. Sandy Hitchcock owned the mine and headed a group of men involved in selling fraudulent stock in mines and other properties in the county.

Card sharks in every gambling parlor, schemes and scams on every street corner, and no one around to investigate or for that matter, to even care. There were two major saloon/hotels in the mining camp and half a dozen sleazy attempts at a saloon. Card sharks were abundant along with working girls and hangers-on.

Hitchcock owned the bank that allowed certain people to make unrealistic investments and then foreclosed on the investment so it could be sold again. He obtained land and sold it over and over, managed to acquire water rights for mines and ranches that didn't exist, and Sandy Hitchcock was only one of many like him in that roaring mining camp.

"Got some eastern investors coming in, Harvey. We can make some real money this time." Sandy Hitchcock, nearing fifty, overweight, and decidedly short of stature was puffing hard, not on the black cigar he was holding but from the short climb up the hill. "Got 'em primed and want you to join me for supper. There are three of them and they can see gold." Hitchcock would have been the villain in any melodrama with his shaded eyes, pencil mustache, and grim, downturned mouth.

"Which property you gonna be selling these fine moneyed gentlemen? We've got papers on several good ones to offer." Harvey Lighthorse was Lincoln County Sheriff and mining partner of Hitchcock. "Is Boots in on the project? As miner's union boss his word carries a lot of weight with investors."

"Boots won't be with us but Buster Cranston will. We'll meet at the Silver Crystal for drinks at six. Wear your gold, Sheriff." Hitchcock laughed knowing Lighthorse loved to show off his watch fob with the gold nuggets dangling on gold chains. He had sliced elk-horn conchos featuring gold nuggets in their centers on his black leather vest, and a nugget infested ring too. Lighthorse was a showboat, but those in Pioche also knew he would shoot first and be deadly accurate doing it.

Boots Kindle on the other hand came to power in the miner's union honestly. It was as close to honest as the man ever got. He worked underground and came up through the ranks with the political savvy a Roman Senator might envy. His power came in the form of understanding human nature and two iron fists. He rarely carried any kind of weapon, using his brain and brawn to beat back those opposed to him or his union.

The union was fighting Hitchcock on every level, wages, hours, and benefits. Miners in the boom towns were paid well but always taken care of by the companies. Long hours, too many work days, and limited health care facilities in the camps were often the case.

"I want to have these gentlemen invest in the North Pass, Harvey. Cranston is salting a couple of the drifts now. I'll have assays to back it up, too. Won't have to talk much. These boys are primed."

Sheriff Lighthorse kept a tight rein on criminal activities in Pioche by way of running the strongest and most active of the outlaw gangs in the area. His deputies were known to do a bit of strong-arm robberies from time-to-time, and if evidence in a crime had a value, it rarely found its way to court.

All-in-all, the busy little mining camp of Pioche, Nevada was an outlaw's nest where bank robbers, murderers, and con men could feel comfortable. It was rumored that more than ten men had been buried at the cemetery before the first natural death occurred in the town.

There were some, however, who wanted a more peaceful place to live and work. Town Marshal, Three-Finger Jack Daws was one of them. His right hand tangled with some heavy rock one day at the Silver Queen Mine and when the dust cleared, he only had three fingers left and a twisted hand. Daws took that opportunity to leave the mining to others and took to keeping the peace.

He found he wasn't very good as a left hander pulling a pistol but could wield a shotgun with no problem. His weapons of choice were his left fist and a double barrel sawed off shotgun. Three-Finger Jack was not friends with Harvey Lighthorse and had threatened to arrest the sheriff more than once. If Three-Finger Jack was at the bar when the sheriff walked in, tension spread through the saloon like lightning.

"Making your rounds, Marshal? It's a beautiful night for it."

"Just taking a stroll through town before supper, Mr. Rivers. Won't have these early sunsets for much longer. Early spring is my favorite time of the year. Don't forget to lock your doors when you close up."

"Doing it now," Peter Rivers, the apothecary said. "Been two days now without someone getting shot. Understand Rolf Pendergrass is betting we won't make three."

"Sad but true, Mr. Rivers. I'm afraid I wouldn't take that bet." Marshal Daws continued his stroll and turned into the Silver Crystal Hotel and Saloon. The long bar along one wall was almost full, tables were mostly full, and the gambling area was filled. Rolf Pendergrass, owner of the Silver Crystal didn't have working girls, leaving that to Gypsy and other town madams. His upstairs was an actual hotel, but the crafty businessman had the hotel check in right at the bar.

Pendergrass was tall and thin, wore fancy silk vests, was quick to laugh, scowl, or shoot. He wore his emotions broadly. He was behind the bar along with two white-aproned barmen when the marshal came in. "Evening, Rolf. Nice and peaceful, eh? How about a cold beer?"

"Good to see you, Marshal. It'll liven up when it gets dark. Want some whiskey with that beer?"

"Might as well. Seen Tom Blair tonight? He was looking for me earlier." Blair owned the Gold Strike Mine and was a long time friend of Daws. Blair had run for sheriff and many believed that Harvey Lighthorse had stuffed the ballot boxes with votes from people who simply didn't exist. There was more than just bad blood between the two.

It was Sandy Hitchcock who had those ballot boxes stuffed and for more than just the office of sheriff. Hitchcock held sway with the county commission, the appraiser's office, and even that of town marshal even though Three-Finger Daws would argue the point.

"He's in the poker room, Marshal, losing again. He'd probably enjoy being interrupted. Give him another few minutes, Jack. I need the money." Many of those nearby laughed along with the saloon owner.

"Sure you do," Three-Finger Jack chuckled. He finished his beer and whiskey and started to walk toward the poker room when Harvey Lighthorse, Sandy Hitchcock, and several others walked into the saloon from the dining room. Their laughter quieted immediately, and all eyes were on the two lawmen. Was tonight the night?

Tables for drinking and socializing were not wide spaced and Lighthorse took up most of the passageway as the group walked toward the bar. Three-Finger Jack was larger than the sheriff and did not turn to the side to allow easy passing. "Evening, Sheriff. Excuse me," Three-Finger said.

Lighthorse didn't move aside, and the two men stood, face to face, glaring at each other. "Headin' to the bar, Daws. Get out of my way." Lighthorse looked back toward those behind him with a nasty grin.

"Always liked a man with good manners." Daws had a look on his face that told the sheriff he was not going to move aside. And then he got the slightest grin. "My grandmother insisted on me learning and using good manners. I have spent my life respecting the elderly and those older than me, so, please, go right on by, Sheriff."

There were a few guffaws heard and anger flashed across the sheriff's face. His hand was shaking, he so desperately wanted to pull down on this impudence. As he passed he gave Three-Finger a hard nudge with his elbow. Daws responded with an elbow to Lighthorse's jaw, shoving the man back into

Sandy Hitchcock, almost knocking the obese mine owner onto a cocktail table.

"Watch it, you bugger," Hitchcock said, not to Daws but to Lighthorse. "Mind who you're pushing around."

"Damn you, Daws," Lighthorse growled, going for the big hog-leg hanging at his side. Three-Finger Daws slammed the double barrel shotgun into Lighthorse's belly and followed it up with an uppercut with the butt end, knocking the man into Hitchcock again and both men crashed to the floor, taking the cocktail table with them.

Men and boys scattered, more tables were turned, more tempers flared, and fist fights broke out in several places. Buster Cranston, Hitchcock's mine superintendent pulled his pistol and fired off a shot and the fighting ended as fast as it started. While he knew Lighthorse was partners with Hitchcock he was not a particular friend of the sheriff and didn't try to interfere in his current predicament.

Daws stood over the man, holding the shotgun at the ready. "Don't care much for rowdy behavior, Sheriff. Best learn your manners when you're in town." Daws turned to the others, that mean looking scattergun sweeping the air, nodded with a smile, and made his way to the poker room. He used those around him, their reactions, that is, to tell him that the sheriff was not about to shoot him in the back. One gasp from an onlooker would have spun that fowling piece around and instant death to the sheriff of Lincoln County, Nevada.

CHAPTER 2

"Looking at this map, Judge, this mining camp of Pioche is out of your jurisdiction. Pioche is in south eastern Nevada, in Lincoln County. That's Utah Federal Court jurisdiction." U.S. Marshal Bull Morrison and his deputy, Slim Calhoun were in Federal Judge Timothy Baker's office, in San Francisco, to get their next orders.

"It is, Morrison and that's the problem. According to Judge Olsen, his marshals are involved with Indian problems and Pioche is about to explode. It's open warfare down there with mines having their own armed forces, the sheriff taking sides based on how much is being paid, and people dying faster than the grave diggers can dig. Olsen has asked for help."

"Sounds like our kind of country, Bull." Slim Calhoun stretched as he stood up from an overstuffed wing-back chair and walked to a large window that looked out on San Francisco Bay, partially hidden in a thin veil of velvet fog. "Bet there's plenty of sunshine in that country. I'm tired of cold, wet fog."

"I've made rail reservations to Elko, but then it's a long ride south. Here is everything Olsen has on the situation. He believes that someone in his office may have connections with the sheriff or some of the mine operators. You'll be on your own, no back up, nobody to share information with. Olsen would enjoy it very much if you could root out his problems as well."

Baker stood up and joined Calhoun at the window. "I want you boys to be more careful than you've ever been."

"Don't let Judge Olsen or anyone else know we're coming. We'll find enough to deal with. If people know we're coming the danger factor multiplies some," Calhoun said. "Read some nasty things about that camp."

Morrison took the large leather wrapped pouch from Judge Baker. "We'll leave first thing in the morning. Steamer to Sacramento and the train to Elko. Seems I've read something about Pioche recently."

"In the paper last week, Bull," Calhoun said. "Seems they buried forty people before they buried the first person to die a natural death. Gotta be a fun place, old man." Calhoun had a wry grin on his ruggedly handsome face, brushed back wavy hair that hung almost to his shoulders, and held the door for his partner of many years.

"Steaks and whiskey, Slim, and we'll make some plans. How is it we get these jobs? We on somebody's bad list? Done bad to some clerk somewhere?" Bull Morrison was just that, a bull of a man. He carried a scar from a knife fight that extended from above his right eye to well past his chin, and when he got excited, angry, or just slightly upset, it became a scarlet slash.

Morrison lived to fight, even if it meant he had to start the fracas. Slim backed him up as a part of his daily routine and federal judges in the west asked for their services on the hardest and most dangerous jobs. "I think it has something to do with getting you out of town, Bull. When we're on the job it gives some of the saloon owners a chance to rebuild."

"Go to hell, Calhoun." The two marshals made their way

to the docks, the most dangerous area in the entire bay area. Three-masted sailing ships stood off at anchor and skippers and first mates were often seen seeking crews. Sometimes, the art of the Shanghai came into play.

"Snake Eyes Malone's got the biggest steaks and meanest whiskey in Frisco and I want my fair share."

They took a table and ordered steaks and a bottle and Bull Morrison opened the leather pouch. He handed half the papers to Calhoun and kept half for himself. They sipped whiskey and read the reports while waiting for their steaks. "Mean damn crowd down that way," Morrison snorted. "Don't much care for law and order, eh? I've always said that if you meet a man who is rude, he probably would also likely have criminal intent."

"I think we've been set-up, Bull. I haven't read or heard a word about Indian trouble in Utah or eastern Nevada. That judge simply wants us to find out who's supplying information to the bad guys in Pioche. Doesn't trust his own people. Olsen is playing with us and I don't much care for that."

"Got the same thoughts, Slim. Gotta play it out, though. Washington sent Olsen to Utah to keep an eye on things and he's become part of what he's supposed to watch. Our best bet is to do what Baker said. Just us. Don't trust nobody. I don't know a soul in that country. You?"

"Nope. Take the train to Wells, though, not Elko, and ride south for several hundred miles, through Shoshone country. Just a couple of drifters coming in lookin' to strike it big." Calhoun had a little boy's grin on his face and watched Bull Morrison do his best to smile. It isn't easy for Bull to smile. Some say it hurts, way down deep when the marshal smiles.

"Just eat your steak and drink your whiskey," Morrison muttered.

Lincoln County Deputy Sheriff Lonesome Gary Thompson, a tall and thin Texan, was drinking tequila at Gypsy's bordello, working up the courage to make himself feel bad. The girls at Gypsy's shirked from the man, often forced him to bathe first, at an added four bits, please, but willingly drank with him. Today it was Gypsy herself at his table.

Gypsy had girls of every size, color, and background, and ran as straight an operation as could be found in the west. Velvet curtains, burgundy in color, covered the windows, comfortable couches and divans were spread about on the main level, an open bar provided its benefits, and miners and buckaroos actually spoke to each other, waiting for further gratification.

"How is it, Thompson, that you have mail coming here?" Gypsy stood six feet and four inches before she put her boots on, weighed a solid two-fifty, and had orange hair, dark skin, and blazing gray eyes. She said she was born of the world when asked about her background, then gave out a deep, convivial laugh along with a wink or two.

"Don't be tellin' people," Thompson said. "Got a side deal cooking with some people in Salt Lake. Sure as hell the sheriff, judge, and half the faro dealers would want to be in on it. Let's just let this be a little something between us," the deputy said.

Thompson took the offered envelope and ripped it open. Scrawled with a heavy hand were these simple words: "Marshals coming soon. Don't know names." Thompson tucked the note in his shirt pocket and got up to leave.

"Let's not get me involved, Mr. Thompson unless the pay end is involved as well. You run your little gambit but not through my doors. Tell your people in Salt Lake to send their missives somewhere else." There wasn't any anger, but Thompson got the message.

"I should have asked. Won't happen again." The deputy slipped into his buckskin jacket.

"Not staying for some pleasuring, Deputy? Sissy will be disappointed. I think she loves you."

"Ain't no love within five miles of this place," Lonesome Gary said. "Ain't much pleasure, either." Sissy took his money, put up with his lack of personal cleanliness, and did what she could to suggest he find another girl, maybe at one of the other houses. From the day he was born Thompson had never taken a bath on his own. Every one of them had been forced on him and those who found themselves nearby often moved away.

Thompson made the two-block walk to the Silver Crystal hoping to find Sheriff Lighthorse. *Somebody looking to bring marshals here? Bet the sheriff don't know that. Bet that damned Three-Finger sent for them. Wonder which ones?*

Lighthorse was standing at the crowded bar when Thompson wedged his way in. "Got a note from Cedar City, Sheriff. Two federal marshals will be coming our way."

"Who cares? Couple of those fools from Salt Lake City? That judge up there is just as crooked as Sandy Hitchcock." He nudged the man next to him and laughed right out. "Let 'em come, Thompson, we'll give 'em a party when they get here. Maybe a necktie party, eh?"

Deputy Thompson couldn't keep his eyes off the bruised and scraped chin, black eye, and sour look on the sheriff's face. He also had better sense than to ask. "If these are real marshals, Sheriff, it could get dangerous. Maybe we ought to get ready for them." Thompson wanted to be a tough guy, was able to throw his weight around because of Lighthorse, but had deep fears about death and dismemberment. "Isn't there something we should do before they get here?"

"There is, Thompson, now that you mention it. Let's you and me walk up to the Lucky Lady saloon and keep the peace. I hear it's been mighty rowdy there, recently. Might get lucky, too. Need to bust some heads." His set-to with Marshal Daws was still seething deep in his belly and Thomas Blair was a good friend of Daws'. Mine owner Blair was known to be a friend with Lucky Lady owner Spike Loring. *Tonight is a good night for a little payback, I think. Marshals coming to town? Bet Daws sent for them. Time to make a play, I think.*

The spring night was cold as the two lawmen walked the streets of Pioche. Thompson nodded and spoke to several, Lighthorse scowled and growled at anyone who came close. "Best bet is to let people believe it's the ranchers who killed the marshals when their bodies are found. Keep that in mind."

CHAPTER 3

"HOW'S THAT ARM FEELING, SLIM. NOT BROKEN, IS IT?"

"It'll be fine, Bull." Slim Calhoun was nursing some painful bruises to his arm and ribs, and not in a good mood to take some joshing from the marshal. "There ain't nothing in my marshal's contract that says I have to protect you from flying piano benches. Next time you start a fight, I ain't gonna protect you."

"I told you, I didn't start it. Man tripped over my boot and fell into the piano. He was most drunk, Slim. I pulled the bench off of you before he threw the chair, didn't I? Well, didn't I?"

"You did, Bull, you did." Slim Calhoun rubbed his arm but couldn't hide the grin on his face. "We got a four- or five-day ride and I'm already bruised. We got five pounds of side meat, coffee, beans, and a bag of hard tack tucked in behind our saddles. No mules on this ride. We put our feet in the stirrups and go, sunup to sundown. I gotta burn off a little anger."

Morrison chuckled as he stepped into the saddle. He was reliving the altercation from the night before. "Hell's bells, Slim, when you got up off the floor, you lit into that mucker like a Nebraska twister. Why, Deputy Marshal Calhoun, you hit him three times before he got one swing in. I'm just proud you bein' my partner and all."

"Thank you, Bull. Thank you."

"That cocktail girl patched you up nice, didn't she?"

Calhoun smiled again. "Oh, my, Mr. Marshal, Sir. She was most kind."

"The man was a criminal at heart, Slim. Rude. That's what he was. Rude." The two men made sixty miles a day, conversations like this one going on constantly. It was a hard ride, they took few breaks, and spent hours discussing what they were riding into. "If what those reports we read are any true indication of what's happening in this camp called Pioche, we might end up needing help, Slim. Don't like to say things like that, but we may need help."

"Worrying on that, Bull. When the law-dogs are outlaws, it makes things awkward. That sheriff ain't no lawman. Hope we find at least a couple of people we can trust." Slim Calhoun had as many doubts as Bull Morrison about finding help at the local level. "Pioche has the worst reputation of any camp in Nevada."

It was nearing mid-day on the fourth day when they looked up from a water crossing and saw the smoke from a mill-site. "Up on the side of the hill, Bull. Must be Pioche. All mountains. Don't see nothing level."

The road they were on led right into the center of the rowdy mining camp. The streets were a muddy mess from a recent early spring thunderstorm, and heavily laden wagons were pulled by teams of mules, oxen, and horses with their teamsters howling profanities at the top of their lungs.

"Commerce doesn't seem to be affected by the criminal element," Bull observed. "We've seen this before, Slim. Working men get into mischief, maybe a fight or two, but it's the fat cats that cause the big trouble. They make a pot full of money and discover it ain't enough. Gotta have more, even if it hurts the people working for 'em."

"Lucky Lady Hotel, Saloon, and Dancehall, Bull. Looks like we're home." Slim pointed out the two-story building in the middle of a long commercial block. "That must be the county courthouse back that way." Calhoun hollered at a passerby, asking where the stables might be.

"Up the next block and the stink will lead you right to it," the man said.

"Why don't you get us a room, Bull. I'll put the animals up and bring our kits down. Need to find a decent restaurant, too. I'm through with trail food for a long time. We passed a couple of nice-looking ranches along that creek. Should be able to find some steaks around here."

Pioche sat on the side of a steep mountain range and the valley below, well watered by creeks and streams was filled with active ranching and farming. "Looks like nice country down there. Grass is high for this early in the season."

Bull stepped down and handed the lead rope to Slim. "Don't be gettin' in no fights. Just get the horses stabled," he said. He was laughing loud as he stepped up on the boardwalk in front of the Lucky Lady Hotel. "You'll find me in the saloon."

Slim had to chuckle as he rode uphill to the next block and turned to the stables, which, as described, were fragrant and muddy. "You run mule trains out of here?" He asked the man in front of large doors. Corrals were filled with forty or fifty mules. Far more than would normally be found at a town's stables.

"Three times a month goin' out and three times a month comin' in. Them's contracted, and I do special freighting, too. What can I do for you?" Along with a large commercial stables, the man was obviously a blacksmith as well. Not so tall as he was muscled and heavy, bald but with a massive mustache, bushy black eyebrows, and gnarled hands that spoke of strength.

"Gonna be here for a spell," Slim said. "Need to keep our horses with you. Got a couple of dry stalls?"

"Just happen to. Name's Jacob Overby, bring 'em on in." Overby turned and walked through the open doors into a large barn with stalls along one entire wall. "Looks like three and four are open. Fifty cents a day and that includes feed. Three dollars a week if you pay in advance. Where you from?"

"Coming down from Boise," Slim lied. "Me and my partner hoping to make a fair strike. Hoping to find some warm and dry country to work in. Sure ain't dry here."

"Got one of them early spring boomers. Just sat on top of us yesterday. Every summer they boil up from the south. It'll be hot tomorrow."

Slim shook his head. *This is his idea of summer? Spring in the mountains is cold.* He gave the man money for a week for the horses, got them rubbed out, and gathered their kits for the short walk down to the hotel. Overby watched him for a moment before heading into his little office. *Ain't never seen prospectors coming in without a mule, without a pick, shovel, pan, or pike. Wonder what their game is? Paid in advance gives him good standing with me.*

BULL MORRISON BOUGHT ROOMS FOR A WEEK AND HEADED INTO THE busy saloon for a long desired cold beer. "Beer," he thundered at the barman. "And keep 'em coming, if you please."

"Comin' atcha," the barman said. "Dry trail you've been on?"

"Four days of dry, my friend. Whiskey's good, even good for you, I think, but it's beer that makes the day worthwhile. Here's to you and yours," Bull said, taking about half the flagon down.

He wiped his hand back and forth across his grand mustache and took a few minutes to give the saloon a good look. Long bar along the south wall with a few tables set around on the street end. Gambling tables were set up in the back along with a stand for piano and banjo players.

There were more than ten men standing at the bar, maybe more at the faro and poker tables, and a few of the drinking tables were occupied as well. "Got yourself a little gold mine, here," Bull said when the barman brought another beer. "Wouldn't mind having a place like this, someday."

"Ain't mine," the barman said. "Wish it was. Spike Loring has the honors there. What brings you to Pioche?"

"Gold," Bull said. He laughed and took a long drink of beer. "Lookin' to fill our pockets."

"Our pockets?" The barman looked around.

"Partner's puttin' up the stock. Name's Morrison. Friends call me Bull."

"Lassen," the barman said. "Jimmy Lassen at your service, Bull Morrison."

"Gimme some whiskey," a man said, trying to shove Bull aside.

"Mind your manners," Bull snarled, pushing back hard. The man spat out some serious vulgarities and pulled a large skinning knife. He whipped it back and forth and went into a crouch, ready to spring at Bull. That garish scar across Bull's face was scarlet when the man lunged.

Bull stepped to one side, ignored the knife, and grabbed the man by his winter coat and whirled in a circle. Men up and down the bar were pushed and shoved by the move and the man with the knife found himself flying across a table three feet behind him. Before the knife man could gather himself up, Bull kicked him twice, once in the head and once in the hand that still held the knife, which went flying.

"Pull a knife on me, gutter rat, and it's time to meet your maker." Bull jerked the man to his feet, planted a hard left to his groin and let him fall into his own puke. "Don't much care for men with bad manners." He walked over to where the knife was and picked it up. Things happened so fast that no one had moved. "To the victor go the spoils," he laughed, tucked the knife in his belt, and walked back to his beer.

"Know that jerk?" He had his back to main floor of the saloon as if he knew that no one would attack. The low rumble of conversation eased back but no loud voices coming to the defense of the downed man.

"Sure do, Bull. His name's Buster Cranston, mine superintendent at the North Pass Mine. Works for Sandy Hitchcock." He pulled a bottle up and poured Bull a glass of whiskey. "Calls for this, doesn't it?" Jimmy Lassen had a big smile on his face. *Ain't never seen Cranston go down like that. Hope this Bull character sticks around for awhile.*

"What's going on here?" The man stood close to six feet tall and carried considerable muscle under his frock coat. Buster Cranston was trying to get to his feet, slipping in the slimy vomit, cussing as loud as the finest mule can sing. Spike Loring looked back and forth at Cranston and Morrison.

"Man knocked me down and stole my knife," Cranston said, wiping an arm across his face.

"That true, stranger?" Loring towered over everyone. He had a wry look splashed across his rugged face, as if to understand that Cranston wasn't telling the whole truth and nothing but.

"No doubt, mister. Yup, I shorley did knock this poor dumb bastard on his ass, and got his knife stuck in my belt as we talk. Ain't that the truth, Jimmy Lassen?" Lassen had a smile as he nodded.

"The truth is, Mr. Loring, Bull Morrison here knocked Cranston on his ass after Cranston pulled the knife on him. Took him to the floor with one punch, he did." Jimmy was almost clapping his hands in glee.

"Yup," Morrison said. The marshal picked up the glass of whiskey and drank it down. "So, you're the owner of this fine establishment. I was just telling Jimmy here that I wouldn't mind having a place like this sometime. That's when Mr. Cranston here got all pushy with me. Don't cater to bad manners."

"Nor do I," Loring said. "Go get cleaned up, Cranston, and don't come back until you've cooled out some." Loring looked over to Bull. "Buster Cranston runs the North Pass Mine for Sandy Hitchcock, so you've just made yourself a couple of enemies. What brings you to Pioche?"

The two watched Cranston make his way out of the saloon before Bull answered. "Gold, Mr. Loring. Looking for gold."

"You don't much look like a prospector, if you don't mind me saying so."

"You're right. Speculator would be more like it. That's my partner coming in the doors right now."

"We have an abundance of gold and speculators in Pioche. Enjoy your drinks, Mr. Morrison, and don't be whipping on my customers," he said. "Unless they're asking for it." He bowed slightly, the grin he offered was obvious, and Loring moved back through the crowd. Lassen chuckled and poured another whiskey for the marshal.

"Looks like I might have missed something," Calhoun said. He watched Spike Loring make his way through the crowd as it broke up. "Can't leave you alone for a minute, can I?"

"Just a rude mining man, Slim. That big gentleman walking away owns this place. Told him we were speculators, so we need to ride with that. Probably learn a lot if people think we're part of the problem."

"We have always been part of the problem, Bull." Calhoun motioned for Jimmy Lassen to bring him a cold beer and a glass for whiskey. "Where would a couple of trail weary boys find a good steak?"

"Ginny Whipple's café, across the street and south half a block. Her father's ranch provides her beef. Best in Lincoln County," Lassen said. "Serves breakfast, dinner, and supper. Busiest little girl in Pioche."

"Sounds like you have a stake in the project," Slim laughed.

"Kinda would like to, I guess. Sure do like her."

"There's a bathhouse at the back of the hotel, Slim. Costs a cartwheel. Don't know where they get their prices, but we need a bath."

"We do, and then a couple or three whole beeves." They finished their drinks and made for the bath house. Lassen noticed Three-Finger Jack Daws follow the boys out.

CHAPTER 4

"YOU TELLING ME A TRAIL BUM WHIPPED YOU? BEAT YOU DUMB, TOOK your knife, and you're standing here talking about it?" Sandy Hitchcock didn't know whether to laugh at the man, feel sorry for him, or kick him in the head. "Mine boss of the richest little operation in Nevada's meanest camp, and you're whipped in public? Might want to think about this the next time you get pushy with a stranger, Cranston."

"Ain't you gonna do something about it?" Cranston almost whined.

"I didn't lose my knife," Hitchcock said. He was laughing as he turned and walked toward his office.

"Bastard." Cranston barely whispered the word and walked out of the mine's office building. "I'll think about it all right. I'll think that big bastard right into his grave." Cranston was furious that the boss wasn't going to issue orders for the stranger's death, wasn't going to back up his mine boss. A thinking man would have understood that it was his actions that caused the beating and would be his responsibility to do something about it.

It was on the long walk back to town that he remembered the new investors being in town, buying into the mine because of how he, Buster Cranston, had salted those two drifts with gold dust and small nuggets. "Maybe I can get even, Mr. Hitchcock, maybe I can. You won't have the chance to laugh at me again."

"A HOT BATH, CLOSE SHAVE, AND FRESH CLOTHING GIVES A MAN A GOOD outlook on life, eh, Bull? Now for some tender beef and a pile of potatoes."

"Did you notice that feller who followed us back toward the baths? Never made an approach, though."

"Watched him careful, Bull. Think he was a friend of the man you accosted?"

"I fought off the one who accosted, you boozer," Bull thundered. "No, the feller following us wanted to make sure we were taking a bath. Didn't want to make contact."

"Meaning, Bull Morrison, he might just happen to be in our rooms going through our kit." Slim Calhoun was at a full run, bounding up the stairs and down the hallway before he stopped talking. The door to his room was ajar and Slim slammed his way in, driving the intruder back and across the single bed.

Calhoun's pistol was cocked and aimed at the man's head before Bull made it into the room. "What have we got, Mr. Calhoun? Ah, a sneak thief, a taker of other's goods, a man destined for an early grave."

"Yup," Slim snickered. "Want to tell me your name before I shoot you?"

"Name's Daws, Jack Daws. I'm Pioche City Marshal so it would be to your benefit not to shoot me. We do need to have a chat, though." Three-Finger Jack looked back and forth at the two men. "I assume that you, sir, are Marshal

Bull Morrison, and you," he said, looking at Slim, "must be Deputy Marshal Calhoun."

Neither marshal said a word nor looked at each other, but both were wondering what this was all about. *So much for nobody knowing we were coming.* Calhoun got a little grin on his face and looked over at Bull. Bull nodded, and Calhoun jammed the revolver up Daws's nose. "Only two men knew we were coming, Jack. Which one do you work against, cuz you sure don't work for either one."

"There's a federal judge in Frisco and a federal judge in Salt Lake knows we're here. The one in Salt Lake thinks there's a leak in his office." Bull Morrison looked over to Slim. "Seems he might be right, eh Slim?"

"Seems so," Calhoun snickered. "So, City Marshal Jack Daws, who is that snitch in Salt Lake? Mess with me and I'll blow your head off. You're already under arrest for breaking and entering. Might as well go for attempted escape."

"Don't shoot. There really is an answer to this." Daws's eyes slowly closed as the gun was eased back in its holster. "I do get information from a man who works for Judge Olsen, but you're making it sound like that man ain't supposed to be telling me stuff."

"According to the judge, he ain't." Calhoun walked around the room, saw where their kit bags had been gone through and emptied on the beds. "We were sent here to root out criminal activity by lawmen, by city and county officials, by some in the general population." Calhoun took a long breath and glared at Daws. "We were to be undercover because Judge Olsen's marshals were well-known and too many people would know they were coming. Just look what we've found in our first hours in town."

Slim chuckled and straightened a chair before sitting.

"First criminal we find is the town marshal who also gets his information from a slum dog in the judge's chambers. Me and Bull don't have long attention spans, Marshal Daws, so you need to start talking and in a straight line. You go off in circles and I'm gonna just start shooting. Got it?" He caressed his Colt and had a nasty grin on his face.

"We're gonna start off with why you broke into our rooms, why you went through out kit, and why are you getting this information? The clock has started," Bull Morrison said.

Three-Finger Jack started talking and didn't stop for at least half an hour, during which neither Bull nor Slim asked one question. It was as if Daws had been waiting for such an opportunity and when he finally stopped talking, he was sweating profusely. "I've actually got most of this written down but have been afraid to show it to anyone."

"I understand the trust issue," Slim said. "Why do you trust us?"

"Partly the threat to shoot me." Daws tried to chuckle but it didn't work well. "Mostly because you're federal marshals. That means something to me."

"Sure would have been better if you had just come to us." Bull Morrison wanted to believe what Daws had said. *Dumb bastard carries a badge, knows we're marshals, and breaks into our rooms. I do not have the least trust in this mucker.* "Even though you have told us all this, it's because we had to threaten you to get it, that gives me trust issues now. You forced us to threaten you."

"Yup," Slim said. "How many people know we're coming? How many have you told?"

"I haven't told anyone. I don't trust anyone in this camp, except for Tom Blair at the Gold Strike Mine."

"What about Spike Loring here at the Lucky Lady? Trust

him?" Bull Morrison took a great like to the man following his exchange with Buster Cranston. "Seems straight arrow."

"He and Rolf Pendergrass at the Silver Crystal seem to roll with the tide. Don't take sides, but that doesn't mean they ain't involved in one side or the other." Daws said.

"Best bet, Marshal Daws is to stay away from us. If we need something or want your help, we'll come to you." Bull Morrison stood up and walked to the hotel window. "If it's of ultimate importance, put it in a sealed envelope and leave it with Jimmy Lassen. What you've told us is pretty much what we already know, have notes on most of the people you talked about, so our work is now complicated by you knowing we're here."

"What Bull means is, don't get in the way. If you give the slightest hint that you know who we are, I'll shoot you ten times in the head." Slim Calhoun said. "Get out of here without being seen and stay away from us."

Three-Finger Jack Daws was a hurt man as he slipped out of the hotel room. *Bad scene, Jack. Damn, and they're right. Should simply have gone to them. I need help, they need help, and now they don't trust me. Got to get their trust.*

Daws was standing at the bar having a large glass of whiskey when Lonesome Gary Thompson walked up. "Share your bottle?" He motioned for Jimmy Lassen to get him a glass. "Been looking for the sheriff. Seen him?"

"Haven't," Daws said. He rarely had anything to do with the sheriff or his deputies, considered them to be a major part of the criminal activity in Pioche. "Sure. Have a shot."

"Ran into Buster Cranston down the street. Looks like hell." Thompson laughed. "Said a trail bum whipped on him, even stole his knife. Wanted to file charges, but that would be with you not the sheriff."

"He picked on the wrong man this time," Jimmy Lassen said.

"Go wash a glass, Lassen. This is man talk," Thompson said. "Lawman talk." He laughed, drank the whiskey down and refilled his glass. "Little jerk's probably right, though. Cranston more than likely started whatever happened." He drank the glass empty and moved off.

Bastard didn't even say thank you. He and Lighthorse won't like it when those marshals come calling. Got no reason to talk to Jimmy that way, either. The entire Lighthorse gang is an arrogant bunch start to finish.

Thompson wondered why he didn't say anything to Daws about marshals coming to town. Lighthorse often spread the news when outside lawmen were coming. He decided not to go back. *Dumb jerk will find out soon enough.*

SLIM AND BULL TOOK A TABLE NEAR THE FRONT WINDOWS AT GINNY Whipple's eatery. "If that beef tastes half as good as it smells cooking, I ain't never leaving this place," Slim said. The little café was fit out like it was in a warm and friendly home somewhere. Light colors of yellow and orange, set off with dark brown leather on the chairs.

"Even got us a tablecloth, Bull. Camp food ain't never gonna make it after this."

"Here you go, boys," Ginny said, setting two large platters down. Each held a massive rib steak, a mound of mashed potatoes with a puddle of butter in each mound, and steamed squash. Ginny Whipple was all of five feet tall, skinny, with flame red hair and five thousand or more freckles. Her green eyes sparkled with life and her smile was warm. Slim knew for a fact that her lips were made for kissing.

"Don't you be leaving none. That would make me feel bad."

"Ain't gonna be leaving none of this," Slim said. "I go out of my way not to make a pretty girl feel bad. Do you bake pies, too?"

"I hope you like apple pie," she giggled. "Also peach cobbler with gobs of heavy cream, too."

"I'm in heaven," Slim said. Ginny giggled again and scurried into the kitchen. Slim enjoyed the swing and sway of her long dress and let his eyes follow her all the way. "Nice girl," he said.

"Hmmph," Bull snorted.

GINNY WHIPPLE MOVED SOME POTS AND PANS AROUND ON THE MASSIVE wood stove in her kitchen but her mind was on the long tall stranger in the front room. "Those eyes are more than I can stand. Hope that big boy is nice, hope he sticks around, and hope more than anything that he isn't part of Harvey Lighthorse's gang of ruffians."

Ginny's father had a ranch down in the valley, less than ten miles from Pioche, worked with other ranchers to wrangle enough water for their grass crops and the farming that was needed. The mines and mills up on the mountainside were taking far more than they were allocated and doing so with the blessing of the local sheriff.

Hank Whipple, Tom Donovan, and Quincy Pierce held the largest of the ranches and were under constant attack by the mine owners. Threats of open warfare were heard often at the county commission meeting when water allocation was discussed. Several ranchers had already been chased from the valley and sold out for pennies on the dollar.

"WHAT DO WE DO ABOUT THIS DAWS FOOL?" BULL MORRISON ASKED. "Sure as hell, he'll mouth off to somebody about us."

"I'm not sure he's really the fool that he acted. He made a mistake going through our kits instead of coming straight to us, but I think he's going to be fine. He knew what he was talking about, and then some."

"We need to get on this Harvey Lighthorse character. My stomach growls when I know about crooked lawmen. He's a big man and his deputies are outlaws, killers, Slim. Maybe all of that will lead us for a drink at the Silver Crystal after supper."

"One thing about Daws, though. He's a lawman, carries a badge that says so. Why hasn't he made any arrests if he knows all this? He seems sincere on the one hand and less than stellar on the other. He ain't really with it, Bull."

"No, he ain't. Now, my fine deputy, let's go drink."

CHAPTER 5

"GAUDY JOINT, ISN'T IT?" SLIM WAS STANDING JUST INSIDE THE BAT-wing doors of the Silver Crystal with Bull already heading for the bar. "Coming dear," he whispered, catching up. "That is one dude standing near the poker table, Bull. Haven't seen anyone wearing that much gold since we were in Denver."

"Fits what we've been told about Harvey Lighthorse. Got bail money in case I get carried away?"

"Always do," Slim chuckled. "That must be Sandy Hitch-cock with him. They're inseparable according to Baker's notes and Daws's account. The sheriff standing behind one of the players and Hitchcock is playing. I hate it when people do that." Slim Calhoun said. "Think he's passing information? Baker said Hitchcock would stand on a pair of deuces in five card. Gambling bug's got him bad."

"Daws said he has the North Pass Mine for sale. Why don't you get in that game, Slim, see if you can get a rise out of the fat man. I'll stand quietly at the bar." Bull Morrison lived to fight. If no one was willing to start a fight with him, he'd go right ahead and start one on his own.

"That'll be the day," Slim said. "Wish me luck." He walked over to the poker table and found an empty chair. He pulled some bills out. "Table open?"

"It is," the dealer said. "Table stakes, sir. If it ain't showing on the table it can't be bet. Ante's a dollar, gentlemen." The dealer was thin, wore a silk vest that Slim was sure carried a little single shot weapon in one of its many pockets. His straight black hair was slicked back, his brown eyes shaded by heavy black brows, and he wore the thinnest mustache Slim had ever seen.

Calhoun tossed his dollar onto the table and the dealer dealt the first cards out. Face down. The hole card. "I'm in," Hitchcock said. "Another dollar to get it started." Everyone called and the dealer put the next cards around, face up. Hitchcock got a king of hearts, Slim a jack of diamonds, there was a six of clubs, an eight of clubs, and a deuce of hearts.

"That king's good for five dollars," Hitchcock said, putting a half eagle on the table. Slim called, the six and eight stayed as well, but the deuce folded. The next round gave a queen of spades to Hitchcock, a ten of diamonds to Slim, a ten to the six, and a seven to the eight.

"Some nice hands showing," the dealer said. "The king-queen bets."

"Another five just to see things along," Hitchcock said.

"I'll see the five and add ten to it," Slim said. The eight and six folded and the dealer waited for the mine operator's response. Sandy Hitchcock got a hard look across his face and stared at Slim Calhoun.

"It's ten dollars to you, Mr. Hitchcock," the dealer said.

"I know what the hell it is," Hitchcock said. He took a look at his hole card and threw forty dollars out. "Raise you thirty, stranger. That jack ten ain't got nothing behind it."

Harvey Lighthorse had moved slowly around the table as the cards were dealt and Slim could almost feel him standing directly behind him. *Want to know my hole card, eh? Ain't gonna get away with that, Sheriff.*

"A raise of thirty dollars to you, mister," the dealer said.

Slim started to lift the cards for a look at the hole card, knowing that Lighthorse had to be almost leaning over his shoulder, and let the cards fall back. "I'll see that thirty, and my jack ten is telling me it's got some strength left. I'll raise twenty." No smile, not even a look toward the mine owner.

Hitchcock looked at his hole card again, which told everyone at the table that he didn't have any strength. Would he try a bluff on this stranger, who seemed to be sitting almost pat? "I'll see the twenty," he said, slipping a double eagle out.

The next cards weren't good for either player. Hitchcock got a three of hearts, "No help," the dealer said. He flipped one toward Slim. "And a five of clubs. No help. King-queen bets."

Hitchcock looked up toward the sheriff, still standing behind Slim, and pulled a bill from his stack. "Good help with that card. It's worth a hundred."

"Bet's one hundred dollars," the dealer said. "To you, stranger."

Slim turned slightly. "Would you move back some, please? Your Bay Rum is overpowering." He again reached for his cards to take a quick look at the hole card.

"Who the hell do you think you are, talking to a gentleman in that tone of voice?" Sheriff Lighthorse got his feelings hurt. "Bay Rum," he snorted. "My aftershave is imported from France. Impudence."

Slim Calhoun snickered, enjoying the show. "The gentleman uses too much," he said. "I'll see that hundred dollars and raise a hundred." Ten twenty-dollar bills were pushed out.

"One hundred dollars to you, Mister Hitchcock."

The active betting, the outburst from the sheriff, and attention was drawn. Bystanders were gathering, wondering who the tall, good-looking stranger was. Why did the sheriff snap at him? Would Hitchcock strip him of every dime he had? There were side bets from many of those standing around the table on many possibilities including gun play.

Hitchcock pushed a stack of double eagles onto the table. "Table is good. Last card, gentlemen." The dealer was enjoying all the action. After all, he got a percentage of every round. He dropped a three of clubs to Hitchcock. There was an almost audible groan from the crowd. They liked it when Hitchcock won at the tables. It usually meant at least one round of free drinks.

"And," the dealer said, flipping a five of diamonds at Slim. "A five to the stranger. A pair of fives bets."

"Damn it, mister, give me room to breathe." The sheriff was almost leaning on Slim and he wasn't going to take it. "My pair of fives rules. I bet another hundred."

"Don't you talk to me that way," Lighthorse said. He reached out to grab Calhoun and found himself sailing across the saloon, smashing into a table full of North Pass miners, spilling all the beer and whiskey.

"That's a pretty serious game of cards being played out. Ain't no time to make trouble, mister." Bull Morrison was staring down at the beer drenched sheriff. "Now, let's watch and see how it's played out. No more petty trouble from a dandy, eh?" Bull laughed stepping back to the table, ignoring the man.

Two of the hard rock miners jerked Lighthorse to his feet and the sheriff took two steps toward Bull Morrison only to be stopped by Rolf Pendergrass, the owner of the saloon. "That's enough, Harvey. You know my rules around the tables. No interruptions, no cat calls, no kibitzing. Being sheriff doesn't change my rules."

Pendergrass turned to Morrison. "And no fighting." He got a pained smile from Bull and looked at the dealer. "Table good?"

"Table is good, Mr. Pendergrass. Pair of fives bet a hundred to you, Mr. Hitchcock."

"I know, damn it." Hitchcock looked at his hole card and smiled. Was this the bluff? He set the cards down and shoved twenty double eagles out. "See your hundred and raise another like it."

Slim noticed that now he had both Bull Morrison and Rolf Pendergrass standing behind him. He let the card lay, checked his stash and noted that he didn't have enough to see and raise. He knew table stakes rules and did the only thing he could. He shoved the last one hundred he had on the table out.

"I call. Let's see these prized cards of yours." The crowd moaned. They wanted to see a lot more money flow across that table.

Hitchcock turned his cards over. "A pair of kings." He started to reach out when Slim showed his hand.

"Not so quick. A pair of fives, and oh, yes, some back up in a pair of jacks. Thank you," he said, gathering in the take. "We'll have to do this again, some time." He took the leather pouch that Morrison offered and filled it with bills and gold coins. "I need a drink."

"Let me buy you and your friend one," Rolf Pendergrass said. "Haven't seen you before." They walked through the crowd and stood at the end of the long bar, Slim on one side of the saloon keeper and Bull on the other.

"Just got into town earlier," Slim said. "Who was that dandy who kept pressuring me?" Slim knew full well who Lighthorse was but wanted to hear what the saloon keeper would say.

"County Sheriff," Pendergrass laughed. He turned to Bull.

"You probably just made a big target of yourself."

"Wouldn't be the first time," Bull said. "Sheriff, eh? Might need to spend some of that money on learning the law instead of gold to wear. Rude," Bull snorted.

"What brings you to Pioche? Sure isn't gambling," the saloon owner said. He looked at Slim. "You played that mighty close to the chest. Most gamblers would have gone for Hitchcock's throat."

"We are looking for gold, just not from gambling, Mr. Pendergrass. We're looking for some decent investment opportunities." Slim saw Lighthorse and Hitchcock walk out of the saloon. "Understand there are some available," he chuckled.

"Investment opportunities, yes. Decent ones? Do your homework, gentlemen," Pendergrass said. "Assay reports can be altered but mill reports are generally fairly accurate. Stocks can be manipulated but dividends are more accurate."

"Sounds like a man who has been educated by delving into the game," Bull said. "Why would you accept a mill report?"

"If the mill is operated by the mine, I wouldn't. If it's an independent, I would simply because they need to maintain a good standing with the producers. You might want to have a chat with Tom Blair at the Gold Strike." Pendergrass nodded to the barman to pour again for the marshals and walked off across the saloon floor.

"Interesting that Sheriff Lighthorse didn't respond in any way after you knocked him on his butt," Slim said. "Ain't the way most in the business would."

"Pendergrass seems to have some strong influence around these parts, Slim. More than is in our reports or noted by Marshal Daws. Lighthorse never said anything after Pendergrass got on his case. Maybe he has something on the sheriff, maybe he's the sheriff's power in the first place. Let's head back to the

Lucky Lady and ask about this Tom Blair fellow."

"Hitchcock is a strange one, Bull. Everything we have suggests that he is behind most of the scams and schemes, has tremendous influence over the county officials, but acts like a jerk at the poker table. We're dealing with curious people, Bull. Curious."

CHAPTER 6

"YOU SHOULD HAVE SHOT THAT BASTARD, HARVEY. YOU ARE THE sheriff, aren't you? Look at you, covered in beer and whiskey, smell to high heaven. Go home, we'll talk in the morning." Sandy Hitchcock turned to walk the short distance to his large Victorian home, set up on the hillside two blocks from the main street. *The man was nothing more than a hired gun when we made him sheriff, now he's nothing more than a city dandy. Thought we had a real man, instead just another stupid outlaw thinking he's something special.*

Lighthorse made his way north to the sheriff's offices, a building housing offices and a jail, next to the Lincoln County Courthouse, a structure that had been under construction for years. *That big bastard's gonna die next time I see him. Pendergrass should never have called me off. Maybe I need to make some adjustments around here. I did better busting banks and trains than I have doing these fools' dirty work.* Of course as an outlaw he didn't wear half a pound of gold, didn't eat for free at any restaurant in town, except one, and rarely drank for free either. His gang now wore badges instead of those wearing badges chasing him. None of that entered his mind, only that he had been humiliated because of Hitchcock again.

He found two of his deputies sitting in front of the wood stove drinking coffee. Billy Benson was wanted in Texas for cattle rustling and murder and Larry Owens was a wanted killer out of New Orleans. In Pioche, their stock in trade was intimidation. Benson was close to five ten and weighed more than two hundred pounds while Owens was shorter and lighter. Both believed a bullet or two in the back was more effective than a face to face encounter.

"What happened to you, Sheriff?" Owens jumped to his feet when Lighthorse came through the door.

"Not important," Lighthorse snarled. "While I'm home changing, I want you boys to find two strangers and chase 'em out of town. One is tall, calls himself Slim, and the other is short and squat. Goes by the name of Bull. Troublemakers. Card cheats, too. No arrests. They either leave town or stay, permanently, in the cemetery."

"That one called Bull beat the crap out of Buster Cranston earlier today at the Lucky Lady." Billy Benson stood up and filled his tin cup with coffee. "Put on a good show. Even took Cranston's knife from him. He and the other one are staying at the Lucky Lady. Saw Three-Finger Daws meeting with them."

"That so?" The Sheriff found a flask in his desk and took a long drink. Lighthorse had to think about that for a moment. *Daws is going to make a big mistake if he gets tied up with a couple of saddle bums.* "Serious troublemaker, that Marshal Daws. The other two? What do you think? Should we get Pizon for back-up?"

That was almost a slap in the face. Sherman (Pizon) Oakley was another of Lighthorse's deputies and a cold-blooded killer out of Arizona Territory. He was a loner, seldom called on to work with any of the other deputies. When local dignitaries disappeared, it was generally accepted as fact that Pizon did it.

"No, Harvey," Benson said. "Those two will be gone by morning, one way or the other. Let's take a walk," he said to Owens. "Lucky Lady first, eh?"

A cold wind blew down the mountainside as the two deputies made their way through the cold mud of the main street. "Saw the big one take Cranston out," Benson said. "He won't be easy. Best bet is to provoke him and then just shoot him dead. The other one will be easy."

"Sheriff was whipped in public, Billy," Owens laughed. "Whipped in public, given a beer bath, and calls on us for help. I wonder how long he'll be wearing that tin badge? I'm making plans to head for Denver and go back to the old ways."

"Lighthorse was always a fool. There's a lot of banks in Arizona that haven't met me," Benson laughed. "Time for me to introduce myself."

They stood on either side of the swinging doors giving the interior of the Lucky Lady a good look before entering. "They're at the end of the bar. That's Blair they're talking to. Lighthorse would be a happy man if we took out Blair, too."

"One problem at a time, Benson," Owens said. "Let's get fairly close and listen for a couple of minutes. Follow my lead when we make our move. We'll get a good fight started, yell 'gun', and shoot all three."

The two were chuckling when they pushed their way to the bar. None of those shoved knew better than to argue with the deputies. "Whiskey, Torres, and clean glasses," Owens said. Chago Torres, the night barman, frowned but got a bottle and went way out of his way to wipe two glasses clean.

"Clean enough for you, Deputy?" Torres said.

"Watch your mouth, boy." Larry Owens grabbed the bottle and ripped the cork out. "Keep close watch on your back getting home, boy." Lots of emphasis on the word boy.

Torres was a big man, hired partly because of his size, partly because he knew how to use his size. "Yeah, you're good at shootin' from the back side. Ain't that right, Deputy?" He turned to walk to the end of the bar when Slim Calhoun motioned for him and Billy Benson reached across the bar, grabbed Torres and jerked him back. His revolver was swinging toward Torres' head when the barman wrenched free.

Bull Morrison took three fast steps and drove a massive fist into the side of Benson's head, driving the man into Larry Owens. It happened so fast Owens was taken by surprise. Bull didn't let up, and with Benson trapped between him and Owens, Morrison twisted the big gun from the deputy's grip and used it to knock the man out.

Bull Morrison stood over the unconscious body glaring at Larry Owens. "You part of this play, too?"

Slim and Tom Blair were right behind Bull and Calhoun saw Chago Torres standing behind the bar with a shotgun in hand. "He was going to bash my head in," Torres said. "They might be wearing badges, but these two men are nothing but street scum and outlaws working for Lighthorse."

Owens was in the worst position he had been in for a long time. Torres would shoot him in a second, this big sumbitch would tear his face off given half a chance, and now he could see Spike Loring coming down the stairs from his upstairs office.

"There better be a good reason for this." Loring was glaring at Bull. "Second time we've met, second fight you've been in my saloon. Don't much care for this, Mr. Morrison."

"Man tried to attack your barkeep, Loring. Doubt if you cotton to that, either." Bull laid Billy Benson's bloody revolver on the top of the bar."

"Where do you think you're going?" Slim Calhoun said,

reaching out and grabbing Larry Owens by his coat as the deputy tried to ease away from the scene. "Ain't through talking to you." Calhoun reached out and opened the coat, seeing the deputy's badge. "Well, well, well. Just looky, Bull, he's carrying a tin badge."

"The man you hit, Morrison, is also carrying a badge," Spike Loring said. Spike looked over at Torres. "That true what Morrison said. Benson tried to attack you?"

"It is, Mr. Loring. Grabbed me and was swinging that revolver there," and he pointed at the gun laying on the bar. "I pulled free just as Bull here beat him down."

Owens had heard enough, could see nothing but trouble coming, and made a dash for the saloon doors. A crowd had gathered around the scene, Benson was trying to get his senses back, and Calhoun was held up trying to make a chase. Owens was well out the door before Slim broke free of the crowd.

Slim stood on the front porch of the Lucky Lady looking up and down the main street, not seeing anything out of the ordinary. A few people out walking, a horse or two being ridden, but no running man trying to get away. "Damn it," Slim muttered. Spike Loring stepped up next to him.

"See anything?"

"Not a thing, Loring. Not a thing. I'm gonna have to have a talk with that feller floundering around on the floor in there. Wearing a badge? Trying to bash a barkeep? Got a lot of questions for that feller."

"Why would you even want to know?" Loring and Slim walked back into the saloon. "Ain't none of your concern."

Damn me. Just about give it up there, Slim old boy. Better come up with some kind of explanation. Gotta quit thinking like a marshal in front of these people. Damn fool. "Well, damn me, but you're right, Loring. Maybe I'll just have another drink or two. Sure does seem strange, though, don't it?"

"Maybe where you're from, but not in Pioche these days.," Loring said. He was still chuckling when he called for Chago Torres to pour some drinks. Bull Morrison had Billy Benson on his feet and gave him a shove for the door.

"Might want to watch your partner's back over the next few days, Calhoun. He's whipped on a couple of people that don't take kindly to being whipped on." Loring downed his drink and walked back upstairs. He didn't even know that Bull had destroyed the sheriff in public.

"At least this time you didn't tell me you weren't gonna get in a fight," Slim said. The ironic grin said much more than that. "I sure wanted to talk to those two." Slim nodded toward Torres. "Where'd you get that name Chago?"

"Short for Santiago," the barman laughed. "Where'd you get the name Slim?"

"We'll do better talking to Tom Blair," Bull snorted. "According to Judge Baker's notes, Blair is one of the few straight shooters in Pioche." Bull Morrison was slowly coming down from his high of a good fight and needed some quiet talking time. "Might learn something, although it seems all we have to do is stand still and all the trouble comes running right at us."

CHAPTER 7

"HE BEAT THE HELL OUT OF YOU AND TOOK YOUR GUN?" HARVEY Lighthorse, all cleaned up, wearing a silk shirt under a fine calf skin vest, and gold hanging everywhere glared at Billy Benson and Larry Owens. "And you," he got right in Owens' face, "just stood there and watched this little piece of theater?" Lighthorse turned to the third deputy lounging in front of the wood stove.

"I suppose you think this is how we run things around here?" Lighthorse poured some coffee into a cup half filled with whiskey. "Find Thompson and be quick about it."

"He's at the Silver Crystal," the man said and high-tailed it out the door. It was a fast two block walk down to the saloon and he found Lonesome Gary Thompson talking to Toby Smith, the gambler who dealt the cards at the game most of Pioche was now talking about.

"Boss wants you, pronto."

"Made a fool of himself here," Thompson said. "What's he done now?" Thompson, unlike the others in the sheriff's gang had no respect for Lighthorse, felt he should have that office, and was doing what he could to make that happen. There was money to be made as Sheriff of Lincoln County. Prestige,

money, women, and more money, Thompson dreamed every
time his head hit the pillow.

"Benson and Owens got their butts kicked by a couple of
strangers they were supposed to run out of town. I don't know
the whole story," he said.

"I think I do," Thompson laughed. "Yes, I do believe I do.
This might just turn out to be my night to howl."

"WELL, NOW, MR. BLAIR, WHERE WERE WE?" BULL SAID, TRYING
to get settled at the bar. "Don't much care to see things like
what just happened."

"Sheriff only hires thugs and wanted men. I'm sure
that Sandy Hitchcock and Rolf Pendergrass arranged for
Lighthorse's election. I've sent for help many times but that
feisty old judge in Salt Lake City always has some excuse
for not sending any."

This time it was marshals worrying about Indian trouble.
Slim Calhoun said to himself. *I wonder how long Judge Olsen
has been on the take? How many other communities are having outlaw trouble because of him?* He caught himself up short
when another thought came through. *I wonder if our judge,
the honorable Mr. Baker found out and needed us to get proof.
It would be his way.*

Blair stood about five-nine and weighed in at a hefty one
eighty. His shoulders and arms spoke of many years of hard
and heavy work, his hands were well worn and featured
gnarled and scarred knuckles. His hair was coal black, and
his eyes were a piercing steel gray, shielded by heavy brows.
Bull Morrison had already sized him up and knew he would
be a tough customer hand to hand.

"What kind of help?" Slim asked but knew Blair was

talking about marshals.

"Federal marshals would clean this mess up in a hurry." Blair said.

"How deep does this mess, as you call it, go? With a county sheriff and a town marshal, it seems the bad guys would almost be outnumbered." Morrison was going to lead Blair into outlining the problems and naming the names.

"The sheriff is an outlaw, Mr. Morrison. You saw that firsthand. And Three-Finger Jack Daws stays in office at the mercy of the other outlaws. Pendergrass and Hitchcock saw to it that Lighthorse is sheriff, and as long as Daws only worries about a town drunk from time-to-time, he'll stay as city marshal. Hitchcock has more mining scams going than the bank has."

"You're a mine operator, Blair. Where do you stand in all this?" Calhoun took a drink of whiskey. "Seems like there should be a few people in this camp who are tired of the constant killings and robberies."

"Jack Daws is one, and I guess I'm the other one," Blair laughed. "Sick as that sounds, it's just about the truth. Everyone's out to skin a cat, I'm afraid. Any way they can."

"If marshals should arrive, Blair, what would you tell them? Where would you want them to start cleaning house?" Morrison asked. "Me? I'd put the sheriff out of business and then work on the schemes and scams, straighten out the crooked businesses, and keep a close eye on the bankers."

Calhoun enjoyed watching Bull work Tom Blair into lining out how best to deal with all the trouble in Pioche. *Bull is already planning how we're gonna bring these people down, but he might just learn something with these questions.*

"Sandy Hitchcock owns the bank, Bull. Many people don't know that. The bank supports many of the schemes and criminal mining ventures. Pendergrass knows and that's why he's so cozy with that grifter. Spike Loring does what he can to stay aloof from the illegal stuff but has been known to back Hitchcock on a few scams. It's money, Bull, just plain old money that drives all these fine enterprises."

"Always the case, Blair. Always, eh, Slim?"

"Yup," Slim said. "On the surface, then, Hitchcock is making most of it, and the others want their share."

The conversation lasted another hour and Blair said goodnight. "One more and we call it," Bull said when the miner left. "I wonder if he's really as straight as he wants us to believe? He knows too much not to be involved some way."

"I was thinking the same thing, but he's definitely afraid of the sheriff and his honchos. We need to concentrate on getting the sheriff out of the picture. He and his men are too dangerous to ignore."

"I'd kinda like to have a chat with Daws again," Bull said. "Lots of fingers pointing at Hitchcock and Pendergrass, and I'd like to know about others. It still rankles me that he carries a badge and hasn't arrested a soul."

"I'VE GOT A JOB FOR YOU, JOHNSON. YOU KNOW WHERE PIZON IS?"

"Probably down at the hot springs. He runs a small saloon and bordello down there. Quite the squire now," he laughed. "I don't much care to be working a job with him."

"Don't care what you care," Lighthorse said. "Go get him and the two of you eliminate these two strangers. Make it a public execution if you want, but I want those two dead."

"And?" Lonesome Gary Thompson said.

Lighthorse scowled, took a quick look around, and said, "And two hundred for each of you. Now git." Harvey Lighthorse knew he wanted more to drink and knew he was shamed at the Silver Crystal. "Spike Loring owes me a drink or two, particularly after you two made fools of yourselves earlier." He drank what was left in the cup and walked out.

It was a short walk to the Lucky Lady and he nodded to the few souls out on a cold night. *Two strangers ride into town, say they are looking for investment property, and beat the hell out of everyone they come across. How does their meeting with Three-Finger Daws fit in all this?*

He had his mind wrapped around his thoughts and didn't even see Bull Morrison and Slim Calhoun at the end of the bar when he walked in. "Gimme a whiskey, Chago. Understand my boys roughed you up earlier. Gotta watch your mouth, boy."

Chago Torres humphed and turned away to get a glass and bottle. "I'd say the dandy in silk and satin is the one with the bad mouth," Bull Morrison said from the end of the bar. "A sheriff with no manners ain't much of a man in my book. A good man behind the bar needs to be shown proper respect in my book. You might dress pretty but you don't got my respect, no sir, you sure don't."

Sheriff Lighthorse took a fast look around, knew he was alone with these two saddle bums and decided to play it as a tough guy. "I'm the sheriff of this county, stranger, and you've just worn out your welcome. Pack up your gear and leave out, boys." Lighthorse turned toward Bull and Slim, letting his right hand settle on the grip of his side-arm. "Now, gentlemen."

"Can't do that, Sheriff. Rooms are paid for through next week," Bull said. Slim had to hold his chuckle in and Bull kept it up. "Unless of course you'd like to refund our money. I know Spike wouldn't want to."

"Smart talk ain't gonna get you nowhere. Pack it up, boys. Ain't gonna tell you again." His grip on the pistol tightened as Bull took a long step toward the outlaw. It was a left that came straight out of his shoulder that sent Lighthorse flying across the saloon, landing in a heap under an empty table.

Bull reached down and took the sheriff's pistol, rolled him over and relieved the man of a knife. "Need to know how to use these things if you're gonna carry 'em." Several patrons had gathered around, staring at the inert body sprawled on the plank floor. Muted comments about a lucky punch, about Lighthorse getting what he deserved, and questions about who this stranger was, were heard.

Bull eyed the knife and Colt. "This is one well-made knife. Might just want to keep this one, too." Bull motioned to Chago. "Tuck these away somewhere safe, Chago, and I sure could use another drink." He put the gun and knife on the bar and turned in time to see Spike Loring hurrying down the stairs.

"Again, Morrison? What now?"

"A lot of people in this old town don't have much for manners, Spike. What's your relationship with this fool who calls himself Sheriff? He and those men who work for him are nothing but outlaws with a badge. I'm gettin' tired of fightin' them off. He wanted you to give us our money back from the rooms and leave town. You wouldn't do that, would you?"

Loring coughed slightly. "Let's sit at a table, Bull. Chago, bring us a bottle and glasses and keep the sheriff away from us when he comes to. Gentlemen?" Some of those at the bar were pointing at the sheriff but unwilling to get involved. "Leave him lie, Lem," one old-timer said. Another stepped over the body to order a beer.

Loring walked the group to the far back of the saloon, in a darkened corner, and took a table. "Something tells me you're a lot more than what you seem to be, Bull Morrison. I'll tell you my story, but I want to hear yours, too."

No one paid any attention when an old man limped out

of the Lucky Lady and made his way to the Sandy Hitchcock mansion, two blocks up the hill. A few eyed the sheriff on the floor but no one offered help of any kind, they just walked around him.

IT WOULD HAVE BEEN A TWENTY-FIVE-MILE RIDE TO THE HOT SPRINGS, it was pitch-black of a cold night, and Lonesome Gary Johnson said to hell with that. It would be warm, slightly friendly, and safe at Gypsy's, and he wouldn't have to pay for every drink. "Mexican's got it right. Mañana will work just fine." The ladies shuddered when he walked through the door with a wide smile on his face. "Evening, girls."

Gypsy stood at the bar talking with one of the ladies and motioned Johnson over. "Heard some talk of a couple of strangers in town, Deputy. Hear they are responsible for some trouble with the sheriff. Something you might want to talk about?"

"Don't know what you heard, Gypsy, but there are a couple of fellas been raising some dust." Johnson said. He had to snicker when he told her that Buster Cranston got whipped, and that deputies Benson and Owens were busted up. "Sheriff wants me to run the strangers out of town. Might just hold off on that for a bit. Let them have their fun."

"You talk loud and mean in here, Deputy, but I ain't seen any of that on the street. What else you heard about these strangers?" She was not wearing her normal warm smile and Johnson tightened up at her nasty comment.

"That ain't so, Gypsy. Why, your ladies appreciate me being a protective type when I'm in here. The two strangers are asking a lot of questions, but that's all I know." He turned away from the madam, angry at her comment.

He bought a bottle and nodded at Shirley Simpson. "Need

some serious help, little lady, and you're the chosen one."

"I'll draw a bath, Deputy. Bath first, always." He was a dolt, but his gold was good and if he had a bath, he was tolerable. Besides, Shirley needed the money. Opium was a costly habit. He could make the ride to the hot springs in the morning.

THE HOT SPRINGS WERE ON A RANCH ABOUT TWENTY-FIVE MILES SOUTH of Pioche and Pizon Oakley made it his. The brothers who owned the ranch lived in Texas and had never seen the property. The ranch manager had a deal with Pizon, and the party was on. The girls were paid well, the ranch manager got his take, and travel from Pioche was easy enough to bring in the miners on weekends. There were no real lawmen in the place.

Sherman (Pizon) Oakley was short and skinny, had a bad attitude every day, took great pleasure in seeing suffering in others, and had more than hatred toward Harvey Lighthorse and his uppity attitude toward his deputies. His game had always been intimidation and blackmail coupled with a good bank job if funds ran low.

He had been in Pioche for two years and spent a great deal of time learning as much as he could about the people who ran things. He used that information from time-to-time to make good money before letting someone discover the mutilated body. His arrangement with Lighthorse came from Sandy Hitchcock knowing too much about Sherman Oakley.

There was a letter somewhere, Oakley didn't know where, that went into great detail about how Oakley operated and who he had murdered. As long as Pizon Oakley worked with Lighthorse, the letter would remain hidden.

Lincoln County Deputy Sheriff Gary Johnson rode into the hot springs complex of small cabins and steaming pools later the next day. "Howdy, Pizon. Sheriff wants to see you. Wants us to do a job."

"Us, Johnson? No. Maybe wants me to do a job with you helping some. You're starting to sound like Lighthorse. Heard our fine tough old sheriff got his clock cleaned by some stranger. That the job?"

"Bad news travels fast, eh?"

"Rider came in late last night tellin' all about it. Is this part of it?" He asked again with some sharpness to the question.

"Probably. Benson and Owens got whipped on, too."

"Let me get my stuff and we'll light out." Pizon hollered at a guy near one of the hot pools. "Be back in a day or two. Keep an eye on things."

CHAPTER 8

"I KNOW IT'S LATE, MR. HITCHCOCK, BUT YOU SAID IF IT'S IMPORTANT I should come." Tony Murphy was breathing hard after the long climb, his ravaged right leg aching from the effort.

"Murphy, my goodness, man, come in." He held the door open as Murphy limped into the living room and almost fell into a well cushioned chair. Hitchcock poured a glass of brandy and handed it to the old man. "Must be important to get you up this old hill of ours. Drink some brandy, catch your breath and tell me all about it."

It was one of those strange relationships that develop between men sometimes. Murphy had been a lead-man working one of the rich drifts in Hitchcock's North Pass Mine a few years ago when a blast went off early, wrecking the man's right leg. They were using black powder and fuse cord, and the threat of what they called a "runner" was always present. Fusing generally burned about a foot in forty-five seconds or so. A runner was just that, burning hard and fast, blowing up the black powder before the men could get out of the way.

Hitchcock had tremendous respect for the man, saw to it that he had a pension, a place to live, and asked him for favors from time to time, such as keeping him informed of interesting happenings.

"Just saw two men get in a fight with a couple of Sheriff Lighthorse's deputies and an hour later those two drifters, well, one of them, beat the devil out of the sheriff. Just let him flop on the floor of the Lucky Lady, and took a table with Spike laughing about it."

Hitchcock was sure he knew who those two men were and for the first time in years felt the beginning pangs of fear. *Have to be the two men at the poker table. Why? Are they specifically looking to take out the sheriff or is there more to it? There have always been rumbles that someone would call in the marshals, but old Judge Olsen is well paid. He always wants more, but he's taken care of.*

Hitchcock was trying to work up a plan but it wasn't there. Could he use Murphy? A cripple? Yes, maybe he could. "You still stay in touch with some of your old crew, Murph?"

"Sure, and some of the new hard-rockers, too. These young-uns are fun to talk to. Not afraid of nothing, but not us old boys. They're all fired up over the union, the miner's union."

"I'm wondering who these two troublemakers are who have come to town, Murph. They may be here to cause trouble in the mines. Could be working for the cattlemen, you know. That water is ours, we need it for ore reduction, but the cattlemen are trying to cut us out."

Hitchcock poured them each another glass of brandy and settled down in a nearby chair. "Maybe you could see what you can find out. Be discreet, old friend, but find out who these tough guys are. You need anything? Pension holding up? Maybe a couple of double eagles would come in handy, eh?"

"Well, Mr. Hitchcock, if you insist." Murphy smiled. He pocketed the gold and hobbled out into the cold. "I'll keep you informed, sir."

"THERE'S A LOT MORE TO YOU TWO THAN JUST STARTING FIGHTS IN MY saloon." Spike Loring said after everyone got settled at a table. "There's also a level of expertise involved in the way you fight, Bull. Don't suppose you'd like to talk about this?" Loring wanted to bring up the questions that Slim wanted to ask but decided to save that one, for the time being.

"I learned to fight a long time ago, Spike. It just comes naturally," Bull said. He tried to smile but that ugly scar across his face destroyed the effort. *Is it time to let Pioche know who we are? Is this the right person, or maybe it should be Tom Blair?*

Bull Morrison had made these decisions many times over the years, but these first days in Pioche seemed different. They learned a lot, but they made several scenes, something that shouldn't be done if you wanted to gather information. *It's hard to remain discrete and unknown when you bluster into saloons and start fights with those you're investigating, Bull, old man.* Bull did his best to hold in a chuckle by looking away. *Damn but I do love a good fight.*

"What about you, Slim? You're mighty fast with that gun, awfully quick to back Bull, and have some interesting questions about who you're fighting." Spike spent hours watching people, saw every angle of society in his saloon and gambling parlor, and was fascinated by these two drifters. Were these questions because of that or did he have other reasons?

Bull Morrison made the decision without discussing it with Slim Calhoun. He looked at Slim, just nodded his head, slightly, and took a long drink of whiskey. "Before I get all involved in things I don't want to get involved in," Bull said, "I have a couple of questions for you."

"Good," Spike Loring said. "I think we might just be on

the same team."

"We'll soon know that," Slim said. "Looks like the sheriff is coming around. Hope Chago still has his gun and knife. I'll be right back." Slim walked up to the bar, saw the weapons behind the bar, and stepped up to the groggy sheriff. "You got a bad attitude, Sheriff, and you've got my partner all riled. Ain't good for him to get riled like that. You gonna make it home?"

"Get out of my way," Lighthorse said. He lurched the few steps to the bar and motioned Chago to get his gun and knife.

"Maybe in the morning, Sheriff," Slim said. "Time to go home."

Lighthorse spun on Slim but held up quickly when he found himself looking down the barrel of a big Colt. "Home, Sheriff, before things get even more ugly than they are." Slim didn't put the gun away until Lighthorse was all the way out the doors. Slim eased his way back to the table and poured a drink.

"That man's a slow learner, Bull. You'll be conducting classes again, I'm sure. Now, where were we?"

"We were about to let Spike know a little bit about us." Bull sat back in the chair, pulled the stump of a well-used cigar from his vest pocket and started chewing. "Why don't you do the honors?"

A quick look around the saloon, just to make sure there weren't extra ears out and about, and Slim cleared his throat with a quick sip of whiskey. "Guess the best place to start is to tell you we aren't speculators, Spike. I'd like to introduce you to U.S. Marshal Bull Morrison. I'm Deputy Marshal Slim Calhoun, and we're here to investigate some allegations of federal law breaking."

Spike Loring took a quick and deep breath, grabbed his glass and drained it. The saloon owner looked back and forth at the two men. To say he had been taken by surprise would be hard to deny. "Oh, brother mine, was I ever wrong." He started laughing, softly at first, and it built to full bore gayety. Spike quickly refilled the glass and kept looking back and forth at the two marshals.

"I'm a gambling man, Bull, and I would have lost my shirt on this one. The mines have been in a fight with ranchers in the area for some time over water. Ranchers need it, miners need it, and there's only so much available. Human nature says both sides feel their fair share is more than the other fellow's. I was sure you were troublemakers brought to town by the ranching consortium." The laughter rang through the half empty saloon. "Who knows this besides me?"

Bull was trying his best to smile and the ugly scar fought him off, but he did get a good chuckle out of the scene. "Nobody but you, Spike." He looked at the smiling Slim and took a long drink. "You mentioned sides, Spike. Still want to talk with us?"

"To see Lighthorse taken out of office, to see Sandy Hitchcock stripped clean, to see a level of honesty and fair play invade our little camp? Yes, I do believe I do. I find it interesting that you told me all this but didn't tell Tom Blair. Blair's one of the men fighting for changes along with Three-Finger Daws."

"Three-Finger is all talk, Spike. He knows who is involved and where to look for criminal activity and doesn't do anything about it except talk." Bull looked to Slim for back-up.

"That and the fact he is the city marshal gives us too many questions. Tom Blair seems to be determined but not quite willing to get fully involved. Maybe a touch of fear and that should be considered. The men we're investigating, when Bull isn't starting fights in your saloon, are known to be dangerous, the least of whom is the sheriff."

"You've got your work cut out. Sandy Hitchcock runs

enough stock fraud conspiracies to keep several investigators busy, his bank finances considerable shady projects, including not making loans and other banking available to ranching interests, and fighting for all the water in the area for his mills. Word is more than one judge is on his payroll."

"And Spike Loring?" Bull quietly asked.

Spike smiled. "Yup. And Spike Loring. I'm not involved in the scams and conspiracies, as such, Bull. No, I'm not. On the other hand, I've not raised my hand or voice against most of the activities, either, but if there are those willing to, I would join them. Timid? You might say so. I say careful of my best interests, which happen to be this saloon and hotel. I also am very aware that Pioche has a bad reputation and people are afraid of investing in business or land because of it."

"Will you keep this under your hat until we make it well known who we are and why we're here?" Slim asked.

Spike nodded. "Good," Bull said. "This has been one hell of a day. How about joining us at Ginny Whipple's for breakfast? Late breakfast."

"See you there. Get a good night's sleep. Can I make part of our deal that you don't start too many more fights in my saloon?"

Laughter followed Loring up the stairs to his office, and Bull and Slim to their rooms.

CHAPTER 9

"Get Boots Kindle over here, Cranston," Sandy Hitchcock said. "For the first time, I think this angry mine owner might want to talk with the Miners' Union. I think those trouble-makers are gun-slingers hired by the ranchers." The obese gentleman had a nasty look on his face and his snicker would have been a warning to anyone other than Buster Cranston.

Two major economic powerhouses needing the same natural resource was a fight that probably started before history was being written. Agriculture and mining, both producing valued and needed products and both using large amounts of precious water. The age-old battle didn't give a damn if Pioche was being over-run by outlaws.

Hitchcock knew the value, understood how much it meant to his mines and to the ranchers. Get a fight started and he knew too, that he would win. The ace up his sleeve just happened to be a judge. If the miners' union thought their mines might be shut down by the ranchers who brought in gunslingers, the war would start.

Buster Cranston was the foreman at the North Pass Mine, also the muscle behind Hitchcock's empire. Many of the employees were more apt to be found knocking heads than searching underground for gold and silver.

"There was a big rumble at the Lucky Lady last night. Sheriff got the hell beat out of him. Those goons, Benson and Owens got whipped on bad, too."

"Heard all about it, Buster. Heard the two got all cozy with Blair and Loring, too. Time to go to war, my friend. Find Kindle and get him over here."

Cranston left the mine office and walked down several blocks to the Miners' Union Hall located in a two-story rock building half a block from the court house. Kindle was standing near a pool table, beer mug in hand, talking with Seamus O'Neil, mine boss for Tom Blair's Gold Strike Mine.

Many eyes turned when Cranston walked in. Two mine bosses in the union hall? Talking to the union boss? It was their building and they were proud of it. The hall featured a fully stocked bar, pool and card tables, and a few over-stuffed chairs scattered around. The upper floor held offices and a large meeting room. Meetings between the union and mines usually took place on neutral ground.

"Most interesting," Kindle said. He had the look of ironic smugness on his face. "The mine bosses of two leading mines want to talk with the union boss. About time your handlers have seen the light. One at a time or do you want to gang up on me?"

There was little humor in the way it was said and one could feel the tension. Many of the men tightened up, some slowly moved toward where Kindle was facing off with the supers, and it took a wave of Kindle's hand to put a calm to the air.

"Hitchcock wants to see you, now," Cranston said. He gave the union man a glare and turned to O'Neil. "What are you doing here?"

"I'll go where I want, Cranston." O'Neil was straight out of the deep Cornish mines and stood with his miners, not necessarily with Tom Blair, although Blair's miners were treated far better than Hitchcock's. "Got a problem with that?"

"Hmph," Cranston said. "Better get up to the office, Kindle. Hitchcock doesn't like someone being late."

"I work on my clock, not his. Hurry back to your master and tell him I'll try to drop by later. Remember, Buck-o, this is the Miners' Union Hall, not fit for gentry." He nodded to O'Neil and walked away.

Seamus O'Neil turned and headed out the door leaving Buster Cranston alone at the pool table. Anger flushed his face, but he knew he couldn't do or say anything inside that building. The fires of Hades would be tame compared to angry miners defending their space.

"That's what he said, Mr. Hitchcock. Don't know what he and O'Neil were talking about. By the way, I saw Deputy Thompson and that slimy murderer Pizon Oakley riding in when I left the hall."

"Pizon is a hired killer, Buster. Lighthorse is probably bringing him in to get the drifters. Letting him do it might be the better way. To hell with Kindle and O'Neil and their uppity ways. I'm going down to the Silver Crystal if anyone asks. Going to sign some stock certificates for those fine gentlemen from Boston. I love Boston money."

How soon the fight over water was replaced by the search for more money.

"WELL, DON'T YOU LOOK DANDY," PIZON OAKLY LAUGHED. "ALL bruised and cut up. I assume the other feller's dead." The killer enjoyed calling attention to other's flaws and problems and prodded as often as possible.

"Go to hell, Oakley, and sit down. I need your services, not your foul mouth. There are two men who rode into town and I want them eliminated. One's stocky, bad scar across his face, and mean. The other's tall and thin, quick as hell with his gun. Kill 'em, Oakley. Take Thompson with you. He knows what they look like."

"I think you know what they look like, Sheriff. That why you don't want to go with me?" Pizon would prod the sheriff until the gold flashing sheriff pulled down on him, something Pizon knew would not happen. He was sure the sheriff was involved with Hitchcock in holding those letters hostage. Lighthorse spat some tobacco juice at the brass spittoon, growled something inaudible, and left the office.

Pizon forced the sheriff to take a step around him to get to the door, rocked back on his heels, and glared at the man. *If I shoot you, I can't get those papers and you know it. I'll get you alone some day, Lighthorse, and then I'll get them.*

He turned back to the deputy. "Don't get in my way, Johnson. In fact, don't come with me. Find something important to do like having a chat with one of ladies at Gypsy's." He made a lewd move at the stove, laughed, and walked out of the office. *Since Lighthorse didn't mention a price on these heads I'm chasing, I'll make my own price. Five hundred dollars for each head and a bundle of letters should be a fair price.*

"Good food and good company, Bull. Glad you invited me." Spike Loring had enlightened Morrison and Calhoun about the political intricacies of Lincoln County and the dangers that lurked the streets of Pioche.

"Our pleasure, Spike. You are aware of the danger being seen with us is, I assume."

"Oh, yes. We have caught the eyes of many, sitting here in the middle of the morning." He swung his head and took in a quick breath. "Pizon Oakley riding right through town and with one of Lighthorse's deputies too. Watch out for that man at all costs, Bull. He's a hired killer that Lighthorse uses to eliminate his enemies and the enemies of those he answers to."

Bull and Slim gave Pizon Oakley a good look up and down and burned his face into their memories. "Oakley, Slim. Pizon Oakley. I've seen paper on him. Arizona Territory, California, and Utah Territory. Busy man."

"His face is carved up almost as bad as yours," Slim said. "Won't forget that face. The way you said that, Spike, makes me believe he doesn't live in Pioche."

"Spends most of his time at the hot springs south of town. Runs a small saloon and whore house. Miners love the place on their days off. Doesn't do my business any good at all. Pizon has made the place open to all and talk is it's an outlaw's nest down there."

They said goodbye to Loring as Ginny Whipple returned with Bull's change. "Heard some interesting stories about you two. You're mannerly and kind in here but the town is saying you are very nasty when you're drinking." There was a hint of humor in the way she said it that made Slim chuckle.

"Nasty? No, not us. It's just that we don't tolerate bad manners, Ginny," Slim said. He gave her a smile and a wink. "Keep your ears open and you might hear even more stories in the next few days. What's on the menu for tonight? Those steaks last night were the perfect end for a long hard day."

"Roast shoulder of pork, big guy. I'll save a whole one for you two." Her tinkle of laughter followed her across the café.

"The reputation of this whole area is well deserved, I think," Slim said. "I think it might be time for us to have another chat with Three-Finger Daws, Bull. He's bound to have heard of your escapades last night."

"Not funny, Calhoun. But, you're right."

Spike ducked back in. "Forgot to say thanks and also to tell you that the ranchers will be at the courthouse later to-day. You might want to meet a couple. This water fight will get nasty soon."

"See you later, Spike. No talk." Bull said.

Spike Loring laughed, nodding his head, and watched the two marshals walk out of the restaurant. *I wonder if anything frightens that man. If the mines hold up and those two get the criminal element under control, I might need to add another level to my hotel.*

The city marshal's office was half a block from the court-house but on the other side of the street. "I think it might be better if we leave a note with Jimmy Lassen instead of just walking right into Daws' office, Bull. If his attitude is wrong, it's sure gonna look funny."

"Right now, Slim, I'm the one with an attitude. Lighthorse obviously called in a hit on us. I don't care who knows that we're marshals. It might put the snakes in hiding, but we'll know if anyone is with us. This is gonna be a big fight all the way and we're gonna be big targets." He got a nod from Slim but wasn't through.

"This new problem of a water war between the mines and ranchers is gonna gum up the works, too. The criminal ele-ment loves that kind of war. They can profit from both camps. We are in for it, I think."

"Yup,' Slim said. "I think we are. That's Daws' office, right over there."

They started across the street just as Pizon Oakley walked out of the sheriff's office. "Get back, Slim," Bull said, pushing the two into a shaded doorway. "That's Oakley." They watched him walk all the way down the street and into the Silver Crystal. "That saloon draws 'em in, Slim. Let's see Marshal Daws and then have a cold one at the Silver Crystal." Both men had smiles on their faces, Bull looking for a fight, Slim looking to back him up.

They stepped out from the doorway and were hailed by a large man across the street. "That's Jacob Overby, the blacksmith," Slim said. "Good morning, Overby, how are our critters doing?"

"Just fine, Mr. Calhoun, just fine. For a couple of speculators, you have made quite a name for yourselves." He turned to Bull. "Especially you, Mr. Morrison. It's not often that a land speculator comes to town and gets in fights with the sheriff, twice in the same day."

"Sheriff forgot his manners, sir," Bull said. No smile. No friendliness. "Have a good day, sir, and keep our animals well." Bull turned to Slim, nodded, and walked off toward the marshal's office.

"Testy gentleman," Overby said.

"It takes time to get to know him, sir. He had a rough day yesterday."

"I heard a rumor that instead of being speculators you actually work for the ranchers in the valley. That you're here to stir up trouble."

"Well, most rumors are just that, Mr. Overby. I wouldn't put much thought to that one. Have a good day," Slim said. He caught up with Bull just outside Daws' office door. "Just found out people think we work for the ranchers and their water fight. Might account for some of what the sheriff has done and said."

"Yup," Bull said. He was about to say something else when

Three-Finger Jack Daws opened the office door. "Good morning, Marshal, we were about to visit you."

"Good, because I was about to try to find you. Sheriff Lighthorse visited me early this morning. Wants me to arrest you."

"Good," Bull said. "Let's step inside and talk about that. I think I might want you to arrest the sheriff."

The office was spare to a fault with just a wood stove, desk, and one chair. A gun case hung on the wall with one rifle and one shotgun in it, and there was a door opposite the front door that may have led to holding cells. "Don't get many visitors I take it," Slim said. There was a coffee pot on a shelf, not filled and on the stove, and one clean tin cup hanging on a hook.

The small pot belly stove stood cold in the center of the room and there was no obvious heat source nearby. "Don't spend a lot of time in here." Daws said. "What do you mean arrest the sheriff? You started the fight according to witnesses."

"Which fight?" Bull said. Calhoun laughed and caught Bull trying to hide one of those ugly smiles of his. "I think you need to sit down, Marshal. We do have something to talk about." Bull said.

"Yes, I think we do," Three-Fingers said. "If you are hired guns for the ranchers I'm telling you right now, leave town. Pioche has enough problems without your kind mucking things up more." Daws settled into the one chair and glowered at Bull and Slim.

Bull looked at Slim, looked over to Daws, and reached in his shirt pocket for a half-chewed cigar. "To be truthful, Marshal, we are hired guns, as you very well know. Hired by the government of this fine country to straighten a few people out. The thing is, we weren't hired by the ranchers, we weren't hired by the mine operators. Seems as though we were hired many years ago by the federal government You know damn well that I'm U.S. Marshal Bull Morrison and he is my deputy, Slim Calhoun." He chewed off a chunk of that black twisted cigar and leaned over the desk. "Got it?"

"I know but you can't be walking around town beating up on people." Daws said. It was almost a whine He slumped back in his chair. "Finally. That whore of a judge finally sent us some help and that help starts more trouble than the outlaws."

"And you want to arrest that help because the outlaw sheriff asked you to?" Bull was storming around the office. "If you have the least sense, you'll see this picture is hung crooked. You got your priorities twisted, mister, and I'm about to untie the knot."

Slim tightened up knowing that Bull was getting riled. "Understand something, Marshal Daws," Slim said. He knew he had to start talking or Bull would destroy the building. "We are here and we are going to do our job. If you get in the way, so be it. If you have other places to be, it would be best. If you're not with us we will act as if you're among the criminals and you will go down hard."

Bull Morrison was fully under control and was using his anger to his advantage. "Among the things said to us by you, Marshal, was that you wanted Pioche cleaned up. Another thing you said was how Federal Judge John T. Olsen was taking bribes. You," he said, and jammed a finger in Daws's chest, "better make up your mind right this minute. You work with us or you get the hell out of the way. I have the authority to put you in your own jail, to arrest those I feel are breaking the law, to conduct this investigation. Do not challenge me again."

Daws sat in his chair, didn't move, even flinch, or say a word. It was several seconds, with both marshals glaring at him, that he found his voice. "Sheriff Lighthorse is an outlaw, Marshal, but you look and act like one. I've come close to drawing down on Lighthorse, I've threatened him with arrest, but never done it."

"Why?" Bull thundered the question at the man.

"The sheriff and the whole damn camp has you buffaloed, Marshal," Slim Calhoun said. "You have as much or more knowledge of illegal activities in this town as we do and you've done nothing but wish that marshals would be sent to clean it up. Wearing that badge carries a heavy burden of responsibility, Daws."

"Time to grow into that badge, Marshal," Bull said. Bull and Slim were good at double-teaming and they were not going to let up on this man who wants to be called marshal. Bull kept up the attack. "With us or not, we are taking over this office. As U.S. Marshal, I have that authority. See to it there is wood for the stove and coffee for the pot. Get more chairs in here and make damn sure those cells back there are ready for customers."

"Questions, Marshal?" Slim asked.

"I'm with you," is all Daws said. "Just tell me what to do."

"That will start happening soon, sir. Soon indeed," Bull Morrison said. He looked around the bare office and back at Daws. "You are the only local law, Marshal. I want to see you help clean up this little camp." Bull turned to Slim. "Silver Crystal time?"

CHAPTER 10

PIZON OAKLEY STRODE DOWN THE MAIN STREET OF PIOCHE DARING anyone to alter his straight-line course. The town's reputation of lawlessness was in the man's eyes. It wasn't the organized crimes of Sandy Hitchcock that created the reputation, it was killers and burglars, card sharps and knife men, that drove the news accounts. Death was writ large on Oakley's face.

Women and children, miners and riff-raff ducked out of his way. Scarred, angry, scowling, and not giving a tinker's damn what anyone thought, he was after blood and to hell with the world. The Silver Crystal was busy at mid-day when he walked up to the bar.

"Cold beer," he growled at the barman. Sandy Hitchcock and Rolf Pendergrass were sitting at a vacant poker table, but Pizon couldn't see either of the two saddle bums he was looking for. He would have felt better if he could take a shot at Hitchcock, but that wasn't to be.

"Seen those two troublemakers come to town?" He asked the barman when he got his beer. "Hear they stirred up some dust in here."

"Whipped on the sheriff, one of them did," the barman chuckled. "Never seen Sheriff Lighthorse back down as fast as he did. Never put up a fight."

"Spineless bastard," Pizon said. "I see Hitchcock but not Buster. Cranston been around?"

"Coming in the door now," the barman said.

Pizon motioned for the mine boss to join him. "Do you ever actually go into that mine that pays you? Ain't even got any rock dust under your fingernails." Cranston was probably the only person that Oakley might consider a friend. "Lookin' for them two drifters kicking up trouble. Seen 'em?"

"Nope, but I'd like to see that big one. Blind-sided me, Pizon. Gonna kill him on sight."

"I'd rather you leave him to me. Money and all." Pizon said. "Maybe I'll wander up to the Gold Strike. Join me?"

"They spend more time at the Lucky Lady than anywhere. Seem to have an in with Spike Loring."

THREE-FINGER JACK DAWS SAT RIGID IN HIS CHAIR AFTER BULL Morrison's comment. He looked back and forth at Bull and Slim and didn't say a word for a long time. "I still find it hard to believe that you are really here." He almost gasped, shaking his head.

"What did you mean by that comment about a judge?" Bull stood next to the stove and leaned toward Daws. "Were you talking about Federal Judge Olsen in Salt Lake?"

"Who else?" Daws said. "I truly believe that some people here in Lincoln County carry the man on their payroll. Petitions have been sent but are turned away for one reason or another. I'm sure John T. Olsen works for Sandy Hitchcock and the criminals in Pioche."

"I don't suppose you have any kind of evidence to back that kind of claim?" Slim Calhoun was far from being a saint, but a charge of this kind against a sitting federal judge was hard to swallow, particularly when it was that judge who was responsible for you being where you were.

I've never met Judge Olsen but Daws seems to believe what he's saying. It would be one hell of a black mark on the judiciary. We're sworn to protect federal judges and courts, and this would create a serious problem. Me and old Bull gotta work careful on this one.

"You don't suppose that old codger got his angel's wings do you? Saw the bad ways he was headin?" Bull said. "It is because of Olsen that we're here, Daws. That's a strong charge, one we will have to follow up, and it is certain to have an effect on our investigation."

Three-Finger Daws hadn't moved in his chair and just continued to stare at the stove. "I'm not much of a drinking man but I could sure use a drink right now. Hitchcock brags about owning Olsen, has kept Boots Kindle and the Miner's Union from being strong by manipulating the judge, has water rights issues in his favor by way of Judge Olsen."

"Sounds good, Daws, but we got to have a whole damn carload of evidence to take down a federal judge." Slim was already working on how to proceed. "You're the town marshal, Lighthorse is the sheriff, but I haven't heard anyone talk about a local judge. A justice of the peace or a county judge. Who hears your cases, Jack?"

"Dewey Schaffer is justice of the peace and Greg Mallard is district judge for three counties, so he's only in town every few weeks. Schaffer handles most of everything except for major crimes, and even then he hears the evidence first."

"I assume he's elected," Bull said. "Owned too?"

"He's an old man, fought in the big war between the states, fought in Indian wars, fought in Mexico. I doubt he's owned, but he does accept favors from the mining crowd, and I don't know if the ranchers even offer favors. He's a crusty old man, quick to anger."

"Sounds like an older Bull Morrison," Slim laughed. "I'd like to meet this man. Where does he drink?"

"Doesn't. Not even a sip of wine. His home is a small cabin tucked up in Ruby Gulch. He has goats, hogs, chickens, and a good kitchen garden. He lost his wife two years ago and is almost a hermit. Holds court on Monday every week."

"Doesn't sound like a man on the take, Slim. Let's take Mr. Daws for a drink at the Lucky Lady and see what else we can learn. I want to visit this justice of the peace, too. We can ride up Ruby Gulch later."

The idea of breaking up the Silver Crystal was put aside for the moment. Bull Morrison had to have a little time to digest all of what Daws had said. Judge Olsen on the take? Maybe they were on a chase put together by Judge Baker. Baker was senior judge for the entire west coast, but Olsen held forth in Utah and southern Nevada which almost stood alone in the federal judiciary.

The three men left the marshal's office and walked the short half block to the Lucky Lady Saloon. *Federal marshals. Damn me, I'm about to drink with two marshals. I really didn't believe them when they caught me in their room.* Daws was more than impressed but was worried about being with Bull, who scared the hell out of him. *Makes me one big target in the minds of a lot of people, but I've prayed for this day, petitioned for their coming. This isn't the time to duck and run. Time for me to stand up, and I ain't done that in a long time.*

Only Three-Finger Jack Daws noticed Bull Morrison's shoulders being a bit more squared up, his head sitting a touch higher as they filed through the bat-wing doors of the saloon. He couldn't have any way of knowing that for Bull, walking into a saloon was like walking into a warm living room. He was home.

Spike Loring watched them walk up to the bar and knew that death would soon foul the air of the place. It was Bull who was first to see Pizon Oakley standing at the end of the bar with Buster Cranston.

"Careful, Slim. Troubled waters flowing at flood stage ahead." Bull gently shoved Three-Finger Jack Daws more off to one side and Slim Calhoun moved slightly wide on the other side as they walked to the bar. Jimmy Lassen was behind the oak planks and saw the heavy clouds spread across Bull's face.

"Best have a bottle, three glasses, and three cold beers to wash the whiskey down," Bull said. His voice was loud and carried down the bar, bounced off the back bar, and rumbled through the smoke-filled air. "Swamper must not have worked last night, Jimmy. Place has a distinctly bad smell this morning. Something putrid near the end of the bar, I think."

Pizon Oakley swung around, his hand reaching for that heavy iron hanging at his side. Bull didn't wait for the move, took one step down the bar and smashed a fist into Pizon's face, knocking him into Buster Cranston. Pizon was still fighting to get his gun out when Bull rammed another fist into his face, driving him to the floor.

Pizon was not a large man and the two heavy fists to his face took him out of the fight. The gun came free, and Bull kicked it across the saloon floor with one foot and fell on Pizon, driving fists, knees, and his head into man. Slim took two steps down the bar, revolver in hand, aimed at Buster Cranston. "Their fight, Mister. Not ours." Cranston glared but couldn't do anything but watch Pizon get the hell beat out of him.

Blood flowed freely from Pizon's nose and ears, his lips

were split open and bleeding, and his eyes rolled back into his head. The bad man was down and out. "Ain't got no fight in him, Slim. These people were wrong. He ain't no mean killer. Never swung a fist," Bull said.

Bull outweighed the killer by a considerable amount and the fight was one sided for the short amount of time it lasted. Bull jumped to his feet, the nasty scar across his face bright red from the effort, and jerked Pizon to his feet. The man was groggy and bloody, and Bull shoved him into the bar.

"Lighthorse is paying you to kill me, Pizon Oakley. Well? What do you have to say about that?" He slapped the man, opened handed. Oakley didn't say anything and Bull slapped him again. "How much is he paying?"

Oakley couldn't talk. He was unconscious and pinned to the bar by Bull. "Lighthorse sure picked the wrong one, eh Slim? Would have been nice to know how much we're worth, though." Morrison turned his attention to Buster Cranston. "You part of the deal, mining man?"

Bull let go of Pizon Oakley and watched him crumble to the floor. He stepped up close to Cranston. "I asked you a question, mining man. You part of Lighthorse's deal?"

"No," Cranston said. "I'm just having a friendly drink." All the big talk was gone and some of the pain from his own fracas with the marshal returned. Anger and frustration spread as a tornado when he saw his own knife hanging at Bull's waist. *I have to kill him. Have to.*

"Then get the hell out of here before you get hurt," Bull said. Buster Cranston stepped back, turned and walked out of the saloon without looking back.

"That's a pitiful sight," Slim said and put the revolver back in its holster. "Ain't a lot of man left there, Bull." He took the drink that three-Finger Daws handed him. Bull already had his down and was reaching for his beer.

"Was that the third or fourth fight you've started in my saloon?" Spike Loring asked. "You just beat the hell out of the meanest and most dangerous man in Pioche, my friend. Lighthorse is going to be in a rage when Cranston runs to tell him." Loring motioned for a couple of men to drag Oakley's inert body out of the saloon.

"Good," Bull said. "Let's take a ride, Slim. I want to meet this Dewey Schaffer. Spike, you and Three-Fingers have a lot to talk about while we're gone. I'm going to depend on both of you to do what's right and that includes cleaning up this camp." He turned and marched toward the swinging doors. "Felt good, Slim. Does a man good to whup on someone after a big breakfast."

Jacob Overby reluctantly gave them directions to Ruby Gulch. *I should have sent them packing. Bastards are gonna either offer old man Schaffer a bribe on behalf of the cattlemen or beat him up. Shoulda just sent 'em off. I gotta let the sheriff know where they're heading.*

The road led the marshals into the mountains covered in piñon, cottonwood, and aspen with a fork that led them into Ruby Gulch, far more a sparkling narrow valley with an active creek flowing down the middle. The mountains were rough edged, rocky and steep, pock marked where prospectors blew holes in outcrops, looking for that elusive gold. Prospectors called them coyote holes and more than one had become home to losers.

There was meadow on either side of the creek with grasses and brush. Someone had taken the time and effort to plant fruit trees about and there was a small herd of goats watched over by a large white dog. The dog was spending time watching the men on horses, too.

"Hell, Slim, I'd be a hermit, too if I lived up here. Stream for water, timber for fire."

"Yup, Bull, all of that, but you wouldn't have anyone to fight with." Both were chuckling as they followed the two-track into the forest at the far end of Ruby Gulch and found a cabin with smoke slowly curling from the native rock chimney.

"Looks like the old justice is home." The two rode up to a cedar pole fence stretched across the front. There was a rack to tie off near a gate. "Hello, the house. We come in peace, Judge." Morrison and Slim sat their horses waiting to be invited to step down.

After a brief amount of time the door opened and a bulky man stepped out. "Come in peace? Then come on in. I'm Dewey Schaffer, late of Boston, Mass."

"I'm pleased to meet you, Judge Schaffer. I'm U.S. Marshal Bull Morrison and this fine gentleman is my deputy, Slim Calhoun. May we bend your ear for a time?"

"Marshals, eh? Well, well." He held the door open and the two walked into a warm and nicely furnished cabin. "My, my. Last time I met a marshal was down in the territories. A couple a real nasty men in the eyes of the outlaws. You got that kind of reputation, Marshal?"

Schaffer was a jovial man, and Bull noticed right away that he had had a rough life. He stood almost six feet tall and weighed well over two hundred pounds. His nose had been broken more than once, his large hands were rough from work and fighting, and he had a crooked smile from split lips.

"More than likely, sir. Seems as though I'm looking at a man who has stood for something important more than once."

"Carried a badge in El Paso, Marshal. And in Tulsa. And in

Denver, before I discovered that being a JP was easier on the body. All that was after a good many years doing army duty."

"Judge Advocate Corps?" Bull asked.

"No. I'm infantry all the way, Marshal. Left the army as a colonel. They were afraid to make me a general."

"So that's our future," Slim laughed. "Just might be looking forward to that. Justice of the peace? Yes sir."

Schaffer had been busy stoking the fire and getting a pot of coffee boiling. "Let's have a cup and talk, then, shall we? Pioche has been in need of federal marshal visitations for some time. Who sent you? Surely it wasn't Judge Olsen."

"You're the second person to tell us that, Judge. Actually, Judge Olsen sent a request to our district judge who sent us. This is our first venture into Pioche and southern Nevada. We're looking into some serious federal crimes including mining scams, banking scams, and now, we find out, water issues."

"You've got a busy schedule, boys. I can probably add to that," the old man chuckled. "I've been praying for the day you would come. John T. Olsen is as criminal in his actions as Sandy Hitchcock is in his. Welcome to Pioche."

Schaffer sat back and looked the two marshals up and down. "Old man Pioche found some gold and silver and founded this camp, and the Indians ran everyone off. What you're seeing is the second coming of Pioche. Maybe this time it'll be the marshals to run everyone off."

"Only the bad ones, Judge," Slim chuckled. "That's quite a bunch of goats you have out there."

Schaffer got up and went to a cupboard and pulled out a plate. "This is one reason, Marshal." He cut several slices of firm white cheese. "White cheddar, Marshal. Have some." Bull took two leaving one each for Slim and the judge.

"I vote for the goats," Bull said. "Getting late, Slim, gotta go."

BUSTER CRANSTON WAS SITTING IN A CANE BACK CHAIR NEXT TO THE pot-belly stove listening to Harvey Lighthorse scream obscenities. "You just stood by and watched Pizon get whipped? Then walked out and left him with that butcher? What kind of man are you?"

Cranston stepped forward fast, his fist swinging wide and hard, catching the sheriff solidly on the jaw, sending him sprawling to the floor. "Don't never talk to me like that, Lighthorse. I'll shoot you dead if you ever do again."

Cranston turned to leave when Jacob Overby hurried into the office. "Sheriff! What the hell?"

"Got himself a bad mouth, Jacob. What do you want?" Buster Cranston poured a cup of coffee, not even looking at the man on the floor. Lighthorse slowly climbed back to his feet, glared at Cranston, almost went for the heavy iron but changed his mind when he saw Overby looking at him.

"What do you want, Overby?" He said. He slumped in his chair behind his desk and found a flask in a drawer. No longer self-assured, no longer filled with self-importance, Lighthorse had been whipped by two men in two days. He could feel his world crumbling around him and the fear tasted of bile.

"Come to tell you about a couple of strangers might be looking to do some harm to Dewey Schaffer. What the hell happened here?"

"None of your damn business. What are you talking about?"

Overby spent more time with mules than men, didn't take nonsense from them, but this? The sheriff bloody and bruised, Buster Cranston not offering help? Overby wanted to turn and leave but also was sure harm was about to come to Schaffer.

Overby took little time telling them about the two men

he believed to be hired gunmen out to do harm to the justice of the peace. "I should have sent them packing but came to tell you instead. Sure as I'm standing here, they're gonna do harm, Sheriff."

"They already have," Lighthorse mumbled. "All right, Overby, I'll take care of it. Go on back to your stinking mules." He looked at Cranston as Overby shuffled out. "Get out, Cranston." Lighthorse stood up and walked back toward the holding cells to find deputies Benson and Owens.

"Got some work for you," he said. "Those bastards that whipped on you are making a move to hurt or kill Justice of the Peace Schaffer. Want you to ride up there and kill them. No arrests, boys. Kill those two on sight."

"Thought you already had them killed, Harvey. Didn't you send Pizon Oakley after those two?"

"Oakley isn't the man we thought he was. That big one, they call him Bull, beat him senseless according to Buster Cranston. Cranston, the cur he is, just stood there and watched Pizon go down. You kill those two."

Both men were still suffering from the abuse they took from Bull and Slim and had ugly smiles on their faces as they walked from the office. "From the condition of Lighthorse's face I'd say somebody whipped on him this morning. Think he and Cranston got into it?" Benson was almost laughing, thinking about it.

"He's gonna have a sore jaw for a while, I think." Larry Owens said. "The big stranger's got into it with him twice, bested him twice, and now Cranston? That boy's gonna be carrying some serious anger for a long time."

It was afternoon and warming nicely as the two rode from town and into the western mountains. "Looking forward to killing that big one, Owens. Ain't never had no man do that to me. Gonna kill him long and slow." Billy Benson was a sadistic killer, seldom got into gun fights or even fights. He was the kind to sneak up on his prey and subdue then torture.

"Word is, those two work for the cattle ranchers and are here to put Sandy Hitchcock out of business. They're hired guns, Benson, they beat the hell out of us, whipped Lighthorse, and now, beat up on Pizon Oakley. We need to just ride in and start shooting. Don't wait for nothing."

"What about Schaffer? Gotta be careful." Benson said.

"Why? If Schaffer gets in the way of a bullet, so what? We'll just say we were too late and those two had already killed him. No, sir. We just ride in and start shooting. Don't want to give those two any chance."

CHAPTER 11

"TALK YOU BOYS INTO STAYING FOR SUPPER? SHOT A COUPLE OF SAGE hens before you got here and can roast 'em up for us. Have plenty of beans and spuds to go with 'em." Dewey Schaffer hadn't had long talks with interesting men for a long time and didn't want to lose this chance for more.

"Mighty kind of you, Judge, but we'd better be getting back to town. Still have a few people we haven't had a chance to talk to." Bull Morrison didn't want to leave but didn't want to have to ride back to Pioche in the black of night, either. "I hope this won't be our only visit to your lovely valley. Or to your courtroom, either."

"Feel free to come visit any time you want. If I can help with your investigation, please ask. Some of the people who have been hurt, honestly, have asked for the hurt. Stupid people fall first for these scams, but even so, the scam is wrong, the people doing the scamming are wrong, and I'm glad you're here."

"Thank you, Judge," Slim said. "We'll do our best to keep you advised." The marshals rode out of the homestead slowly, enjoying the late afternoon sun and shadows playing across the little valley. "Could almost taste roasted sage hen, Bull."

"Yup," was all the big marshal said. "The notes we got from Judge Baker in San Francisco say almost the same things Three-Finger Daws, Spike Loring, and now, Judge Schaffer say. We know who the criminals are and we know what crimes have been committed. Our only job seems to be proving all of that."

"Simple, right, Bull?" They chuckled thinking about the rather monumental task in front of them. Slim stood up in the stirrups, bringing his horse to a stop. "Looks like a couple of riders coming this way, Bull. They're coming fast." He was pointing at rolling dust a mile in front of them.

"Only the blacksmith knew we were coming out here," Bull said. "Let's get off the trail and see who this might be." They rode thirty yards or so into a stand of pine and aspen and waited in the shadows for the riders. A small stream dribbled its way through the trees to join the creek running the length of the valley.

"Don't think this would be Overby," Slim said. "He is among those who think we're hired guns for the cattlemen, but he doesn't strike me as one who would look to kill us."

"Might have told somebody we were coming out here. He gave us directions, remember," Bull said. The two pulled their rifles, checked the loads, and watched two riders emerge from a small cloud of dust.

"That's those two deputies we tangled with," Bull said. "Let's mess up their party, Slim." He put the spurs to his horse, charging out of the trees right at Billy Benson who was in the lead. Slim had his horse right behind and swerved to charge Larry Owens. The two deputies were taken by complete surprise and tried to shy away from the charge.

Bull drove his horse into Benson's, swung the rifle barrel and knocked Benson to the ground. The deputy fell into the little creek and flailed around in the mud. Bull was off his horse and jumped on the deputy before the man could collect himself. Fist after fist pounded Benson's face until the deputy lay still in the cold mud. Bull grabbed the man's revolver and got to his feet, brushing mud, leaves, and other debris away.

"Get up," he bawled, grabbing the killer by his coat and jerking him up. Benson's legs weren't going to hold him and Bull just let him fall back into the creek.

Owens saw Slim coming hard, turned his horse harder and set his spurs. The chase lasted about fifty yards at best as Slim's horse was much faster. Slim saw Owens reach for his gun, turn, and fire as they rode through sage and other brush. Slim felt the bullet drive through his boot but stayed in the saddle. He brought the horse to a fast stop, pulled the rifle up, despite the pain in his foot, and put a heavy chunk of lead through the middle of Owens' back.

The man was flung from the saddle and tumbled into the dirt, dead. "Didn't want to do that," Slim mumbled. He brought his horse near the body and looked back at Bull. "Took one in the foot, Bull. I'm out of the fight," he hollered. "Owens is dead."

"Good. My man's not much good at fighting." He led his horse in one hand and all but dragged Benson with the other to where Slim still sat on his horse. "Watch this jasper, Slim, and I'll gather the horses for the ride back to town. You make that ride?"

"I'll make it. Gonna be out of action for a spell, I think. Might want to send for help."

"No, we'll be fine," Bull said. He gathered the outlaw's horses, tied the dead Owens to his, tied the still groggy Benson to his, and the four rode off at a walk into the gathering dusk.

"A fair hunt, I'd say." Bull joshed, jabbed Benson with a rifle barrel, and tried his best to smile. "Think we should take these two to the sheriff's jail or Marshal Daws's?"

"Daws' for sure. Then, my dear friend, we need to find me a doctor."

"No whining, Slim. Ain't good for our image."

"YOU'RE THE TOWN DOCTOR, TOO?" SLIM WAS AMAZED WHEN ONE OF the men on the street directed them to Ginny Whipple's little café for treatment."

"Close as this camp has to one," she smiled. "Can you walk?"

"Nope and I'm feeling just a bit fuzzy, too. Gonna need help getting in there." He was still sitting tall in the saddle, but Ginny Whipple could see he wasn't focusing very well. Bull pulled his deputy down and helped him into the living quarters behind the café. Ginny handed Bull a knife with an almost saw blade on it.

"Need that boot cut off, Mr. Morrison," Ginny said. Bull handed the knife back, drew his own Bowie, and quickly had the boot off. "Gently, Mr. Morrison," Ginny said as Slim howled out his pain. "We want to save the foot."

"I'm going back to Daws' office, Slim." Morrison just shook his head and looked at the charming lady doctor. "Take care of this gentleman, please." Bull gave Ginny as good a smile as he could give, nodded to Slim, and walked out. *Puts a crimp in things for sure. Slim is good deciphering paperwork on these kinds of crimes. Best back-up I've ever had. He'll have to do all that work and I'll have to get him the paperwork. And he won't have my back.*

Three-Finger Jack Daws had Larry Owens' body laid out

on a cot in one cell and Billy Benson nursing head wounds and a massive headache in the other. "Many people in town are going to consider you heroes for this," Daws said.

"Sounds like maybe you don't," Bull said.

"Man was shot in the back."

"After he shot my deputy. No wonder criminals run amok in this camp. You got your necessaries going the wrong way, Daws. You were standing right there when Benson told me that he was sent to kill us by the sheriff. Now you're questioning my deputy defending himself?" Bull was letting his anger grow and turned and walked out of the cell area and into the almost empty office area.

"You got a flask in your desk?" He hollered. *You better have. Question my deputy's intentions? I'm gonna start whipping on somebody real soon here.*

"Second drawer down on the right," Daws answered. He came into the office. "You're right, Bull. I wasn't thinking right. Is Slim going to be all right?"

"Slim's going to be fine. How do I get in touch with the district judge? I need to get word to him about this, need to get word to my judge in San Francisco, and I'd rather the whole camp doesn't know about it."

"Can't get Judge Mallard by wire. Have to send someone. The telegraph operator spends more time working for Hitchcock than he does the wire company. Talk to Spike Loring. He has men working for him who can get things like that done for you."

"All right, Daws. Now, you listen to me hard. I have arrested Billy Benson on numerous charges and am entrusting him to your care. Understand this, Daws. By law, you are required to see to it that Benson remains in that cell and is protected. Lighthorse is sure to demand his release and you better not cave to that. Tell me you understand."

"You're being mighty strong, Bull. I understand, and I'll take care of him. You'll need to have the undertaker come for Owens' body. He can't stay back there."

Bull spun and walked out the door. *Lighthorse will eat that man alive, damn it. Got to get word to Mallard and Baker. I think Slim was right, though. I might need to call in some help.*

"It was almost a parade, Sheriff, the way those strangers rode into town. Owens was draped across his saddle and Benson had his hands tied behind his back, slumped in the saddle and bleeding. Hell of a show," Toby Smith said. Smith was the gambler at the Silver Crystal and had rushed to tell the sheriff all about it. "Everybody at the Silver Crystal saw them."

"You'll see a real show when I find those two drifters. Then you'll see a show." Lighthorse was shaking with anger, or maybe some of it was fear. His words were big, his previous actions weren't. "Where'd they go?"

"Took Benson and Owens' body to Three-Finger Daws' office. The smaller of the two is at Whipple's. Looked like his foot was injured. Couldn't walk."

"All right, Smith. Thank you and get out. I got work to do." He was losing men faster than he could count. Pizon down and out, Owens lay dead, and Benson was behind bars. All he had left was Lonesome Gary Thompson. *Those two gotta die and I don't have any more men. I'll declare them killers, raise a posse, and we'll get 'em dead for sure.*

He left the office for the block-long walk to the Silver Crystal. The first thing the outlaw sheriff noticed was that Hitchcock wasn't there and neither was Buster Cranston. It would have been better if they had been, but he found a good crowd of men at the bar and tables.

Lighthorse stood at the bar, pulled his revolver and pounded on the bar. "Need your attention, men. Pioche is facing a serious situation and I need your help. Two killers have come to our little camp, probably on the payroll of the cattlemen. They killed deputy Owens just a few hours ago, wounded deputy Benson, and are getting help from Marshal Daws."

The sheriff's comments got loud response with calls for action, questions thrown, and the sheriff took his time getting things quieted down. It was this power, this control, that he loved almost as much as his gold. He spent the next ten minutes getting as many lies told as he could think of, getting as many men riled as possible, and called for the death of Morrison and Calhoun. "Two hundred dollars on the head of each, men. You see 'em, you kill 'em, and I'll pay you in gold."

Several men made a quick move for the doors and one of them was Quincy Pierce, the owner of the Lazy P cattle ranch located in the valley east of Pioche. He had been in town for meetings between cattlemen and miners earlier in the day. *Those men don't work for us. Don't know who they are but I've got to get word that there might be vigilantes coming our way.*

CHAPTER 12

"How bad is it, Ginny? Hurts like all get out." Slim was stretched out on a comfortable mattress watching the lovely lady work with wet cloths and medicines. *I've been busted up many times in this job, but never doctored by someone this pretty. One lucky law dog today. Gotta make this last.* "I've seen you carve beef in your kitchen. Sure hope I don't have to see you carving on me."

There was a tinkle of laughter from the petite lady, and she turned to look Slim in the face. "All but one of your toes are fine, Mr. Calhoun. I can't find the missing one. It's the little one on the right foot that's gone astray."

The bullet ripped through the boot severing Slim Calhoun's little toe. The pain had been intense, there was considerable bleeding, but overall, the wound wasn't that severe. "Mr. Morrison cut your boot free and ripped your stocking off. Let's see if we can find that toe, shall we?"

So casual, Slim thought, watching the lady. *As if many days a week she would go looking for someone's severed toe. She's ranch raised and there isn't much of anything that would bother this lady. She is one fine looking woman.* He also saw some ironic humor in the situation. How many deputy marshals have café owners searching for their missing toes?

The mangled digit was still in the stocking but Ginny Whipple was quick to say she was not capable of putting it back where it belonged. "The impact from the bullet separated the toe clean and quick," she said. She whipped her arm about as if using a cleaver.

"When Mr. Morrison ripped the stocking off, what little skin still held the toe ripped loose. There is almost no damage to the foot itself, so I'll just clean this wound, sew everything closed, and within just a few days, you'll be walking fine, Mr. Calhoun."

While she was working, she kept up a conversation. "It's all right to let me know when it hurts," she said. Her smile was all Slim needed. The pain of her stitching the wound closed wasn't as bad as he expected. "There are things going on with you and Mr. Morrison that I don't understand," she said. "I've heard some strange stories about you two."

"The whole town will know in short order, so I guess it's best if I tell you instead of letting the rumor mill build things up. Bull Morrison is not Mr. Morrison. He's U.S. Marshal Bull Morrison. I'm his deputy and we're here to do our best to eliminate the outlaw portion of the town's society."

"My goodness." Ginny sat back with a wide smile on her freckled face. She made that comment several times as she finished sewing up Slim's foot. "This should hurt, Mr. Calhoun. You aren't saying anything."

"Oh, it hurts, Ginny. It hurts plenty."

While she bandaged the wound, she said more than once that people were saying the two marshals were hired guns. "I wanted to like you because you've been so nice, so friendly, even helpful a time or two, but being hired killers frightened me to the bone."

"Bull said it earlier today, Ginny. We are hired guns, but we were hired by the government to go after crooks." He looked at his neatly wrapped foot. "That's a fine job."

"Let's see if you can put any pressure on that, Marshal Calhoun? Not much now. Let's not rip things apart."

He sat up and swung his legs over the side of the bed, easing himself up. Putting his weight on his left foot he slowly added weight to the injured foot. "Whoa, but that does hurt some." He added more weight then took it all off. "Don't think I can walk, though."

"You're feeling more of the bruised foot than the wound itself. A couple of days and you'll be fine. Limping a bit, but fine." *Most men would be crying out in pain and he just smiles and says it hurts. Sure would like to know more about him. Damn those eyes.*

"Any idea how I'm going to get back to the hotel?" Slim had a crooked smile on his face as he sat on the edge of the bed, testing his wounded foot again and again.

"You're not, Deputy Marshal Calhoun. You're staying right where you are for the next few days."

"That won't be very good for your reputation, besides which, it could get somewhat dangerous." He let his smile run rampant, accepting hers right back at him. "I do need to see Bull as soon as possible. I'm asking a lot, but there are some mean and nasty men out there who don't want us around."

"I'll send my kitchen helper, Terry. Where should he start?

"Lucky Lady Saloon would be my first choice. Bull is going to want to talk with Spike Loring, after his chat with Daws. When will I be able to get a boot on?"

"If you had one, probably day after tomorrow if you don't rip things loose down there. I'll be back to check on you."

BULL WALKED HIS AND SLIM'S HORSES UP TO JACOB OVERBY'S STABLES.
"We need to have a little talk, Mr. Overby." He didn't give the
man time to say aye or nay. "Slim tells me you think we're
hired killers, working for the cattlemen. We're not. Don't
interrupt. I'm U.S. Marshal Bull Morrison and Slim Calhoun
is my deputy. Did you send those two killers who work for
Lighthorse after us?"

Overby's look told Bull the man was stunned finding out
who they were. "I told the sheriff you were heading for Judge
Schaffer's. Good God, what happened?"

"Owens is dead and Benson's in jail. My deputy is wounded
and out of action and I'm holding you responsible. Exactly
what did you say to the sheriff?"

"I thought you were going to harm or kill the judge. Everyone's talking about you being hired killers. I thought I was
doing the right thing."

"Maybe anywhere but Pioche going to the sheriff would be
the right thing." Bull had to snicker after saying that. *Isn't that
stupid? Going to the sheriff about potential killers is the wrong
thing to do? This man isn't the problem.* "Doing the right thing
is important to you, Mr. Overby?"

"Indeed. Yes," he said. "This little camp is filled with men
not doing the right thing. I run a freighting business, Marshal.
That's why all the mules. Outlaws are hurting my business. I
run large freight wagons into Cedar City, north to Salt Lake,
and into the Prescott area of Arizona Territory. Those men
hurt my business."

Bull grabbed the double-barreled shotgun from his saddle
and filled a coat pocket with shells. "I have some business that
needs taken care of right away. Would you take care of our
animals, please? In the morning, I'll be here and you and I

will have a much longer talk."

"Very well, Marshal. I'll help you any way I can. How bad was Calhoun wounded? I like that man. Somehow I knew he wasn't a hired killer."

"He'll be fine," Bull said. He walked back down the hill toward the Lucky Lady Saloon. The night was clear and cold with a slight breeze blowing in from the south. "I wonder when spring reaches these high areas?"

There was a loud and boisterous crowd in the Lucky Lady when Bull came through the bat wing doors. He found Spike Loring at the end of the bar. "No trouble tonight, Bull. Please. I got a good crowd and they're spending good money." Bull tried to smile, nodded to Jimmy Lassen that he wanted a cold beer and glass of whiskey.

"No trouble, Loring but we do need to have a long conversation, somewhere where I won't be tempted to start a fight, because I sure do want to."

Loring took them to a table off in the corner, near a window. "Town's talking about you two. Sheriff put a bounty on your head about an hour ago. Got men all riled. I think it would be a good time to let people know who you are. Before they start shooting at you."

"Think you're right." *Best time is right now. Saloon's full and the word will spread.*

He was going to try to catch the crowd's attention when two men burst through the doors of the saloon. "That's him!" One yelled it out, pointing at Morrison. "The killer hired by the cattlemen." The two turned to Loring and Bull and went for their guns. Bull saw it coming well before Spike Loring and shoved the table, so it knocked the saloon keeper to the floor.

Morrison rolled out to his left, brought the shotgun up and fired, first one barrel then the second, destroying the upper bodies of both men. He jumped to his feet, dropping the scattergun and pulled his revolver. "Anybody else?" He looked quickly around the saloon, found everyone standing or sitting as still as they could manage. One move by anyone and more would die.

"Well, good," Bull said. "This is a good time to have a quick talk with you fine folk. Pay close attention," he said, waving the pistol about. Nobody moved, not a word was said, he owned his crowd.

"I'm only going to say this once. I'm United States Marshal Bull Morrison. My partner is Deputy United States Marshal Slim Calhoun. Those in Pioche who have been breaking the law are going to find us bustin' their butts. End of speech."

The silence only lasted a few seconds, but Spike Loring found it more than interesting. "You got 'em with that, Bull. I knew you'd find one way or another to start a fight."

"You know those two jaspers on the floor?" Bull picked his shotgun up and reloaded it. He was about to sit down when a scrawny little man in his fifties walked up to the table. "Don't start something you ain't ready to finish." Bull was tensed, ready to kill again.

"Miss Whipple sent me to tell you that Slim wants to see you. He found his toe."

"What?" Bull looked at the kitchen helper named Terry and looked at Spike, and then back to Terry. "What?"

"Slim found his toe and wants to see you," Terry said, turned, and scurried out of the saloon.

Bull just shook his head. *Found his toe?* He finished his drink, still shaking his head. "I'm going down to the Silver Crystal Saloon, Spike. Let that crowd know who I am."

"Alone?" Loring couldn't believe what he heard.

"Well, yes," Bull said. "Slim can't walk and he's my only

deputy. Don't think I'd trust Three-Finger Daws to back my play." He grabbed the shotgun and made his way through the crowd to the swinging doors. Loring just shook his head, got up, and motioned for some help with the two dead men.

"Let's get these two taken care of, boys. I think there might be more coming along. Billy Boards is gonna be busy with the burying." *Must take a special breed of man to be a marshal. I'm glad I'm not of that breed.* A gambler? Yes, Spike Loring got the money to build the Lucky Lady gambling. He knew also that he was a good businessman, but was he going to back this crazy marshal? Was he a supporter of law and order? Well, he thought, climbing the stairs to his office, *I guess I am, mostly.*

There were few people on the streets and Bull walked the block or so to the Silver Crystal. The wind was blowing and he fought it on the long walk without anyone making a play. *Just how criminal can a sheriff get? He put a bounty on our heads? Loring believes that that other fellow, Pizon, was hired by the sheriff to kill us, too. We came to clean up the town so I guess we'll start with the sheriff.*

It was a noisy crowd in the Crystal when Bull walked in doing his best not to snicker at his thoughts. "Standing at the bar, are you? First some words," he muttered. Within seconds the crowd was all but silent, recognizing the huge man. Would someone go for that bounty right now?

He held the cocked shotgun at the ready and yelled for quiet. The ugly scar across Bull Morrison's face was almost scarlet as he yelled at the crowd. "Got something to say. Sheriff Lighthorse, you in particular need to hear this since you sent two men out to kill me a few minutes ago." There was a stirring in the crowd, comments flashing between friends and patrons. Bull let it continue for a few seconds then held the shotgun up for quiet.

"My name is United States Marshal Bull Morrison. My partner is Deputy United States Marshal Slim Calhoun."

As at the Lucky Lady, a hush descended as a woolen blanket over the crowd. Bull kept the shotgun at the ready and waded through the crowd to where Lighthorse stood with saloon owner Rolf Pendergrass. He shoved both barrels into Lighthorse's chest and there were some loud gasps from those standing close.

"Harvey Lighthorse, you're under arrest. Place your weapons on the bar, slow as molasses." Bull watched Rolf Pendergrass back up a few feet and saw the crowd edge away as well. Would they stand with the sheriff? Would they pull their guns and shoot Morrison dead? Or was that wild play of Bull's enough to keep them at bay? "Now, Sheriff. Won't say it again." He poked the barrels of the big gun hard into the man's chest.

Some in the crowd had seen Bull knock the sheriff on his butt once, had heard about Buster Cranston's beating, and had seen this monster of a man ride through town with a dead deputy sheriff draped over a saddle. Would they now see Sheriff Lighthorse be blown to bits?

Lighthorse eased his revolver out of that fancy black leather holster, the one with gold and silver conchos and fancy tooling and laid it on the bar. "Anything else? Don't let me find a derringer or knife later." Lighthorse eased a little pepperbox out of his inside vest pocket and reached behind his back bringing a knife out.

Bull picked the knife up and admired it. "Took one like it from that mining man, Sheriff. Might just keep this one, too. Let's go now," Bull said. He turned to the crowd. "If you are part of the criminal element in Pioche, Slim and I are here to put you out of business. If you're not, you have nothing to fear from either one of us." He poked the sheriff hard in the back and they slowly made their way to the doors.

They were almost there when a man leaped out from the crowd, gun drawn. Bull turned and let loose one barrel, blowing the man's chest into shreds, throwing the gunman back ten feet or more. "Anyone else want to play dumb?" Morrison pushed the sheriff out the door and they made the long slow walk to Daws' office.

Bull decided to make a show of it and walked Lighthorse down the middle of the muddy street. *A man just has to do something like this once in a while. Slim would have a fit, the judge would cuss for an hour, and I don't give a damn. Come on you cowardly bastards, take your best shot at me.*

With every step Bull anticipated someone shooting him dead. Every shadow could hide an assassin, every building had a dark corner from which the lethal bullet could be fired, and every sound could be someone cocking a weapon. "One of your hired guns come for me, Sheriff, you die too. You overplay your hand again and you'll pay dearly." When he turned the corner at the courthouse relief flooded seeing light in the marshal's office.

"Got another guest for you, Marshal. This one will take some special care. He's incredibly stupid." Bull forced Lighthorse through the door with another hard poke in the back. "You have a friend waiting for you in the back, Sheriff."

"My lord, Morrison. What have you done?" Three-Finger sprung from his chair, looking out the door hoping no one would burst through behind Bull.

"What I've done, Three-Finger Jack Daws is what you should have done some time ago. Sheriff Lighthorse is my prisoner. Search him thoroughly and lock him up but not in the same cell as Benson. Keep 'em separated. I'll be at Ginny Whipple's if you need me." *What is the matter with that man?*

City Marshal and afraid to arrest those who break the law. We're stuck with him, I guess.

Making his way to the café he wondered if he should have said something to Daws about the bounty on his head? Did it include Daws or was that bounty only for the heads of Bull and Slim? Did Daws need to know? By the time he realized he wasn't going to find any answers he was walking into the warm and wonderfully aromatic diner.

"Hello, Marshal," Ginny said. "Time for supper?"

"I'm glad he told you, Miss Whipple, and yes, but not until I have a chat with the man in the back room who talks too much."

"We found his toe."

Morrison stopped and whirled around. "That's the second time I've heard that. What does it mean?"

"The only damage from the gunshot was the loss of Slim's little toe. It was stuck in his stocking. He'll be fine in a day or so. Sore, limping maybe, but fine."

"Good," Bull said, heading for the back rooms. *Found his toe. So glad. I'm gonna need all of him, minus one toe.*

CHAPTER 13

SANDY HITCHCOCK HURRIED TO THE DOOR. "WHAT'S THE MEANING OF all this pounding? Oh, hello Murphy. Come in, come in. My goodness what a ruckus."

The crippled old man made it to a large chair and fell into it, panting. "Bad trouble, Mr. Hitchcock. Sheriff Lighthorse has been arrested by federal marshals." The old man was talking a mile a minute and Hitchcock tried to slow him down.

"Lighthorse arrested? Marshals? Surely you're mistaken, Murphy. Let me get you a brandy, catch your breath, and tell me what happened, nice and slow." He poured two and settled into a chair opposite Tony Murphy. "Now, nice and slow. What marshals? And what happened?"

It took only a few minutes for Murphy to tell what happened at the Silver Crystal. The old man wasn't aware of what happened at the Lucky Lady Saloon. "The big one called himself Bull Morrison and said he was a U.S. Marshal. He named his partner as a Deputy Marshal and called him Slim Calhoun."

"And this Bull character arrested the sheriff? No one tried to interfere? Where is the sheriff now?"

"Jake Johnson tried to shoot the marshal and died hard for trying. Pendergrass just stood by and watched. Deputy Gary

Johnson sat at the poker table, not moving. Somebody said Morrison took the sheriff to Marshal Daws' jail."

"I'm going to write out a message, Tony, and I want you to deliver it to Buster Cranston at the mine. If he's underground, see to it that he's fetched up and give it to him personal. Here's a double eagle for your trouble and for coming to me." It took just a minute for Hitchcock to write a quick note to Cranston and Murphy was puffing and hobbling his way up the hill to the mine. *Everything in this camp is uphill. Ain't nothin' level.*

Cranston was having coffee in front of a pot-belly stove when Murphy wheezed his way into the offices. "Got a note for you from Hitchcock, Buster."

Cranston read the note and sat back in his chair, a scowl spread across his face. "Bad news is it?" Murphy asked. Cranston handed it to him. Murphy read it out loud, one word at a time, slowly.

"Marshals in town. Been double crossed by the judge. Get men, find the marshals, and kill them. Everything lost if you don't, including your life." Murphy handed it back to Cranston. "The big one, called Bull, arrested the sheriff, Buster."

Cranston smiled at Murphy's comment, relishing the thought. "Wish I'd been there to see that, Murph. Old Harvey Lighthorse in irons." Cranston walked to the shaft head and pulled on a rope several times. Murphy recognized the alarm. Cranston's rope sounded bells in lower depths of the mine announcing 'Fire!' Leave the mine. 'Fire!' Hoists began moving fast, bringing crews to the surface. Cranston had them stand together when the last hard-rocker stepped from a man-cage.

"There's no fire, boys. Relax." Fire, underground, was deadly, and every man feared being trapped by one. "There's another problem that might be worse. Two men are in town to shut the mines down. They think they have the authority to do that. They work for the ranchers and they are going to cut off water to the mines."

Grumbling turned to anger, and loud voices called for death to the two and to the ranchers, which was what Cranston hoped for. "Boys, we got to make some serious plans on how to handle this. Come daylight we need to break the sheriff out of jail, find those two killers, and then attack the ranchers. I want you men to go to your homes and arm yourselves. We'll meet at the Silver Crystal Saloon at sunrise. Don't be gettin' drunk. We need sober fightin' men. Don't be going of all cocked and crazy. We have to do this as an army would."

"IT'S STARTING, SLIM," BULL SAID WALKING INTO THE BEDROOM. SLIM was sitting on the edge of the bed still testing his foot. "Lighthorse put out a bounty on our heads. I arrested him but three men have already tried to kill me. They're dead of course."

"Of course" He looked for an attempt at a smile or some reaction and only saw a worried scowl. "It's gonna get nasty, I know, Bull, but we're in this even if I'm out of it for at least another day. What have you got in mind?"

"The whole camp knows who we are now, so some will be with us and some against. Sandy Hitchcock will put together his miners, for sure, and we don't know if Lighthorse has any more paid killers working for him. Loring can give us a couple of people, maybe, Three-Finger Daws is a jerk, and I just hope we can count on his gun."

"What about Overby?" Slim asked. "I know you and he clashed but I think he could come up with some help."

"I'm talking with him first thing in the morning. This is going to be rough. I'm going up to the sheriff's office now and clear it out. That's our new headquarters. I'll have Daws move the prisoners and he'll work from there, too. We'll get you up there in the morning. Where's your toe?"

"Ginny gave it to her dog. Bullet blew it right off my foot. Like taking a chicken leg off. Damndest thing you've ever seen."

"Don't want to. Sleep good." Bull walked into the café for supper, trying to get pictures of toes, bullets, and dogs out of his head. "You gave Slim's toe to the dogs?" He asked Ginny when she brought pork chops, taters, and gravy to the table. She chuckled and walked off leaving Bull to his supper.

WITH A FULL STOMACH AND STRANGE VISIONS OF TOES AND DOGS GONE, Marshal Morrison headed for the Lucky Lady Saloon cradling that wicked shotgun. He'd clear the sheriff's offices in the morning, right now he was going to see if he could find some trustworthy men to help in the coming fight. Many of the men in the saloon took one look at his eyes, saw that bright red scar across his face, and moved out of the way, letting him get to the bar. "I need a stiff whiskey, Chago. It's been one hell of a day."

Spike Loring walked up behind him. "I'm going to make it worse, Bull. Want you to meet some people." They walked to the table by the window to meet with two men dressed as cattlemen, not miners. "These are the men leading the fight for water for the ranchers in the valley. Quincy Pierce has the Lazy P and Tom Donovan the Bar Double X. Gentlemen, meet US. Marshal Bull Morrison."

"So, you're the killer we hired, eh?" Donovan said. His smile was warm, splashed across a deeply tanned face. He wore a full beard and flowing black hair speckled with shards of white. Pierce chuckled at the comment, too.

"That's me," Bull said. The three shook hands and everyone sat down. "I just arrested the sheriff and have him locked up tight. Tell me more about the water problems you and the mines are having. Litigation is far superior to firearms, but what I'm hearing could lead to a water war and that would kill a lot of good people."

Quincy Pierce looked hard at Morrison as soon as the man said the sheriff was locked up. "I like your style, Morrison." *It's been a long time coming and this ferocious looking bastard might just be the man to put things straight around these parts.* Pierce looked at Loring and smiled.

"It takes a lot of water to run a cattle ranch or a farm to raise food. Nevada has water laws as does Utah, and some of our ranchers have property that overlaps state lines. We have legal allocations that are being denied." There was a lot of anger in his voice.

"That's right, Marshal," Donovan said. He was a burly man, heavy with well used muscles and sharp, penetrating eyes. "We have allocations and the mines have allocations, but Hitchcock has convinced the other operators that their allocations come first and if they need more, they have the right of law to take what they need."

"There's more, Marshal," Pierce said. The two men had been waiting for someone with a voice to hear their complaints. Judges have been paid off, the sheriff has been paid off, and this large, mean looking man with a marshal's badge just might be their salvation.

"Hitchcock has a judge in Salt Lake City in his employ, and I mean every word of that. Judge John T. Olsen works for Sandy Hitchcock and our water is being taken from us."

Bull Morrison accepted the drink that was sent over by Chago Torres. "Sounds like half a dozen problems here. I'm a Federal Marshal. Judge Olsen is a Federal Judge. Water law is a state law. Olsen can't make water decisions and I'm not supposed to take responsibility for state crimes. Has anyone talked with or filed suit in Nevada District Court? With Judge Gregory Mallard?"

"Olsen might be speaking for Hitchcock because the water table from which the mines and the ranches draw is on both sides of the state lines. Olsen said because of that, the questions come under federal jurisdiction," Pierce said.

"Whew," Morrison uttered. "All right then, I'm going to proceed based on what you just said, and it better be so. I'm not easy to get along with if I'm lied to."

Pierce tightened up, clenched fists ready to swing at the comment. "I will bring you a copy of the finding," Pierce said. His teeth seemed clenched as well as his fists. "No man has lived through calling me a liar, Morrison."

The two men glared at each other for a short time before Bull ended the brief showdown. Morrison seemed to soften slightly as if finding this rancher, a man he could trust. "You bring that finding or decree, find Judge Mallory and bring him to Pioche, and with some luck we'll save a few lives. I'm thinking Judge Olsen is right because of the water table, but why that should give the mines more access than their allocations isn't. In the meantime, I have another half dozen federal laws that have been broken around here."

He took a moment to take a long drink of his whiskey. "Have any of the ranches been, let's say, illegally foreclosed on by Hitchcock's bank?"

"Threatened, yes. Regularly," Donovan said. "Hitchcock never takes it past a threat because of Justice of the Peace Schaffer and Judge Mallory. Hitchcock doesn't own them."

"Yet," Pierce said. He was going to say more when Seamus O'Neil came rushing in the swinging doors of the saloon.

"Where's this marshal? I need to talk with this marshal,"

he yelled out. "There's trouble coming."

"Right here, O'Neil," Bull said. He waved at the man.

"Thank God." He rushed to the table. "Buster Cranston at the North Pass Mine has just told his men that you and your partner are here to shut off all the water to the mines. He told them to meet at the Silver Crystal at sunrise. They plan to free the sheriff, kill you and your partner, and start raiding the ranches in the valley. Cranston has to be working on Hitchcock's orders."

O'Neil, the mine boss for Thomas Blair, grabbed the bottle and poured a quick drink. "Just how is it that you know all this?" Bull asked. "Blair isn't exactly on Hitchcock's favorite person list. Why would Blair know this?"

"A couple of our men were in the Silver Crystal when North Pass men came in talking about it. Cranston has them fired up and ready to attack the jail and the ranches."

"Exactly what I feared," Bull said. "Where do Tom Blair and some of the other mine owners stand?"

"Blair sent me to find you. He's organized a meeting with our men, asked union boss Kindle to be there, and would like to be at the jail in the morning when Cranston brings his mob."

"No," Bull said. "We don't need a full bore war in the middle of town." He sat back and took a long look at the ceiling. "I think it best if you get Boots Kindle up to the jail now." Morrison turned to the ranchers. "I think you men need to head back to your ranches and set up for protection. With some luck I'll prevail and you won't need it. I'm going to the jail now."

He flagged Loring over. "Get two or three men you trust to bring Slim Calhoun from Ginny Whipple's up to the jail. Might want to go with them. Slim might argue. Then meet me at the jail."

"We'll get him," Donovan said. "Want to see this sheriff of

ours in irons, then we'll head for the ranches. I can send one of my men for Mallard, but Schaffer is almost here in town."

"He knows what we're doing," Bull said. "Spike, can you get word to the judge?" Spike nodded.

"I'm not going to just sit at the ranch and hope things work out here in town," Pierce said. "I'm going to have some of the older men stay at the ranch and bring the rest back to town. Hitchcock won't be talked down, Marshal. Tell him I'm right, Donovan."

"I'm sure he's right, Marshal. I'm going to do the same. Hitchcock always gets his way. One way or the other, he'll have his men attack that jail, save his sheriff, and kill you."

Morrison only thought about what was said for seconds before nodding in agreement. "Don't want war. I demand that if you and your men come that Hitchcock or one of his men has to be the one to fire the first round. This is now my war, gentlemen, not yours."

CHAPTER 14

BULL OPENED THE DOOR TO THE SHERIFF'S OFFICE AND FOUND GARY Thompson in the sheriff's chair. He had a fire in the stove, coffee boiling, and a smug look on his face. "Been expecting you," he said. "I'm Lincoln County Deputy Sheriff Gary Johnson."

"That so? Marshal Daws will be here shortly along with a couple of prisoners. Take me into the cell area and if you do something dumb, I'll shoot you dead," Bull said. The shotgun was held at the ready and Thompson's eyes were fixed on the cocked hammers.

"You don't have to threaten me, Marshal. I want to do what's right. Court clerk Moody sent me a note that you would be coming." He stood up and motioned for Bull to follow. The cells were through a door at the back of the office. "We have six cells and each will hold up to four men."

Court clerk Moody? Moody works in Olsen's court. Why would this deputy get a note from Moody? We've run into riddles at every step we take. Bull looked hard at this deputy trying to see if the man was playing with him, just stupid, or if he meant what he said.

"Tell me about this Moody person. Why would a federal judge's court clerk be sending you a letter and not the sheriff?"

Morrison found the leak in Judge Olsen's office but now had even more questions. If there is a letter it should have come from the judge and it should have been sent to the sheriff. "That would be most unusual, Deputy."

"Sheriff Lighthorse is more outlaw than lawman, Marshal. I'm sure you're aware of that and Judge Olsen does the bidding of Sandy Hitchcock. I've known KC since school days, that's what he calls himself now, his name is Kevin Clarke Moody, and he's been helping me get word to the Marshal Service for help. Guess it worked."

Thompson was trying to get everything out all at the same time and Morrison motioned for him to slow down. "Take it easy, Deputy. We have a lot to discuss." Bull took a quick look around the empty cell area and the two walked back into the office.

"What exactly do you mean that you and this Moody feller have been getting word to the Marshal Service? Don't mess with me, Thompson. Sheriff keep a flask in that desk?" Bull pulled a tin cup from a rack and filled it half full of boiling coffee. *What a damn mess. I've got to get a partial report to Judge Baker pronto. He needs to get Olsen in irons before this thing explodes. Does Baker even have that authority?* Thompson found the flask in a bottom drawer.

"I helped Moody put together a portfolio of criminal activity here in Pioche and he sent it to a federal judge in San Francisco under Judge Olsen's name. Olsen doesn't know about any of this."

"I'll just bet he doesn't," Bull said. *Moody and this arrogant Thompson need to be horsewhipped on the one hand and handed medals for bravery on the other. I'd like to punch this self-righteous fool five times then pick him up and give him a hug. What the hell is Baker going to do with what I'm going to send him?*

Bull took in a quick breath. Would this have an effect on the admittance of evidence? Have these two men muddied any future findings? *I gotta get a wire off to Baker.*

Bull had a million questions for this deputy but before he could get started, Three-Finger Daws came in with Lighthorse and Benson, followed immediately by the ranchers, half carrying Slim. Bull got up so Slim could have the swivel chair and motioned for Thompson to help Daws get the prisoners, in irons, to the cells.

"Separate cells, Deputy. Don't take any guff from either one. I'm putting one hell of a lot of trust in you, Thompson, and I will shoot you dead if you turn on me." He turned to Marshal Daws. "Well? Help him, Daws. Get those bastards locked up." He was as keyed up as a man could get, had half a dozen jobs lined up in front of him and was trying to prioritize his moves.

Slim watched the little play and had to smile. "You got quite a bunch of helpers there, Bull. Mr. Donovan brought me up to date on what Hitchcock is planning. We got to get word to Judge Baker as soon as possible."

"I know," Bull said. "I've learned even more in the last half hour." He turned to Pierce and Donovan. "Thank you, gentlemen," Bull said. "Better get back to your ranches. I'm still not sure it's the right thing to bring your people, but I know you're going to. Just remember, we don't want a war if we don't have to have one."

"We don't either, Marshal," Tom Donovan said. "Hitchcock will make that decision, I'm afraid." He started for the door and turned back. "How are you going to get word to your judge? Hitchcock owns the telegraph office here."

"I can send one of my men north to Cedar City," Pierce said.

"Would that help?" Cedar City was a large iron producing city across the Utah border.

"Yes, it would," Bull said. "Slim, rifle that desk and find me writing paper. This will take a little time, Pierce, but if you'll wait I'll write a quick summary of what's happening and your man can send a wire from anywhere but Pioche."

SEAMUS O'NEIL WAS SITTING IN BOOTS KINDLE'S UPSTAIRS OFFICE AT the Miners' Union Hall telling him what his men heard at the Silver Crystal Saloon. "That's what they said, Boots. I know we haven't always been on the same side, but this time, we better be. Cranston wants the North Pass miners to meet at the saloon at sunrise and they're going to march on the jail."

"I'm not sure I'm against the idea," Kindle said. "Lighthorse is a crook, an outlaw, and like so many, works for Hitchcock. These two hired killers are mucking up the water, O'Neil. Not sure about a lynching, but if they're working for the ranchers, and the plan is to cut off all the water to the mines and mills, then I'm probably in favor of what Cranston is doing. Blair ain't thinking right to try and stop the attack."

"That's just the point, Boots," O'Neil said. "Those two men who have been raising hell around town aren't hired killers. They are United States Marshals." Kindle stood straight up at the comment.

"Marshals? Here in Pioche? Hah!" Boots Kindle walked around the desk, shoved his hands in his coat pocket. "Why?"

"Blair says they are here to put Hitchcock out of business. That's why. Three-Finger Jack Daws has been working with them, that's why Spike Loring has been so friendly with them. They ain't killers, Boots, they're marshals."

"Well, just damn me all to hell. Marshals in Pioche. I want

to meet these two. That one big one has whipped on everyone in town, I think. It'll be sunrise in another hour or two. Let's go meet these marshals."

The Union building was almost next door to the still-building courthouse and the jail was next door to that. Lights were burning bright at the sheriff's office when O'Neil and Boots Kindle walked in. "Morning," Seamus O'Neil said. "I brought Kindle like you asked, Marshal."

"Good. Slim, do the honors. I got to finish this report to Baker. He isn't gonna believe a word of it."

"Find some coffee," Slim said, "and let's talk. I'm Deputy U.S. Marshal Slim Calhoun and the big feller is Marshal Bull Morrison. Mr. Kindle, we're here to put Sandy Hitchcock and all the other criminals in Pioche out of business and in jail. Hitchcock is bringing a gang of his miners this way in the next hour to set the former sheriff, Harvey Lighthorse, free and to kill Bull and myself. Oh, and all those standing with us."

"I've had it in the back of my mind that at some point real lawmen would ride into Pioche and clean up this putrid stink hole. The men working for Hitchcock are scammed right along with everyone else," Kindle said. He shook his head and scowled. "They have money withdrawn from their wages to invest in mines that don't exist. They'll show you the stock certificates. Most don't even know they're being fleeced."

He reached in his coat pocket and came up with a shiny engraved flask and took a sip. "They put in ten hours underground but are docked portage fees, which amounts to two hours per day. Two hours to ride up and down on the lifts. I'll help any way I can, Marshal." He took another and longer drink from the flask.

"Yes, Marshal Calhoun, I'll stand with you, but you better understand that you will be facing fifty or more men who believe you're here to take away their jobs. They will think they are fighting a righteous war."

Bull folded the three pages of handwritten notes and slipped them in an envelope. "Here you are, Pierce. If this gets in the wrong hands a lot of people could die. After you get this to the telegraph, make sure you get it back. I want this back in my hands. Understand?"

"I do, Bull. Donovan and I will return as soon as we can. It will be well after daylight, of course, but we will be back. I won't lose your report. Come on, Tom. Let's ride."

"The return telegraph from the judge in San Francisco will come to you, Mr. Pierce. It's imperative that it gets to me as quick as possible. We've arrested the sheriff but in the next several days, Slim and I will be filling this jail. A federal judge is sure to be appointed to handle all of this and it won't be John T. Olsen. Stay safe, you two. We'll need both of you at trial, too."

CHAPTER 15

SHADES OF GRAY DOMINATED THE SKY AS SANDY HITCHCOCK STRODE into the Silver Crystal Saloon. It was filled with men who had been drinking for more than an hour. Strident and angry voices filled the smoky air and Hitchcock wondered if Buster Cranston had done the right thing, allowing the men to drink freely. He found his mine boss at the bar.

"Unruly mob you have here, Cranston. Let's not let this get out of hand. A drunken mob can forget its primary purpose, which is to wipe out those two killers. I'm not looking for a riot, Buster."

Buster Cranston looked questioningly at the fat man. *It was a riot you called for Hitchcock and now you see what one looks like just before it gets started. I'll play your stupid game but you are the one that called for this.*

"They'll do as they're told, Mr. Hitchcock. A shot or two of whiskey just adds to their resolve," Cranston said. "If you give 'em a good pep talk, they'll be fine. Rowdy? Hell yes. After all, they will be defending what it is that keeps them working. Water."

Hitchcock snickered as he pulled a chair over and stood on it, challenging the very hardwood it was made from. The obese mine owner was waving both hands at the cheering crowd. *Cranston's a bigger fool than I thought. He should know how I'm manipulating this water question for heaven's sake, he's helped me right along. Well, if he's bought into it, I'm sure the men have too.*

More than fifty men were screaming obscenities, howling for blood, and more than one had ideas about killing the sheriff if the chance happened by. Unseen by Cranston or Hitchcock were several men who had kerosene soaked torches waiting for them outside.

It took Hitchcock several minutes and a couple of rounds from his side-arm to get the men quiet enough for him to speak. "Men, these two vile hired killers have come to our little camp to take us out of business. The greedy ranchers have sent these killers to shut off the water supply to our mines. Without that water, you will be out of work. You won't have a home. I don't think I have to say anything else."

The yelling and screaming could be heard two blocks away at the jail, could be heard throughout Pioche. Spike Loring had closed the saloon earlier and now put braces across the closed front doors. Ginny Whipple decided not to open the café that morning, after all. And at the jail, Slim simply said, "It's about to start."

Old man Appleby, the apothecary, was awakened by the noise, made several unseemly remarks to the Mrs. and tried to go back to sleep. "Damn fools will want me to cure their headaches later," he said.

"Let's save our water, save out mines. Now, men, let's protect what is ours," Hitchcock yelled out, stepped down from the chair, and with Buster Cranston alongside, led the men out of the saloon. Within moments, several torches were seen to add light to the rising sun as the crowd made its way down the main street to the courthouse and jail. It was a rowdy procession with drunken men howling, screaming, voicing their obscene thoughts.

There was no plan as neither Hitchcock nor Cranston had discussed how they should make their attack. When the mob was still half a block from the complex one of the men with a torch ran up on the boardwalk and broke a window at the apothecary's. "No!" Cranston ran hard and tackled the man, knocking the torch from his grip.

He slammed his fists hard, knocked the miner out and grabbed the torch. "No!" He shouted it again. "We are not burning this town down. Our purpose is to save our water, men. On to the jail, now." No one could hear Appleby's anger.

There was a lot of grumbling. A good fire is fun to watch when you're drunk and don't give a damn whether there's water for the mines or not. "That bastard charges us too much for our medicines," one man yelled out. "He needs to be burned out."

There was considerable support for the idea and Cranston pulled his revolver and fired a shot, quieting the crowd some. "To the jail, men. Get those hired killers. Save our mines." The mob surged forward again and Hitchcock's worries were coming true. These men were not in any kind of control and sure as gold gleams in the sun, something will burn before the morning is over.

BULL LOOKED AROUND THE SMALL OFFICE. IT WAS HE, SLIM, Three-Finger Daws, Gary Thompson, Seamus O'Neil, and Boots Kindle, the bunch holding shotguns at the ready. "Six of us against them, gentlemen. Remember, no one fires a shot until one of them shoots. Mr. Kindle, most of these men are members of your union and I'm depending on you to do your best to get us out of this."

"I know most of them, Marshal, have worked with many of them, but I'm also sure that they have been filled with lies from Cranston and Hitchcock. All I can do is try my best."

Bull and Slim opened the door to the office and stepped out onto the wide boardwalk. The rest of the group filled out around them. Boots Kindle watched the men slopping their way through cold mud and stepped out in front. He raised his arms high, the shotgun in one hand and called for the men to listen.

"Get out of way Kindle," Cranston said. "Move aside or die."

"Men," Kindle cried out, shaking the scattergun. "You've been lied to again by these greedy mine owners. Listen to me. You know I'm on your side, I'm one of you. Hitchcock and his cheating foreman Cranston lie to you every day of the week and this morning is no different. These two men," and Kindle pointed at Bull and Slim, "don't work for the ranchers. Listen to me, these men are United States Marshals."

There was the slightest hush that fell at those words. Marshals? In Pioche? Kindle wouldn't lie, would he? The momentary hush fell to cat-calls, more screaming, and Kindle had to turn to threatening with the shotgun to get the men to listen.

"That's right, these men are marshals and they are here, not to shut off water to the mines, but to keep men like Hitchcock and Cranston from stealing from you, from robbing you of your wages, from keeping them from taking your jobs. Go home. There is nothing here for you."

Shift bosses, lead-men, and others in the group saw that Kindle had to be right. He'd never lied to the men before, the shift leaders started using their positions to move the men away from the jail area. "Kindle's never lied to us, men," one yelled out. Another shouted something about Kindle being a friend of the miner, not the ranchers, so what he said is right. Kindle pointed at different men, giving the high sign with the shotgun and smiling.

It all came together when Cranston charged Kindle, screaming about saving water. Kindle almost let him get too close and finally smashed the mine foreman in the nose with a hard straight left. He followed that up with the butt of the shotgun sweeping up and into the man's groin, dropping him into the mud. The crowd was almost silenced.

"I've never lied to you, men. Neither Hitchcock nor Cranston can say that. Go home. Make your next shift. There will be water."

It took a long time, but slowly, and in groups of two or three, the mob broke up. Many did go home, but there were those who made their way to the Silver Crystal. The men with the torches led the way to the saloon having been denied what they hoped would be a fine conflagration. Muttering about who was lying, asking if those men were really marshals, why was Kimble standing up for the ranchers, and some wondering why the sheriff was even in jail.

In any large group there will always be those who don't behave, who won't take direction, and who take great delight in seeing to it that someone is hurt. They are usually the ones who drink heavily and are bullies by nature. Many of that ilk filed into the Silver Crystal Saloon with no intent of making their next shift, but rather, making as much trouble as possible.

It would take strong men to counteract such behavior. Buster Cranston wasn't that type of man. He could give orders when told what orders to give. He could whack a man across the side of the head, beat one down, but wasn't able to see trouble coming. Hitchcock on the other hand could, but would he?

Hitchcock pulled Cranston aside as they slowly walked back to the saloon. "I'm holding you responsible for this, Buster. You did a poor job preparing these men for an assault. You should never have allowed them to get drunk. Kimble should never have been allowed to be there. You fouled this up, Buster, and you'll pay for it."

Cranston didn't say anything, just watched as the rich old mine owner turned off the main street and started up the hill to his mansion of a home. *You'll see what I'm capable of, old man. Take your fat butt up the hill, you bastard, and watch what happens just a little later today.*

"IT ISN'T OVER," BOOTS KINDLE SAID. THEY WERE BACK IN THE OFFICE waiting for the coffee to boil. "Cranston won't let this end with him face down in the mud. He'll take those men to the saloon, let everyone get drunk and fill them with more hate. No, Marshal, it ain't over."

Bull Sorenson knew the union man was right and was trying to figure how best to prepare for the next assault. He thought of asking Seamus O'Neil to bring in men from Blair's mine and nixed that idea. *I want to stop the assault, not add to the problem.* "Slim, let's you and me have a little talk with the sheriff."

As they walked into the cell block Slim saw a glimmer of a smile from Bull's badly scarred face. "You have something on your mind? I do too, but I wouldn't smile about mine."

"All right then, Marshal Calhoun, you go first," Bull said. "And then I'll tell you what it is we're going to do."

"Very funny," Slim said. "I'm thinking that if we can get just a hint of evidence from the sheriff, it's time to arrest Hitchcock."

"That's my plan exactly," Bull said. "Didn't know you were a mind reader. If we are lucky, when Judge Baker gets my wire he's going to send us some people and in a hurry. Probably those marshals from Utah that may or may not be chasing Indians. We have to keep a lid on this camp for at least three days."

"We have Marshal Daws, Bull. He could arrest Hitchcock for attempting to incite a riot. It's a local charge but would hold him until we get evidence of a federal crime. We know it's there, just have to find it. Water of course is the key."

"We'll let the sheriff make that decision, Slim. We want Lighthorse to incriminate Hitchcock and anyone else who comes to mind. Let's not be gentle with old Harvey Lighthorse, partner."

Lighthorse was rather subdued when Slim and Bull entered his cell, sitting on a cot, holding his head in his hands. "What was all the yelling?"

"Don't have any idea," Bull said. He sat down on a cot opposite the sheriff. "Probably just a crowd of angry and ugly miners out to lynch the sheriff." He gave Slim a nod and reached in a pocket for a stub of badly chewed cigar. "That your thought on the matter, Slim?"

"Sounds right. How much of this water situation are you a part of, Lighthorse? We're looking to put Hitchcock in the slammer for a long time, but he insists that you are the one who cuts off the water to the ranches."

"No, no." Lighthorse barked it out, sitting straight up. "No, no. The reservoir is up the mountain and the irrigation lines and mine lines are at the base. It's Buster Cranston who shuts off the ranch water."

"How is it you know that?" Bull asked in an almost soft voice. "Does someone tell him to do that?"

"Well, when Hitchcock needs more water for his mines, he sends Cranston and me. I'm there to keep the peace, keep the miners from interfering. It's all legal. Hitchcock has papers from a judge in Salt Lake."

"You said mines," Slim said.

"Sandy Hitchcock represents all the mines in the district," Lighthorse said. "He controls the water for all the mines, and because of that judge's order, all the ranches, too." Calhoun and Morrison took quick glances at each other without saying anything. "Well, most of the mines, maybe not all. Tom Blair and a couple of others are independent. There's nothing illegal. I go with Buster so that he can shut the water off to the ranches."

"It's Hitchcock that orders the water to be shut off?"

"Yes, of course. He has a court order that allows him to have complete control of all the water in this district."

"Thank you, Mr. Lighthorse. We'll have a few more questions a little later. Breakfast will be late today," Bull said, trying to smile. He motioned to Slim and they left the cell block.

"Certainly matches what Thompson said about Judge Olsen." Slim walked straight to the coffee pot. "We now have enough evidence to arrest Hitchcock, Bull."

"Along with a federal judge," Bull said. "That's the gig, isn't it? We've trolled the waters and hooked a big one." Morrison added more whiskey to his cup, neglected to add coffee. "Let's check mining records when we get a chance. Dollar to a double eagle Judge Olsen is listed as owner of several of these Hitchcock mines. We need to put a lid on today's mob and get to our real work."

"Think Thompson and Daws could handle that? I don't." Slim shook his head and poured more coffee.

"No, I don't either. I'm not sure all four of us could. Maybe the best bet is to get out on the street. The troublemakers will be drinking hard and if some try something stupid we can break heads. Like the good old days," he chuckled.

Thompson was at the desk and Daws was standing at the window looking out on the main street. "See anything out there?" Slim asked.

"There's a group of men outside the Silver Crystal listening to someone. Maybe ten men." Thompson said.

"Let's take a walk," Bull said. "All of us."

CHAPTER 16

"When the fat man speaks, Cranston crawls," George Hannibal yelled out at the men standing around the front of the Silver Crystal Saloon. He had been drinking steadily for hours, his normally angry personality fueled by liquor, the man held an unlit torch and could smell blood. "It's time to go back and attack the jail. Kindle lied about those killers."

He was furious that his union boss took the side of those killers who were going to take his job, his means. "They are hired guns come to shut off the mine water. Cranston isn't man enough to lead us. I am," he cried. "Who's with me?"

There were eight men standing in the cold morning air and they all held bottles. Drunk, boisterous, and filled with alcohol induced bravado, they all yelled their approval. Two of them picked up torches and got them lit, and Hannibal shoved his fist in the air a few times, leading the men off in a disorderly march up the street.

Bull stood on the boardwalk in front of the jail, shotgun at the ready. "Let's go, boys. We got us a fight coming our way. We'll stop 'em first and insist they go home. If they don't break up, we break 'em up. Stay away from your guns if you can."

The four lawmen, walking abreast down the middle of the

muddy street toward the rowdy gang of torch bearing miners was a sight to see, and Ginny Whipple was wishing she wasn't seeing it. *No, Slim, don't do it. Look at him, limping, scowling, carrying that shotgun almost like a club. Don't get hurt, big boy. Don't.* She couldn't watch any more, turned, and almost scampered away from the window and back to her kitchen.

There were other eyes, too. The apothecary, Appleby, was cussing under his breath, watching the angry miners coming one way and the lawmen coming the other. "Beat those bastards down," he muttered before continuing to clean up the broken glass in his little shop. "Take those torches from those men and whip them bloody."

Hannibal saw the four lawmen coming and motioned at them. "Those are the two hired guns come to wipe out the mines. Are we going to let them live? Let them collect their blood money from the ranchers? And look who's with them, that fine upstanding town marshal."

He was screaming and the men started yelling taunts, howling epithets unfit for a lady's ears, and began walking toward the four, faster and faster. It only took one man to create the spark and it was George Hannibal who grabbed a torch and gave it a hefty swing, watching it arc through the cold air. It landed on a balcony above one of the dry goods stores.

A man swung the window open and jumped out onto the porch, grabbed the torch and flung it back at the crowd below. One of the drunken miners screamed his defiance, grabbed his pistol and shot the man, knocking him back through the window. The cries of pain from the man echoed along with the sobbing of a woman.

"Let's take 'em out," Bull said. "I was wrong about the guns. Use what you feel you need." He moved on George Hannibal and Slim Calhoun made a direct route for the man doing the shooting. Gary Thompson, with all the strong words he'd uttered about taking on the tough guys, held back some but it was Three-Finger Jack Daws who surprised Bull Morrison.

Daws took on two men, clubbing one with his shotgun and high kicking the other. The kicked man went for his sidearm while falling backward and Daws rolled out of the way of the shot leveling the scatter gun and firing off a shot, blowing the man's face to shreds. The terrible flat sound of that big gun put an instant stop to the foray.

Handguns and rifles just don't sound like shotguns and every man-jack one of those on the street knew what that sound meant. Someone just died a horrible death, peppered deep with heavy lead shot. The crowd was silenced.

Morrison jumped at the sudden quiet. "Put your weapons down. Drop those torches. You," and he pointed at George Hannibal, "are under arrest for inciting a riot. You," and he pointed at the man with the gun. "You, my friend are under arrest for murder. Marshal Daws, Deputy Thompson, take your prisoners to jail. The rest of you drunken fools, go home or go to jail. Your choice."

"Put 'em all in jail, Marshal," Appleby yelled out through the broken window. "Hitchcock too." He shook his fist at the men in the street. "Bunch of ignorant hoodlums. Hang the bastards."

Morrison watched the five men slowly drop their torches and holster their weapons. "Any more trouble and the bunch of you will be behind bars. Go home and sober up."

Daws and Thompson took Hannibal and the other back to the jail and Morrison and Slim made their way to Ginny's Café. "Need some help with my foot, Bull. Bleeding I think."

"I'm suffering worse than you," Bull said. "Ain't had coffee or breakfast. Not good for a man of my size. Get your foot fixed, get my stomach filled, and we'll march on Sandy Hitchcock."

"Better plan of taking Buster Cranston in, too. He's an instigator."

"Only does what he's told," Bull said. "Seen so many like him. Tough when told to be tough, otherwise working in a fog of emptiness."

BUSTER CRANSTON MADE THE QUICK WALK UP TO HITCHCOCK'S MAN-sion and banged on the door. "Bad news, Sandy. Hannibal and some of the men made another charge on the jail. One is dead, don't know his name, and two are in jail. Hannibal and somebody else. We need to get you up to the mine."

"You just can't do anything right, Buster. Why was Boots Kindle there, earlier? Answer that and then pack it in. You're through as far as I'm concerned. I need a man to run my mine, not someone who bows to the union." Hitchcock turned to show his contempt for the man and Buster Cranston blew up, swung a mighty fist and watched the corpulent mine owner tumble across his living room. One table, an unlit oil lamp, and an elegant needlepoint chair tumbled right along with him.

"You don't talk to me like that, Hitchcock, not after what I've done for you. You want me out? Fine, you fat old bastard. Pay me my share and I'll be a memory."

"Your share?" Hitchcock laughed. He was near the fireplace and trying to get to his feet. "Your share of what?" With his extra weight and a solid punch to his jaw, the old man was having a hard time getting back to his feet. "You got no share of nothing, Cranston."

Hitchcock slipped his hand inside his fine velvet smoking jacket and brought a pepperbox out. "Get out, Cranston. Grab your gear and get out of town. You're finished, done, over."

Cranston glared, started to turn away and instead grabbed the overturned lamp table and flung it at Hitchcock. The gun went off and Cranston fell back with a chunk of lead buried in his left arm, just above the elbow. Hitchcock fell to the floor and Cranston ran from the mansion. He dashed uphill, to the mine, to his cabin. He was muttering and cussing while he tried to make a bandage for his arm. *I got to get out of here but I'm not leaving with empty pockets.*

Cranston, as mine boss, had company housing near the mill site, just below the mine. He ran to the mine office and opened the safe, grabbed as much loose bills and gold coin as he could carry, and made his way to the stables where he saddled one horse and threw a pack saddle on another. A quick ride back to the cabin to load the pack and he rode north out of town.

"I MIGHT HAVE TO STAY IN PIOCHE WHEN THIS IS ALL OVER, BULL." BULL and Slim were having breakfast at Ginny's after she mended Slim's foot. "I like these window seats, I like this diner, never been fed better, never had better medical care, and those wonderful eyes that smile at me when she's near — well, I might just have to stay."

"What did she say about your toe?"

"Ain't got a toe."

"What did she say about your wound? You a lawyer now?"

"Says I'm gonna be fine." Slim snapped it out. "Just shouldn't get in any fights for another week or so. I told her I would try my best." Slim thought that one day should have been enough and was more than unhappy that he had to limp and not put much pressure on the foot. "I'll be fine,

Bull. Let's leave it at that."

Bull scowled, worrying about his partner but knowing this wasn't the time to say anything. He leaned over and looked out the window. "Well, looky there, Slim. That's Buster Cranston. Looks like he's leaving town, Slim. Got a pack horse and all. That's strange."

"Think he got fired or got in a twit with Sandy Hitchcock? Maybe we better pay that mine owner a visit. Maybe he's getting ready to pull out too."

Before they could move four men on horses rode up in front of the café. "That's Pierce and Donovan and a couple of buckaroos. Just in time," Slim said. He almost ran out before the men could get tied off. "Good timing. Buster Cranston just rode out of town with a pack horse, heading north. Think you could convince him to return?"

Donovan laughed, turned his horse and put the spurs to it. Pierce and the cowhands joined the chase. "We'll get him," Donovan yelled out. "Pierce, you better stay, give him the messages."

Pierce turned back. "Probably right." He tied off and the three walked back into the café. "Got a couple of wires back right away, Bull." They took their seats and Pierce dug the wires out of his coat.

"Fast return," Bull muttered. He read the first one and handed it to Slim and grabbed the second one. "Stirred the mud, we did, old man." He read the second one and handed it to Slim. "Let's have one more cup of coffee and then we'll go arrest that mining man."

CHAPTER 17

THE VIEW FROM THE THIRD FLOOR OF THE SAN FRANCISCO FEDERAL building was a gray shroud of fog as Federal District Judge Timothy Baker read the long wire again. That same gray shroud covered the judge's face as well. *You've done it this time, Bull Morrison.* He laid the wire down, shook his head and called for his clerk, Lucius Berry.

"Our intrepid Marshal Morrison is about to have a federal judge and his clerk indicted, Lucius. It's a sad time for the federal judiciary, I'm afraid." He stood up and paced around the large office, stopped at the windows, even though there was nothing to see, and ended up in front of a blazing fireplace. *How many good men have burned in the fires of hades because of greed? Such a sad fate, John T. Olsen, but if what Bull said in that wire is true, you will burn.*

Is it only greed? Is there something inside a man that would turn him in such a radical manner? I've known that man for fifteen or more years, yet, maybe I didn't ever know him at all. From what Bull has said, this is a well planned operation, not just a single mistake on the part of the man.

"Taking bribes, involved in state water issues, involved in questionable mining schemes, and other nasty programs. I've known Judge Olsen for years, Lucien. Years. Read this after you send a return wire that says, proceed at full speed but with caution. When that's sent, I'll need you back here."

Interesting that Olsen had me send Morrison and Calhoun in the first place. John T. was never one to play games, always spoke right out. Well, if he's as guilty as Bull thinks he is, he'll go down hard. But why call for the investigation himself?

Baker has seen more than one man appointed to the judiciary fall to greed but never expected it from his long time acquaintance, Judge John T. Olsen. *That man's been on the federal bench for more than ten years and there's never been the slightest hint of an irregularity. Not to mention out and out criminal behavior.* Baker shook his shaggy old head and reached for writing paper and documents. But thoughts of Olsen interfered.

He's the one who asked for Morrison and Calhoun? Is there something more going on, something that maybe the judge has become aware of? Or has that man got religion and needs help? Knows he's done wrong and can't just confess to an old friend?

Federal judges are appointed for life by the president with confirmation by the senate and come from all walks of society. Most are well known jurists, but there are always simple political pay-offs as well. It is rare for a federal judge to come up short in the ethics department, but it has happened and Baker was seeing one.

The wires hummed and in less than two hours he had marshals in Utah moving toward Salt Lake City, and had the necessary papers wired to the federal attorney for Utah calling for the investigation of Judge Olsen. He also had papers sent to the federal attorney for Nevada who would have to issue arrest warrants for Sandy Hitchcock and "any others associated with the criminal activities involved."

It was the third sheaf of papers that were sent to Morrison that would be the most important. Bull and his deputy were told, in the strongest language, to make sure the evidence they discovered was more than sufficient to convict. Baker sat back in his big chair, stared out the window for some time, and wondered what it was that would make a man, at the height of personal success, trade his good name for a prison uniform.

Money, not prestige, he already has that. I have dealt with crime and criminals for a quarter of a century and at this moment I could not tell you what it is that would change me from a proudly ethical man to a low-life criminal. His thoughts were interrupted by the return of Lucius Berry.

"It's out of our hands now, Lucius. It isn't the first time that the Marshals Morrison and Calhoun have been out there on their own. God help the bad guys." It wasn't really a chuckle nor was it a snicker. Close to a harrumph as the old judge gave the slightest smile to his long serving clerk.

TOM DONOVAN PUSHED THE WOUNDED BUSTER CRANSTON THROUGH the door and into the sheriff's office. "Morrison said to lock this one up. Keep him as far from the sheriff as you can." He was carrying a feed sack and threw it onto the desk. "I counted more than two thousand dollars in there, Marshal." Thompson and Daws were standing near the wood stove. "Marshal wants you, Daws, to join him at Sandy Hitchcock's home. They'll be there by the time you get there."

The burly rancher turned and walked out, mounted his horse and rode for home. *Sure would like to stay and watch that old bastard get arrested but there's work to be done. Been too long away as it is.* It was a pleasant ride back to his sprawling ranch knowing that the water war might really be over.

"Looks like Morrison is going to arrest Hitchcock," Three-finger Jack Daws said to Thompson. "Been a long time coming. Better make a cell ready for him."

It was a short walk up the hill to Hitchcock's mansion and Daws found the front door standing open and the two marshals standing over the inert body of Sandy Hitchcock. "What happened?" He asked.

"Looks like murder, Marshal. Cranston locked up?" Daws nodded and Bull knelt down to look at the head wound Hitchcock suffered. "Was Cranston wounded?"

"Had a gunshot to his arm," Daws said.

"Might be self defense then. I doubt it, though, from the bruises on this man's face. Looks like he was whupped on, tried to shoot his assailant, and got knocked into the rocks here. Take a good look, Slim."

"Gun was fired once, but I found it fifteen feet or more from the body, Bull." Slim was on his knees looking at the body. "Hitchcock's knuckles aren't scraped or bruised but his face is a mess. He shot that man in self-defense, Bull. Whoever Hitchcock shot killed him. I have no doubt."

"Let's have us a nice little talk with Buster Cranston," Bull said.

"Whether it was Cranston or someone else, they spent some time looking for something. This house is as much office as it is home, Bull. The desk has been rifled, the shelves have been swept of whatever papers might have been there, and the file drawers emptied. We'll start with Cranston. Somebody was looking for something."

The discussion continued on the walk back to the jail and a confrontation with Buster Cranston. "The shame, Slim, is that we may never get the entire picture since we can't question Hitchcock. We will need to find the evidence to convict Olsen at Hitchcock's mine or maybe there at his home."

They found Ginny Whipple in the cell along with Gary Thompson. "He gonna live?" Bull asked, sitting down on a cot.

"Bullet went through his arm, clean as all. He'll be fine, Marshal. I'll come back tomorrow and clean the wound again. He's been talking about Hitchcock being in jail, not him."

"I'm sure he has," Bull said. "Thank you, Miss Whipple. Slim and I will take over now. Send your bill to Lincoln County. See the lady out, Thompson and don't disturb us."

Almost gruff, Bull Morrison was torn between being somewhat pleased that Hitchcock was no longer in the picture and upset that he would never have the pleasure of arresting and questioning the man.

"Hitchcock also owned the bank, Bull. His bank manager needs to be in on this search as well. I'd like to start there."

"Good idea," Bull said. "I'll brace this fine upstanding citizen, you tear the bank apart."

Slim took the two-block walk toward the center of town and was intercepted by Spike Loring at the Lucky Lady Saloon. "Heard a rumor that Sandy Hitchcock was murdered by Buster Cranston. That true?" Loring asked. "Not a real loss for Pioche if it is."

"Hitchcock is dead and Cranston is in custody, Spike, but that isn't the end of it. What do you know about Hitchcock's bank? Is it a real bank? Where is it? I haven't seen anything that looks like a real bank in town."

"Come into the saloon, Slim. You look like you could handle a stiff drink about now." Loring led them to the end of the bar and Jimmy Lassen set up the drinks. "The Pioche Bank is a chartered banking institution, legal in its standing, if not in all its dealings. It's located inside the building that houses the Silver Crystal Saloon. There is an entrance from inside the saloon and from the street."

"I'll be damned," Slim said. "Never noticed. Next you'll be telling me that Pendergrass is the bank manager." He took the whiskey down in one gulp.

"No." Loring laughed. "I wouldn't put it past him, though. I'm sure he's involved in some way. Sam Washburn is the bank manager. Seems to be a straight shooter, but my only dealings have been short term loans, none of the mining ventures or land speculations that Hitchcock was into."

"Mining scams I'm familiar with, but land speculation?" Slim motioned for Lassen to hit him again. "Dry today, Jimmy. Keep 'em coming."

"Hitchcock has foreclosed on some ranches and is breaking them up into smaller pieces and selling them to the eastern population as health investments. Very involved and I'm sure very illegal. He's also working to bring a railroad into the valley below us. He's managed to get some eastern funding on that, as well."

"I hope I can find paperwork on most of this," Slim said. "How does he get this land he sells back east." Slim stopped cold. *Is he selling land or just saying he has land for sale? After all, speculators sold thousands of acres of riverfront property along the Reese River and it's not even a creek sized body of water. Saying you have it and selling it far from having it and selling it.*

"I'm sure you will. Well, he foreclosed on the ranches but they are fully operational. He hasn't closed the ranching operations and doesn't plan to. The properties he forecloses on seem to have sufficient water, too." He had to chuckle at the comment.

"He is selling small acreage to east coast investors on land they will never see. Get the picture? The judge in Salt Lake,

Olsen, is his partner in the land and railroad deals." Loring was being hailed by someone at the faro table and nodded goodbye to Slim.

Calhoun spent a few minutes walking up and down the street near the Silver Crystal building, seeing the bank's entrance and limited signage. "Not much interested in street traffic for his bank," he murmured. Instead of using the street entrance, he stepped into the Silver Crystal. There was still a rowdy crowd at the bar and some of the tables.

"Here to start trouble, Marshal?" Rolf Pendergrass was standing near the end of the bar.

"Not in my plans, Pendergrass." Slim nodded to the barman for a cold beer. "Actually looking for the bank manager."

"I'd look in the bank first," Pendergrass said. He snickered and walked off. Slim took his time with the beer, looking at all the action in the bar and locating the bank's almost hidden entrance. It was off to the side of the poker tables.

Hitchcock could play poker and keep an eye on his bank at the same time. Well, let's see what Mr. Washburn has to say about mines, land, and railroads. A dollar to a double eagle I'll have to get a court order. That gives me a fine reason to visit with Dewey Schaffer again.

Calhoun let his mind wander a bit and knew for certain that if he approached the bank manager without a warrant, he would never recover any evidence of wrongdoing by Hitchcock. It would burn or get destroyed. *I'll get the warrant first.*

CHAPTER 18

"LAST TIME WE MET, BUSTER CRANSTON, YOU MADE A SERIOUS AT-
tempt to kill me. Don't think you enjoyed the outcome, eh?"
Bull Morrison was sitting on a cot across from Cranston.
"What happened at Hitchcock's?"

"Don't know what you're talking about," Cranston said.

"You were seen going in and coming out, Cranston. And
when we went in, Sandy Hitchcock was dead, his gun had been
fired, and you were captured running away with a gunshot
wound." Bull poked the wounded arm. "Again, what happened?"

Cranston grabbed his wounded arm. "Bastard. Man fired
me and I beat the hell out of him. He pulled a gun and shot
me and I left. He was alive and yelling some nasty words at me
when I left. If he's dead he wasn't killed by me."

"For some reason I want to believe you. Where'd the
money come from?"

"Took it from the mine office. He owed me and I took it."

"I'm going to let the justice of the peace sort this out,
Cranston. For now, the charges are robbing the mine office,
but that could change fast. Who else might have a reason to
kill the fat man?"

"Just about everyone in Lincoln County," Cranston laughed.

"He buys and sells people and commodities, Marshal. Ask Harvey Lighthorse, there," he said and pointed at the sheriff in the next cell. "He bought you, Sheriff, and wasn't in any hurry to come to your rescue."

"Go to hell, Cranston, but he's right, Marshal. There are a lot of people who would feel they have a good reason to kill the old man. He hasn't made anyone but himself rich and there are many who are destitute because of him."

Bull Morrison nodded and walked from the cell, locking it tight. "I'll be at the Lucky Lady if you need me," he said to Thompson. "You've been a deputy for some time, who did the sheriff hire as jailer?"

"Didn't actually have one, Marshal. Whoever was in the office checked on the prisoners from time to time."

"Sloppy. Anybody asked for the job before all this blew up?"

"The swamper at the Lucky Lady has asked many times. George Abraham Washington. Says he grew up as a slave. Got a million stories to tell but none to be believed."

"I'll send him over," Morrison said. "He's to stay in the cell block and report to me."

"GOOD TIMING, BULL," SLIM SAID. THEY MET ON THE STREET IN FRONT of the Lucky Lady. "I was just coming to find you. Got some good information on the bank and bank manager and want to ride out to see Judge Schaffer and get a warrant to search the bank records. Want to come along? Maybe he'll offer some of that good cheese."

"You go ahead, Slim. I'm about to hire a jailer and track down some people who have serious grudges with Hitchcock. Pretty sure that Cranston isn't the killer. Doesn't add up. Hitchcock has ruined a lot of people in Pioche. Get the goods on

Judge Olsen, I'll try to find our killer."

Slim headed for the stables for his horse and Bull stepped into the saloon for a drink and a jailer. "Morning, Jimmy. Whiskey and a beer, if you please."

Good afternoon, Marshal," Jimmy Lassen joshed. "It's actually mid-afternoon, sir."

"Been a long day," Bull said. "Where would I find George Abraham Washington?"

"Should be at the pisser out back, Marshal. What's he done?"

"Nothing, I hope." He headed out the back door and followed a well worn trail. "You Washington?"

"Yes, sir," the scrawny little man said. He wasn't five feet tall, didn't weigh a hundred and ten pounds, and was blacker than anyone Bull had ever seen. He was stepping from the shack and gave Bull a big toothy smile. "You must be the man been beatin' on everybody. Don't be beatin' on me. I ain't done nothing."

Bull had to chuckle. "You're safe, George. I'm U.S. Marshal Bull Morrison and I need a jailer. Filling up the county jail fast and those people need watching. I understand you've wanted the job."

"I have," Washington said. "Marshal, eh? I knew a man said he'd met a marshal once. Glad to meet you. I'll need some clean clothes to be a jailer. Can't be seen in these rags."

Bull handed the man a half eagle and told him he had an hour to report to Gary Thompson. "I'm the boss, George, and I want those men well taken care of. I also want to know what it is they might be talking about."

"Thank you, Marshal. I'll be the bestest jailer you done ever met." Bull had to laugh watching the man hightail it to the dry goods store for new clothes.

One chore done, three hundred to go. Need to talk with Spike and Jimmy Lassen.

"Hope you don't mind me bustin' in on you like this," Slim said. "Our investigation is moving fast and I need your help."

"Come in, Slim," Justice of the Peace Schaffer said. "Encouraging or otherwise?" The fireplace was blazing and the judge led them to the living room. "The rumor mill doesn't reach out this far."

"I'll tell you what's happened and then tell you why I'm here."

"Then we'll need some good cheese and bread, and some strong coffee to wash it down. Go ahead and start while I get the goods."

Slim told him about the near riots, about people being shot, others arrested, and finally, about the death of Sandy Hitchcock and arrest of Buster Cranston. "You're right, Slim, things have been moving fast. "I'll come to town tomorrow, then and hold court. Most of who you have in custody are there on local charges. I'll either remand them for district court, let 'em go, or find 'em guilty."

He poured the coffee. "There was something else?"

"We've been told of illegal land speculation scams, railroad scams, and water scams being done through Hitchcock's bank. The worst part of all this is, we believe, a federal judge is involved as a working partner with Hitchcock."

"Morrison mentioned that Judge Olsen might be involved. That is way beyond my authority, I think, Slim."

"What I would like is a court warrant to search the bank's records. Can you authorize that?"

"I would hate to jeopardize your investigation, have it thrown out on a technicality, so I must decline your request. You need to talk with Greg Mallard, the district judge for this and surrounding counties. It would be hell if I issue a search warrant and have that destroy the effort to find the judge guilty."

Schaffer walked around the small living room for a long time. "No, Slim, you must get that warrant from Mallard. I'm sorry."

"I am too, Judge, but I also think you're right. Do you hold court right at the jail?"

"Someday, within the next fifty years or so, they'll have our courthouse built, so yes, I hold court right in the sheriff's office. I'll be there at nine, court at ten. When you talk of funds missing, payoffs made, you should include those involved in building the courthouse."

Slim laughed. "I've heard it called the million-dollar courthouse."

It was a long cold ride back to Pioche, despite the beauty of Ruby Gulch and the mountains in the late afternoon sun. *He's right and I know it, but it sure puts a damper on the investigation. I'm not going to talk with that bank manager until I have a warrant. That would give us away worse than we already are. Donovan said he would get word to Mallard. Hope he does and soon. Hope Ginny has some steaks this big for supper, too.*

CHAPTER 20

LIGHTHORSE FELT RELIEVED THAT SANDY HITCHCOCK WAS DEAD. THE information he had could have followed him anywhere. *Dates, times, names of railroads and banks I hit, and he has that information in a sealed envelope. Will it be released to these marshals?*

Lighthorse was sitting in his own jail, under arrest for offering money to anyone killing either or both of the marshals. *This fool of a marshal will never be able to make those charges stick. I offered pay for his death there won't be anyone to help prove that. Hell, the fool killed the men coming for him. Who would dare testify against me, anyway?*

It was that level of arrogance that followed him his whole life. Never smart enough to be quiet after a big hit. Go out and buy the flashy gold and silver, Lighthorse, and then go to the saloon and show it off. No one will put two and two together. Add yesterday's stagecoach robbery to today's flashy jewelry. No, Sheriff, never. Lighthorse feared that letter full of his drunken confessions to Hitchcock would become more than public. Would put him in prison for a long time.

Lighthorse looked over at Washington and found him asleep in that chair. "Cranston, you got any ideas on who it was

you start?"

"Remember the man you beat the hell out of? The one the sheriff hired to kill you and Slim? He would be high on my list. Lighthorse would be right there, too. And, I wouldn't rule out Rolf Pendergrass. There would also be those who owed him money, Marshal, and that would include me."

Slim Calhoun walked in and joined them. "Not gonna get that warrant, Bull, and Schaffer is right not giving it. Need to get it from Mallard. Schaffer will hold court tomorrow morning. Anything new from your end?"

"Yes there is," Bull said. "Spike Loring has named himself as a suspect in the killing of Sandy Hitchcock. Think we should arrest the man?"

"Not before we finish our drinks," Slim joshed. "Have you heard anything from Tom Donovan? He was going to try to send Mallard our way."

"Too early. I expect another wire from Judge Baker, too. Maybe tomorrow. I hate to ignore the bank, Slim. Warrant or not, we should pay the manager a visit. Sure as all get-out evidence will up and disappear."

It didn't take a second nudge and the two walked the two blocks to the Silver Crystal Saloon. "Go in from the saloon side," Bull said. "Like we own the joint." He tried hard to smile but it just wasn't there. "If Pendergrass is at the bar, I'll talk with him and you head into the bank."

"I'm just going to look around, Bull. Sure as hell if I ask questions, don't have a search warrant, evidence will burn as soon as I leave." Bull nodded.

The cold air of the past several days had warmed some as the two marshals slipped through the swinging batwing doors. "There's Pendergrass," Bull said. He watched Slim turn and head for the bank. "Evening, Pendergrass. Wonder if we

could talk for a spell?" Bull nodded to the barman for a cold beer. Pendergrass moved to a table near the front of the saloon.

"What's on your mind, Marshal?"

"I'm sure you've heard that Hitchcock is dead. Killed in his own home." Pendergrass nodded but didn't say anything. "Strange, though," Bull continued. "The place was ransacked, as if someone was looking for something."

"Not really strange," Pendergrass said. "The man was a blackmailer, Marshal. There are many in Pioche who have been attacked by the man. I was under the impression that Buster Cranston was arrested."

"He was but not for murder. What kind of blackmail?"

"He would learn something about someone and have it written out and sealed. If anything happened to him it would become public knowledge but kept in total secret if certain things were done. It wasn't always for money. In the case of the sheriff, for instance, his outlaw background was safely secret if he did the fat man's bidding."

"And you?" Bull asked. He eyed Pendergrass, saw no change in his face or body at the question.

"Oh yes, including me. In the beginning, that is. What he had on me has nothing to do with today, though. The closest I came to working with him is giving him space for his bank. I have my saloon safe right next to his over there. It's a good arrangement."

"Whoever killed Hitchcock was looking for something, Pendergrass. It's going to be a long investigation, I think." Bull saw Slim coming in from the bank and joined him. They walked out onto the quiet early evening street.

"Pendergrass offered something that might help us. Anything coming from the bank?"

"Nothing without a warrant. All I did was say hello and

Washburn, the manager came right out and said he wouldn't even talk to me without a warrant. Just as I feared, Bull. Sure as hell evidence will be gone in hours."

"I might know where it's going," Bull said. "Pendergrass gave that space for a bank to Hitchcock but keeps his own safe next to the bank's. I'd be willing to bet that Sam Washburn has access to that safe."

Slim chuckled softly. "Suppose there's room in that safe to hide some of Hitchcock's secret papers? I hope we make contact with that district judge soon."

"Judge Mallard serves four counties. He could be any-where." Bull said. "Donovan seemed to think he could get word to the man. Tomorrow's another day, Slim."

"Time for supper old man and a long night's sleep. We have court in the morning. My foot hurts."

"Do you think Schaffer was just putting you off? I've heard twice today that Hitchcock was excellent at blackmail. Think he might have something on the judge?"

"No. Schaffer pointed out how our whole case could be thrown out if he was wrong in giving us a search warrant. I think he's as honest as the day, Bull. That Washburn is a weasel, though. Looked like any of a hundred men we'd find behind a faro table anywhere we went. I wouldn't trust him to hold the door for me."

killed Hitchcock? That marshal seemed sure it wasn't you."

"It wasn't. Any of a hundred that come to mind. Maybe Pizon, maybe Pendergrass. Maybe you paid somebody."

As soon as he said Pizon, Lighthorse's heart almost constricted. *My God, those letters.* Hitchcock's evidence against Pizon were sealed in envelopes and in the sheriff's custody. In the event of Hitchcock's death, they were to be sent to a federal judge in Salt Lake City. *If it was Pizon that killed Hitchcock he will figure it out that I have those letters. I got to get out of here and destroy them.*

Most lawmen work hard to see if they could figure out how to escape from their jails but Lighthorse had never been a lawman before. He had never even spent much time back in the cell area. Panic was starting to set in as he looked into every square inch of his cell, searching for the escape answer.

"Lookin' for a way out, Sheriff?" Cranston laughed, and Lighthorse settled down on his bunk.

The cells were cages of woven steel bars the corner posts of which were set deep into concrete. He knew immediately he wouldn't break his way out of the cell, but he knew he was far smarter than that Bull fellow. He would connive his way out. *I'll destroy Pizon's letters, find mine, and ride like the wind for Texas.*

"Fine meal, Ginny. Slim's foot healing up right?" Bull was still in the dining room waiting for Ginny to finish cleaning and bandaging Slim's wounded foot when she came out from the back.

"Coming along fine, Marshal. I know it won't do me any good to suggest he stay off his feet for a day or so."

"Not a chance." Bull said. Slim came out, the limp not as

noticeable. "Good. Let's drop in on the jail before nightcaps at the Lucky Lady. Want you to meet our new jailer."

"We're in a situation, Bull. Not enough people. Wish to hell we could trust the telegraph here in Pioche. Need to know what's happening in Salt Lake, they need to know what's going on here, and we both need to know what Judge Baker is doing. We don't even know the lead Marshal in Salt Lake."

"Before court in the morning, let's drop in at the telegraph office, put the fear of Bull Morrison in the man's heart and soul." The laugh was genuine, but Bull simply couldn't smile.

Lonesome Gary Thompson was sitting at the desk when Bull and Slim got back to the jail. "Coffee's hot, Marshal, and the prisoners have eaten. You run a good jail. I've been on the sheriff for a long time to get a jailer and to feed the prisoners better."

"Thank you, Thompson. Anyone ever escaped from this jail?" Bull asked.

"No. I think it was Jacob Overby who built the woven cells. Don't know how anyone would escape."

"Through a jailer's or deputy's stupidity, Deputy," Slim said. "Those men back there are all capable of deceit, Johnson. Deception, lies, and the ability to kill make them very dangerous. I would imagine that each one is planning how best to con their way out of here right at this moment."

Bull led Slim into the cell area and found George Abraham Washington sitting in his chair reading. "Ah, Marshal Bull. This other must be Marshal Slim. Our guests have had supper and after I read another chapter or two, I'll turn down the lamps, but not off."

"Very good, George," Bull said. "Anyone make trouble?"

"Only with words, Marshal, not with action. With the life I've lived, words don't mean nothin'."

"Get a good rest. Court will be held in the front office at ten. Have these men ready. Leg irons, interlocked, and handcuffs for all."

Bull and Slim never said a word to any of the prisoners, got a nod and smile from Washington, and stepped back into the office. "Quite the man, Bull. Where did you find him?"

"He was the swamper at the Lucky Lady," Bull said. "Loring will probably raise our rent, now." He swept the office with one short gaze, nodded to Johnson, and walked out, Slim right with him. "I can taste some brandy, Slim. And a new cigar. I've chewed this one as far down as I dare take it."

"Have you noticed how many people give us a long stare when we walk in? The looks were anger and hate when we first got here, now it's more subdued." Slim led the way to the end of the bar. "Probably have some of their hard-earned money on how long you are in the building before you start a fight."

Bull Morrison ignored Slim and walked straight to the bar. "Buenos noches, Chago," Bull said. "Brandy, por favor."

"Buenos noches, Toro. Coming right up. Spike will be down shortly, said if you come in to wait for him." He poured two snifters of brandy and passed them across the oak. "Well, well, he must have seen you. Here he comes now."

"Tell me what you know about the telegraph operator." Bull said. "We've been led to believe he works for Hitchcock more than he does for the telegraph. Where would his favors go now?"

"Interesting," Spike Loring said. He flagged Chago over. "Get Stewart down here, Chago. He's at one of the tables in the back." Loring turned back to Bull and Slim. "Paul Stewart is our telegraph operator and he came to me this afternoon with an interesting story you'll appreciate."

Chago came back to the bar with a man in his fifties, maybe

even older. He was heavy, red in the face, and thin in the hair department. "Paul Stewart," Spike said, "meet Marshal Bull Morrison. You were asking about him earlier."

"Marshal," Stewart said, almost bowing. "I'm sure glad to meet you. Mr. Hitchcock is a horrible man, evil. He said if I didn't tell him about every wire that someone wanted to send, before I sent it, mind you, he would kill my wife and burn my home down. If he didn't like what the wire was to say he would forbid me to send it. Sometimes he would alter the words so they seemed to say the opposite of what the sender wanted to say. I had to do what he said. I tried to tell Sheriff Lighthorse what Hitchcock said, and he laughed at me."

"I'm not laughing," Bull said. "Anyone else threaten you?" Bull was having a hard time understanding that almost all the crime in Pioche led back to just one man. The mining camp's reputation indicated wide open criminal activity, but Morrison was seeing a one-man gang.

Hitchcock couldn't do all this alone. Lighthorse isn't smart enough to be anything more than an annoying cog in the wheel. Buster Cranston got things done for the fat man, but there was no thinking, planning, organizing there. Hitchcock had to have partners.

"There's more to this barrel full of crime than one lone man could control," the marshal said right out. "Who else is giving you orders, Mr. Stewart? Don't lie to me, don't try to hide something from me. I'm a far meaner man than you've ever met."

"No, sir." Stewart said. "Others in town have asked for favors but no one but Hitchcock has threatened me or my poor wife."

"The kind of favors an outlaw might ask for?" Slim asked. "We want to be able to send wires, Stewart, and we want to know that you will not be running off and telling the world what we're doing."

"Before Mr. Hitchcock, Marshal, I never, ever, passed on information from my clients. An operator can lose his job faster doing that than anything. With Hitchcock dead, anything you send or receive through my wires will be safe. I've always been an honest man, but I would not let that horrible man kill my wife."

"Very well, Stewart. We'll see you in your office at eight tomorrow morning. Cross the marshal service, sir, and you'll lose more than your job. Your wife will be visiting you in prison for many years."

"Your communication will be secure, Marshal. I promise," the wire operator said. Again, the elderly man almost bowed to Morrison, nodded to Calhoun, and hurried out of the saloon.

"Believe him, Slim?"

"Yup," is all Slim said. "A nice quiet brandy, a long sleep, and we raise a lot of dust tomorrow." Before he could get his snifter in hand a tall, heavy, dusty buckaroo came through the swinging doors of the saloon.

"There a federal marshal in here?" he yelled out. "Need to talk to him."

"Right here," Bull said, flagging the man.

"Tom Donovan sent me. Got a passel of telegrams for you. Donovan also said to tell you that Judge Mallard will be in Pioche sometime tomorrow. Probably late. Long ride. Need a beer." He reached deep in his heavy coat and produced a wad of paper for Bull.

"Thank you," Bull said. "Beer's on me." He motioned for Slim to join him at a table where they could be alone. He spread the various pages out on the table's surface and tried to sort them into some kind of order. Slim took over the process before Bull got angry and just tore them up.

"By date and time, Bull." There were three wires, multi-pages long and Slim read the first one aloud. The Salt Lake City marshal was Peter Flannigan, a long time friend and fine lawman. "Flannigan wants us to come to Salt Lake, Bull. Bring as much evidence as we can find, bring our prisoners if there are any still alive, and the investigation will center on Judge Olsen's activities."

"No," Bull said softly. "No, no, no. The case is mostly federal, yes, but it originates here in Pioche. City Marshal Daws and Deputy Thompson can handle the local law breakers, but we can't run off like that."

"I agree, particularly since we haven't examined anything in that bank vault. We haven't gone over Hitchcock's home with a strong glass either. Not to mention the mine offices." He set aside the wire from Flannigan. "This is from Judge Baker." Slim read the missive quickly. "You are lead marshal, Bull, so Flannigan will follow your lead. He is waiting for an answer from Washington on exactly how to proceed."

"How to proceed?" Bull thundered. "Hang the bastard, that's how to proceed." Bull said. "What does he mean?"

"Washington has to make the decision on which department will hold court, San Francisco or Salt Lake, and which judge will be sitting, Baker or one sent in from somewhere else." Slim set the pages down. "Don't think I'd pick Salt Lake. That's Olsen's home territory."

"I'd pick Carson City myself," Bull said, "and bring in a judge from back east but that won't happen. Baker will swing it for San Francisco and he'll be the judge. You just watch." Bull took another long belt of brandy and harrumphed some. "Long damn day, Slim. Let's call it."

"The reputation of this little camp is gonna increase a

notch or two by the time we get through. The murderers and card sharks will have to move aside for Hitchcock's scams and shenanigans." Slim said. "I got a problem with Deputy Thompson working with Marshal Daws, Bull. Neither one of them is really ready for the job. Neither one really thinks."

"Afraid we ain't got much choice, old friend."

CHAPTER 21

MARSHAL DAWS TOOK OVER THE SHERIFF'S OFFICE FOR THE NIGHT AND sent Lonesome Gary Thompson home. Daws liked the way things seemed to be working out. *Sheriff Lighthorse was nothing more than an outlaw who used his gang as deputies. Well, things are different now. We even have a jailer on board.* Daws stepped into the cell area.

"Just me, George," Three-Finger Jack said. "Everything in order back here?"

"They been snorin' and jabber-talking all night, Marshal." Washington was on a cot in an empty cell, covered in a warm wool blanket. "Marshal Bull said there would be court at ten and to have them fed and ready by nine. You'll have to help me get them properly shackled."

"Miz Whipple brings breakfast at seven, so we'll be fine, George. Get some sleep." Three-Finger Jack turned to leave. "I'm about to make my rounds of town, be gone for a while. I'll stoke the wood stove good when I leave."

George rolled over. *Ain't this just somethin'. Got a bed with a cover, gonna get a hot breakfast brought to me, an all cuz they got some outlaws need watchin' over. Other way around, not that many years ago. Had a man with a rifle keepin' us folks from runnin' off.* George chuckled softly, closed his eyes, and was glad he didn't have dreams of field after field of cotton and white men with guns overseeing every move they made. He never heard Daws stoke the fire and leave the building.

"HITCHCOCK ALWAYS SAID HE GAVE THOSE LETTERS TO LIGHTHORSE to keep. First his house, then the jail."

Pizon Oakley murmured as he tied his horse in the back of the Lighthorse property, which was on the same block as Hitchcock's but further south. The night was dark, no lamp light could be seen inside, and Pizon broke the kitchen door window. He carefully reached in and unlocked it and walked to the stove. "Cold," he muttered. "Good. Means the bastard's still in jail."

Pizon spent a furious ten minutes tearing the kitchen and living room apart, not finding the letter. He worked his way upstairs and ripped the sheriff's bedroom apart as well. "Not a single piece of anything personal. He must keep all his papers and stuff at the office. Fool."

Pizon rode around the dark uphill streets, slowly working his way toward the courthouse/jail complex. It was dark, late, and there were few people out and about.

Three-Finger Jack Daws stabled his horse at Overby's, so was walking the town, shaking doors, calming drunks, and paying his respects at the various saloons and houses of pleasure. Pizon had no way of knowing if anyone was at the jail and didn't care if there was. That letter must be found, must be destroyed.

Lighthorse was too cheap to hire a jailer so if a deputy is in there, he's dead. That fool must keep all his papers in his desk and my letter must be with them. Hitchcock always said

Lighthorse had it. It was the last taunt the fat man made.

He tied his horse under a cottonwood tree half a block from the jail and tried his best to stay in the darkest part of the walk back. He stood to the side of the jail door and listened for some kind of sound. Pizon took a deep breath, had his gun in hand, and slowly lifted the latch, eased the door open, and stepped into an empty office.

"Fire's lit so somebody will be coming back," Pizon muttered, moving quickly to the sheriff's large oak desk. There were three drawers on each side with one in the center at the top, and Pizon started with that one, pulling everything out and strewing the contents about. Some on top of the desk, some on the floor.

"What the hell is that deputy doing out there?" George Abraham Washington came out of a sound sleep at the noise from the office. He slipped out from the wool blanket and walked barefoot to the office door, which stood slightly ajar.

"Oh my," he whispered, moving back from the door. The movement was seen and Pizon rushed through the slightly open door. The confrontation was fast and ugly. Washington ran for the open cell but Pizon was much faster, and slugged the skinny little ex-slave knocking him to the concrete floor. Pizon kicked Washington in the head at least three times before turning his attention to the prisoners, slowly coming awake from the ruckus.

"You, Lighthorse, where is that letter from Hitchcock? Where?" He had his weapon in hand and aimed it at Lighthorse's head.

"Let us out, Oakley. I'll take you to it. Even if I tried to tell you where it is, you couldn't get at it. Let us out."

"No, no, Sheriff. I ain't as dumb as you. Tell me now or I shoot you dead."

"Shoot me and that letter goes public. Let us out and I'll take you to it."

Pizon was about to shoot Lighthorse, not let him out, when Three-Finger Daws came rushing through the door and into the cell area. He had that shotgun at the ready, but Pizon whirled and shot twice, knocking the city marshal down. Pizon took one quick look back at Lighthorse, turned and raced from the jail area to his horse.

"YOU HEAR THAT?" BULL MORRISON JUMPED FROM HIS BED, GRABBING his pants. He yelled into the adjoining room. "Shots, Slim. Sounded like close to the jail." He got his pants, shirt, and boots on, and was strapping his gun on as Slim did the same. They rushed down the stairs and out the door as a rider flashed past them, riding south at a hard gallop.

The jail building door was wide open and the two ran into the office, strewn with papers from the sheriff's desk. "What the hell's going on?" Bull asked and raced for the cell area door. Washington was on the floor near an open cell, moaning, holding his bleeding head, and Daws was inert, bleeding hard.

Slim took a fast count and knew none of the prisoners was missing. "What happened, Lighthorse? Tell me now." Lighthorse didn't say anything, just stood near the bars of his cell. "Damn it, Lighthorse, there are two men seriously wounded here. What happened? Who did this?"

Bull got Washington on his feet and onto the cot. "Somebody came in here looking for something. Who was it?" Bull had the jailer settled and walked to where the cell keys were hanging and opened Lighthorse's cell. He threw his sidearm to Slim and walked into the cell. "Who, Sheriff?"

The fist seemed to come out of nowhere and Harvey

Lighthorse found himself flat on his back with Bull Morrison standing over him ready to pound his head into the concrete floor. "Who, Sheriff?"

"Oakley," Lighthorse mumbled through split lips and broken teeth.

"It's four o'clock, Bull and these men need help. I'm going for Ginny Whipple," Slim said. Despite his sore foot he ran to the closed cafe, woke the lady up by banging on the back door. She was holding a sawed off double barreled stagecoach messenger's shotgun when she opened the door.

"Whoa! Easy now,"

"What do you want?" She demanded, not asked, and Slim backed up half a step and threw his hands up.

"Easy, Ginny. It's Slim." He took a quick breath looking down the massive holes at the end of the gun and told her about Daws being shot and Washington being mauled.

"Oh my," She said. "Come in. I thought you were one of those crazy drunks." Slim stood in the living room and Ginny headed back to her bedroom. He told her what he knew while the lady dressed and put together a small medical kit and they made a fast run back to the jail.

"Take it easy, Washington. Your old head was kicked and stomped hard. Just lay back and don't worry none. Miss Whipple will be here shortly." Only those who rode with Bull ever saw the soft side of the marshal. It only showed if a friend or working partner was hurt bad. The fact that the man even had a soft side was never discussed.

Bull moved to Daws, unconscious and bleeding from two wounds that were sure to lead to death. Both were through the middle of his lower body, wounds that simply couldn't be treated by anyone other than a well trained doctor and even then it was a crap shoot on success.

That rider who passed us in such a rush must have been Pizon. Racing south like that would take him to the hot springs Spike talked about. Why, though? Why want to shoot the sheriff? Why tear up the office? Time for another session with the sheriff.

He left his revolver with Washington, opened the cell door, and stepped inside, closing and locking the door. He tossed the keys out onto the floor. "It's just us Lighthorse and I want some answers. You said it was Pizon Oakley came in here and shot Three-Finger Daws and beat the hell out of Mr. Washington. Why, Lighthorse?" He took one step toward the sheriff who cringed back a step. "What was he looking for?"

"Something from Hitchcock," Lighthorse mumbled. "Hitchcock was holding something over his head. Something important."

"Why would Pizon believe you have it?" Bull's anger was building and he had to do something to get it back under control. Getting one word answers, evading the questions, not cooperating in the least was not in Lighthorse's best interests.

"We're going to come to an understanding real quick here, Sheriff," Bull said. "Court will be held at ten in the morning before Justice of the Peace Schaffer. Judge Mallard is due in town later in the day. You are just hours from being sent to prison. Charges are piling up here, Sheriff. Not answering my questions makes you an accessory to what Pizon did in here. Being in a conspiracy with a man who attempted to kill two lawmen doesn't sit well with judges, Lighthorse."

Morrison reached out and grabbed Lighthorse by the front of his shirt and pulled him right up to his face. "Why?" He pushed the man back hard and the sheriff fell onto a cot.

"All right, Marshal. All right. Pizon was robbing a bank in Arizona Territory and in the process took a woman and her two children hostage. The children were a boy twelve and a girl fourteen. When officials discovered the three bodies they also discovered the terrible things Pizon did to the woman and both children."

"How do you know this?" Bull asked. He was bent over the man, that dangerous right fist cocked and ready.

"Because Hitchcock had newspaper accounts and knew the accounts were about the man known as Pizon Oakley who was responsible. Hitchcock said he would notify Arizona Territory lawmen unless Pizon worked for him. He gave all of that to me to hold."

"And just where would I find these newspaper accounts, Sheriff? Or does Pizon have them, now."

"He doesn't have them. They're in a safe place. What's it worth to you for me to tell you where they are?"

"Your life, you bastard." He took a step back and smiled that horrible smile of his. He was agitated to the point the scar across his face was crimson, and Lighthorse knew he had played the wrong card. Before Bull made a move, Slim and Ginny burst into the cell area.

"Good timing, Calhoun. Another ten seconds and this man would be dead." He pointed at the keys and Slim let him out. "That rider racing out of town was Pizon Oakley who was responsible for these men's injuries. I have to be here for court and Pizon was racing for the hot springs. He's also wanted for murder and horrible atrocities in Arizona Territory. Slim, you need to catch him and bring him back. Dead would be best."

"I'll get him. Hope Overby's there so I can get my horse," he snickered. His limp, aggravated by the running held up and he was able to dog-trot to the freight yard. He found Overby talking with three of his mule skinners.

"Marshal Calhoun, I'm glad to see you moving well," the

blacksmith said. "what's going on this time of night?"

"Need to get my horse, Overby. Pizon Oakley tried to kill Three-Finger Jack."

"That bastard." One of the teamsters said. "Man needs to be put away like the mad dog he is. You're one of the marshals been beating everyone up?" Thomas Tucker, known as Terrible Tommy was bigger and heavier than Bull Morrison and offered a little chuckle with his comment.

"My partner," Slim said. "Oakley's riding hard for the hot springs and I need to either catch or kill him."

"You'll need help, Marshal," Overby said. "You boys ain't scheduled out until tomorrow and this here marshal's already got one wound. Let's take a nice little ride to the hot springs, shall we?"

"He has help down there, Overby," Slim said. "This is going to be dangerous." Overby chuckled along with the skinners, and they all walked into the big barn to saddle up. "Pizon tried to kill George Abraham Washington as well."

"Then it's a fact he ain't comin' back alive," Terrible Tommy said. "My grampa was a slave, too. I don't look like Washington cuz of my gramma, and my ma'n pa. they's all white, but I sure did love my grampa. Old George Washington is a good man."

The other two mule skinners Eric Marston and Zeke Trumple laughed and made rude comments that just bounced off Tucker. They had been friends working together for a long time. Terrible Tommy's background was well known. "Have your fun, boys, but if you ever got some good hugs and squeezes from my old Grampa you'd feel the same."

CHAPTER 22

"Be light in another two hours," Overby said. "Take the main road south, stay at a trot most of the way, and we'll eat up those twenty miles." Three teamsters, one blacksmith, and one Deputy U.S. Marshal were on the road in just minutes. Terrible Tommy, at his insistence rode alongside Slim Calhoun.

"I was in the Silver Crystal the night you beat fat old Hitchcock out of his money and saw your partner smack the sheriff. Pretty good show. I think your partner and I would get along just fine. More'n once I've wanted to punch Lighthorse right in the mouth. Him and Pizon are killers, Marshal. Killers."

"I know, Tommy. When we get back, I'll see to it that you have a drink or two with my partner." Slim had to chuckle thinking about the two of them, Terrible Tommy and Bull Morrison, standing at the same bar, looking for a fight. *I better make sure we're drinking at the Silver Crystal and not the Lucky Lady or we won't have a home.*

"It's comin' sunrise, Pizon," the gambler, Toby Smith, hollered out. "What is it we're supposed to do? Are we riding into trouble or what?"

Pizon had ridden hard through the dark night and gathered the few men who were at the hot springs. Riding hard at night can be fatal, but there was a well used wagon road the entire way, which made the ride much safer. "Damn right we're riding into trouble. Those two dudes are trying to make everyone believe they're marshals but they ain't. They're hired guns riding for the ranchers and they have the sheriff locked up. They even shot Marshal Daws," Pizon lied.

If he gets these men riled to the point of killing the marshals and giving Pizon a chance to beat the tar out of the the sheriff, he'll be able to get those papers and evade the hangman's noose. Pizon was good at rabble-rousing, particularly if he had something personal to gain from it.

"We're riding into Pioche, freeing the sheriff, and helping him drive those two out of town." Pizon had the five men screaming for blood, passing a bottle or two of rot-gut whiskey among them. "Then we might just ride down into the valley and burn a ranch or two." He was yelling, laughing, pumping his fist, getting the men riled more than the bottles of liquor had done.

When I get that fool sheriff out from behind those bars, I'll beat him until he tells me where those papers are. Let these fools ride out and burn a ranch, I'll burn those papers and ride for Virginia City. There's a couple of banks there just waiting for me.

"Find your horses and saddle up, men. I want to be on the road to Pioche in half an hour," Pizon Oakley said. "Make sure your weapons are loaded and that you have extra ammunition." He motioned for Toby Smith to walk with him.

"When we attack the jail, Smith, it's important that we don't kill the sheriff. We need him to be alive," Pizon said. "He's our reason for being there and we are acting as his deputies so everything we do is legal." The lies poured like warm honey and Smith took it all in. "We can save the sheriff, save the mines by wiping out the ranchers, and be safe doing it."

"Are you sure those two men aren't really federal marshals? I saw that one big one beat the hell out of Lighthorse and show a badge after."

"Hell, Smith, I've got three or four badges I've took from sheriffs. They come in handy to fool the foolish. Now get your horse. Remember, we got to keep the sheriff alive."

THE RIDE SOUTH WAS GOING WELL, A FULL MOON HELPING THINGS. Riding at a trot for long distances ate up the miles. "We'll be at the hot springs in less than an hour, Marshal," Tucker said. "We got to ride up and over that cut in the hills up there and we'll drop right down to the hot springs."

"Be a good place to stop and talk about what we'll find and how we'll act," Slim said. "I'd feel best if we can bring Pizon back alive but not at the risk of lives. How far is that pass?"

The sun was shining bright and Tucker pointed out the pass about three miles in front of them. "There's a cold-water spring and some trees at the top. Good place to stop."

The four rode up the slight incline to a stand of cottonwood and aspen wrapped around a flowing spring. The pass was a broad cut in the mountain, and it was obvious they weren't the first riders to enjoy the rest area and fresh water. Some litter, the remains of coffee fires, even some lead rope still hanging from tree trunks. They could look well down the other side into a lush valley.

"Who knows the layout of the hot springs?' Slim asked as the men gathered around him.

"Been there many times," Eric Marston said. "Pizon is a blood thirsty killer but his whores are first class. There are several cabins near the hot springs, a barn, and a couple of other buildings. Two of the cabins are for the working girls, one is Pizon's and one is for the ranch manager to use when he's around."

"You lead us right to Pizon's cabin, Mr. Marston." Slim was about to say something else when Jacob Overby jumped to his feet, pointing at dust a mile or two down the trail to the hot springs.

"We got a mess of riders coming this way, Marshal. Got to be at least five or six."

Slim ran to his horse and got his telescope and used the horse to steady the look. "They found us boys. That's Pizon Oakley riding in the lead." Slim laughed and the others jumped for their horses. "Let's give them a nice surprise. Hide the horses in the trees and take up positions on both sides of the road. Let's not be shooting each other when they get here."

Tucker had his horse and grabbed the lead rope of Slim's, running the two into the trees and tying them off. The horses were tied near a jumble of rocks that Slim was planning to be behind. "Gonna stick to you like a fly to paper, Marshal," Terrible Tommy Tucker said, grinning like a little boy with a licorice stick. "Do we shoot first?"

"No," Slim said. "Listen up, now." The men gathered around quickly. "It's important that I call out who we are and why. Judges don't like it much when we just start shooting, and right now, boys, we're all working for the courts."

Slim, Terrible Tommy, and Overby found good hiding places on the west side of the pass while Zeke Trumple and Eric Marston set up shop on the east side. Slim looked around to make sure everyone was ready, watched the men riding hard close the distance, and prepared for a hard fight. "You are mine, Pizon Oakley."

PIZON OAKLEY WAS LEADING THE LITTLE BAND OF OUTLAWS WITH THE gambler Smith alongside. They were riding up the side of the cut at a gentle lope, not talking. Pizon had his mind on Lighthorse and knew he would have a hard time getting those papers without killing the man. *I made one mistake killing Hitchcock before he could tell me where Lighthorse hid the papers. I can't make that mistake again.*

"We'll be in Pioche in a couple of hours, Smith. I shot Three-Finger Jack Daws so the only ones at the jail will be those two hired guns. We'll go in shooting. Don't hesitate, cuz if you do, you'll die."

"You can count on me, Pizon." Smith said. *I thought he said the marshals shot Daws? Interesting.* Smith was a good gambler, enjoyed what he thought was the friendship of the killer, but deep inside, he knew he had never shot anyone, wasn't sure he could.

When the gang of outlaws rode into the pass, they walked their horses across the flats at the top. Slim Calhoun yelled out. "Pizon Oakley. Stop where you are. This is Deputy Marshal Slim Calhoun. You're under arrest. Stop or die."

Oakley put the spurs to his horse, laid out low across the horse's neck and raced for freedom. Smith pulled his horse to a stop and grabbed for his weapon as did the other three outlaws. Slim ran to his horse and was on the chase immediately. Terrible Tommy Tucker wanted to run with Slim, saw Smith pulling down on the running marshal, and shot the gambler right off his horse. Then he ran for his horse.

Overby, Marston, and Trumple held rifles and shotguns and took the other outlaws, still full of hot liquor, without shots being fired. "Tie 'em tight, boys and fling 'em back on their horses. We'll take a nice ride back to Pioche." Jacob Overby was having a fine time of it. "Don't take no kind of back talk from any of 'em. That gambler dude dead?"

"No, Jacob, but he might be by the time we make town." Marston hefted the wounded man across the saddle and tied the ropes tight. "Don't you think we should help the marshal?"

"We are," Overby said. "He's got Terrible Tommy. He don't need nothing else."

PIZON OAKLEY DIDN'T WANT TO RUN NORTH BUT DIDN'T HAVE ANY choice and was trying to figure out where he could get off this main road and evade the two men chasing him. The only roads were lanes that led to ranches and Pizon knew those wouldn't work. The countryside was mountainous, rocky, and too dangerous to try to ride through at a full gallop.

Slim knew that Tucker was close behind and kept at a hard run, following close behind Oakley. *He's taking us right back to Pioche. Gonna make it easy for us.* Slim was closing fast but knew it would be a long chase. *Horses got a good rest at the top of that cut.* Slim knew less about the road they were on than Oakley and wasn't aware that none of the trails that led off it didn't really go anywhere.

At the pass they were less than fifteen miles from Pioche, and at a full out run, the horses would be done-in well before they reached town. *Gotta keep at this pace and ride Oakley down. Old Boney Back is a far better horse than Oakley's. Come on, big boy, let's get him.*

Oakley's horse was showing signs of being winded, the one Terrible Tommy was riding was slowing as well, as Slim closed on Pizon Oakley. "Gonna take you down hard, Pizon," Slim mumbled.

Oakley kept turning in the saddle, watching Slim close on him. He drew his revolver but didn't try to fire. "Trees," he said right out when he caught sight of a stand of cottonwood. He turned off the road and raced as hard as the horse could go for the trees. Slim was less than twenty yards behind, with Tucker about fifty yards back from Slim.

"Come on, horse. Come on, boy," Pizon yelled out, setting the spurs hard on the winded animal. Could he feel the icy fingers of death? He felt the horse giving out on him, could hear the pounding hooves behind him, and screamed at the horse. They rode through the heavy sage, not around or over, slowing the horse even more. Finally, Pizon raced into the swampy area surrounded by trees and jumped from the saddle. He ran hard for a downed tree and leaped into the mud behind it, revolver in hand.

Slim turned hard to the left when he saw Pizon leap, and jumped from his horse, running for a tree and getting onto the ground behind the thick trunk. He could see where Pizon was but couldn't see the outlaw. *Gotta get more off to the side.* He made a quick dash off to his left and dove behind a large cottonwood.

That's better. I got you now, Pizon. Ain't nowhere to go but prison or the grave, killer. Slim flagged Tucker who jumped from his horse, to the right, and hid behind a tree. With arm motions Slim pointed out where Pizon was and that he was going to advance on him if Tucker would do some shooting.

Tucker saw the dead trunk, couldn't see Pizon, but put a shot across the dead tree, kicking up splinters of dead wood and bark. The shot did its work and Pizon immediately took a shot in Tucker's direction. Slim ran forward to another tree and heard Tucker answer Pizon's shot. Slim ran again to a tree just twenty yards or so from Pizon.

Oakley was reloading his big revolver, too busy to notice Calhoun moving toward him, tree by tree. *Gotta kill these men, gotta get those papers from Nighthorse. Gotta get out of this country.* His mind was racing through all the things he needed to do but wasn't paying attention to what needed to be done immediately. He never saw Calhoun move up to within fifteen yards of so of his position.

I see you, killer. Slim eased the sights onto Pizon's chest and squeezed off a shot, watched as the man was jerked back and face down. "Come on, Tucker," he yelled, and raced for the dead trunk. Pizon was face down in the mud, trying to crawl away when Slim put his foot onto the outlaw's neck.

"End of the line, Oakley." Slim jerked the revolver from the Oakley's hand and rolled him over. The bullet went into the center of Oakley's chest and the blood was coming in hard spurts. Tucker ran up then. "It's a real shame, Mr. Oakley," Slim said, "but I'm afraid I won't have the chance to see you hang."

Oakley's eyes rolled back in his head, he choked once on blood, and slumped back in the dirt. "Ain't no way for a man to die, Mr. Tucker. Ain't heard a good word said about this man since me and Bull rode into Pioche. Probably ain't got nobody to mourn his passing either."

"I'll get the horses," Tucker said. "Good shot."

Slim and Tucker had Pizon's body tied tight when Overby led the others up to the stand of trees. "Anybody hurtin'?"

"Not a soul," Slim said.

CHAPTER 23

"HE ISN'T GONNA MAKE IT, IS HE?" BULL MORRISON WAS PACING around the cell area watching Ginny Whipple work on Daws.

"I'm not giving up, Marshal. The bullets did some serious damage, but all I'm seeing right now is blood, not what would be in damaged organs. Keep that fresh water coming." One bullet passed high on Daws' right side, nicking a rib bone. Ginny had taken care of that one. The other bullet was lower and seemed to simply go through the flesh, not destroying organs and inner systems. "Three-Finger Jack is a lucky man, Marshal."

Ginny had the wounds cleaned and bandaged about the same time that Justice of the Peace Dewey Schaffer arrived. "Looks like this has been a busy place," he quipped, making his way through the papers and stuff still scattered about. "What happened?"

Gary Thompson was right behind the judge. "Damn," he said. He walked to the cell block door and found Marshal Morrison sitting on a cot talking with Washington. "Good morning," he said.

"Busy morning, Thompson." Bull got up and walked out of Washington's cell. "You can start by making a fire, making coffee, and cleaning up that mess up front."

"Judge Schaffer is out there now," Thompson said as he turned back from the doorway and Bull followed him out.

"Morning, Judge. Let's us have a nice talk."

"I think we need to," he said. The wise old Justice of the Peace could see blood and wounded men through the slightly open door, had waded through a mess of papers and other debris coming in, and a solemn U.S. Marshal looking hard and mean. "Where's your partner?"

"On the chase. Grab a chair, Judge. Get that coffee boiling, Thompson, we're gonna need it by the pot." The judge slipped into the chair nearest the stove and Bull grabbed the one behind the desk. "You're here because of what Slim brought to you, but there have been some drastic changes in that."

"Calhoun told me about arresting the sheriff for allegedly offering money to anyone killing either or both of you, the murder of Hitchcock, and needing a warrant to search the bank's records." He sat back in his chair, the slightest smile across his face. "There's more?"

Bull had to chuckle. "I'm afraid there is considerably more, your honor. A man named Pizon Oakley is probably the man who killed Hitchcock but is also responsible for what you see here." Bull spread his arms wide, showing the mess in the office. "My new jailer, George Abraham Lincoln Washington is suffering a severe beating and Pioche Town Marshal Three-Finger Jack Daws might not live from gunshot wounds."

"Washington? A most interesting gentleman." He chuckled. "Actually, his name is George Abraham Washington. He has one of the finest outlooks on life I've run into in this old mining camp. What on earth would have brought all this about?"

Schaffer got up and walked about the office, stuck his head into the cell-block, and walked back to stand next to the stove, his shaggy old head slowly nodding back and forth. "Destruction of personal property, attempted murder..." He let his thoughts hang in the air for a long moment. "Why?"

"Mr. Hitchcock was blackmailing Oakley, we believe. Oakley is wanted for horrible crimes committed in Arizona Territory and Hitchcock had newspaper accounts of the crime and naming Oakley as the criminal. He believed that Sheriff Nighthorse was holding those papers and Oakley came to get them."

"And these other people got in the way," Schaffer said. "Definitely Hitchcock's way. Too often the way, Marshal. Innocents get whipped, shot, even killed just for being in the wrong place." He took the cup of coffee offered by Thompson. "I'm not sure we can hold court, Marshal. Tell me about what kind of chase Calhoun is on."

"Oakley made a run for the hot springs south of here. Slim's on his tail. Been gone several hours and it might be several more before we hear something. Before you make a decision on holding court, we got word last night that District Judge Gregory Mallard will arrive in town late today."

"Calhoun was under the impression that strong evidence of wrong-doing might be in that bank's vault. He didn't go into detail and I'm not asking you to, either. But you should go into as much detail as you can when Mallard gets here. These water and property issues have led to more than one death already."

"I'm fearful that we've already lost considerable evidence, your honor. Sam Washburn probably lit last night's fire with it."

"A federal judge would have thrown it out if I had issued a warrant. It really isn't in my purview. I'm sure Mallard will tell you the same thing. Tell me more of last night. This is amazing."

"A PARADE OF DEAD, WOUNDED, AND STUPID, IS WHAT WE'RE LEAD-
ing, Marshal." Terrible Tommy Tucker laughed as they rode
over a hump in the road and Pioche came into view. They
rode at a slow walk through the late afternoon warmth
drawing the attention of many. Gasps of recognition came
from many, seeing the bodies of the gambler, Toby Smith,
and the killer Oakley.

Slim nodded to Spike Loring as they passed the Lucky Lady
and turned toward the jail. He stepped down from his horse
and knew all the running and jumping had torn loose most
of the good work Ginny Whipple had done. He tied off the
horse and the one he was leading, carrying Oakley's body, and
limped up onto the boardwalk. "Long damn day, Bull," he said
to Morrison as the marshal stepped out of the office. "I could
use a belt of that good stuff you have tucked away."

"Good work, Slim. Good work." He held the door for Calhoun and turned to help bring the living prisoners in. "Need
to get the dead ones to the undertaker."

"I'll take care of that," Jacob Overby said. "It'll be my
pleasure."

Slim found a chair behind the desk and fell into it. He
pulled a couple of drawers open before he found Bull's flask
and took a long drink. "Damn this old foot of mine hurts.
Ginny sure ain't gonna like this," he said. He nodded to Dewey Schaffer talking to another man and moved his wounded
foot back and forth and could feel the wetness inside the
boot. "Ain't gonna like it one bit."

"What ain't I gonna like, Slim?" She walked out from the
cell block. "You look a bit rough, my friend. What happened?"

"Yes, Marshal, what happened?" Schaffer stepped over

to the desk. "Looks like you spent some time rolling around in the mud."

"Had to play jack-rabbit but we got Oakley. Damn fool wouldn't quit though until he ran out of blood." Slim lifted his boot as if to show her. "I wrecked your doctoring, Ginny. Sorry."

"Slim, this is District Judge Gregory Mallard," Schaffer said.

"Judge Mallard. Am I glad to see you."

"Same here, Marshal. Marshal Morrison has told me some fine stories about your time here in Pioche. Glad you're all right. No way you could have arrested Oakley?"

"None. He was shooting at me when my bullet ripped through his heart." Slim looked at Ginny Whipple. "How's our new jailer? That was a nasty hit he took to that head of his."

"He'll be weak and out of balance for a few days but fine. It's Marshal Daws who might give us a lot of trouble. I don't think his internal organs were hit by the bullets, but if they were, there is no way I can stop the infection that will come." She poured a cup of coffee and put it in front of Slim.

"Here, drink this and we'll get that boot off."

"That's a brand new boot, woman. No knives." He was half chuckling and half serious. "Already lost one pair."

"I'll take it off him," Judge Mallard said. Mallard was a big man, spent his early days cutting wood for the army before attending law school, and his arms and shoulders were proof of being a good worker. He lifted Slim's leg and slowly eased the boot back and forth, toe to heel, while gently pulling on it. It slipped right off and the bloody stocking proved Slim's comments right.

"At least you've still got four toes in there," Ginny said. "I hope." She pulled the stocking off and saw most of her stitches had been ripped loose. "This might take some serious needle work, my friend. The healing process was well along, though. I need clean water and some rags to clean up this mess." Gary Thompson ran to the cell block for them.

"I wish Slim was with us but at least he's being well treated," Bull Morrison said as he, Spike Loring, and the two judges sat down to supper.

"I, too," Judge Schaffer said, "but this isn't the time to slow the grinding wheels of justice. Take your time, Marshal, and tell Judge Mallard exactly why you need his warrant to search that vault."

"Actually, Judge Schaffer, it's two vaults. Calhoun wasn't aware of the second one when he visited you." Bull took less than ten minutes to lay out how Hitchcock was able to manipulate the water laws, how he cut off water to the ranches any time he wanted. He went into as much detail as he could on how Hitchcock conned his way into owning most of the mines and mills in the Pioche district, along with farms and ranches in the valley. "He had a lot of help in this, Judge. Help from a federal judge in Salt Lake." He watched the jurist's eyebrows jerk skyward.

"We have that investigation well underway, but what we believe is in that vault should put several people in prison for a long time. I believe documents detailing his and Judge Olsen's manipulation of water and land law efforts are in those vaults."

"Man has quite a little fiefdom on this mountain side," Mallard said. "You're suggesting that Hitchcock did all this with the help of Federal District Judge John Olsen?" Bull nodded and the judge sat back in his chair, looking at the three men with him.

"And you think there is evidence of this alleged criminal activity in the bank vault? The kind of evidence that would send a federal judge to prison?"

"This is another interesting part, your honor," Bull said. "Rolf Pendergrass, the owner of the Silver Crystal Saloon and Hotel gave Hitchcock a large portion of the first floor of his building for the bank. He did this in exchange for him to keep his saloon vault in the bank. I'm sure after Slim's visit with bank manager Washburn much of that evidence was transferred to the saloon vault."

"Having that search warrant in your hands as soon as possible is obvious to me, and Dewey, you were absolutely right in not issuing it. A federal judge would certainly have thrown it out. After supper, Marshal, we'll go back to the jail and I'll write up two of them, one for the bank's records including what's in the bank vault, and one for the saloon vault."

"Thank you, sir."

"Do you have enough men to serve the warrants? Seems to me most of your available help is wounded."

"It is, indeed," Bull said. "Right now, I have the benefit of Gary Thompson. It's worrisome, too. Slim and I are sure that Hitchcock could not have put all this together without the help of someone of equal intelligence, but we haven't found that person. It can't be Buster Cranston, his mine foreman. The man isn't that smart."

"You think that person might interfere?"

"Exactly," Bull said. "I have the authority to deputize as needed, but the corral ain't full of good stock to choose from."

"If I can help, I will," Loring said. "Tom Blair was in earlier and he has some good men working for him, too."

"Good to know, Spike. Thank you."

"Surely there are two or three men in town that you

could deputize," Mallard said. "I'm aware of the criminal
element, but there must be a few." It was almost a question
and Schaffer had to laugh at the judge.

"I'm hoping the ranchers will bring some men with them
when they come back," Morrison said. "Ain't many good men
in this old camp."

CHAPTER 24

IT WAS NEARING THE TEN O'CLOCK HOUR, HE HAD FOREGONE SUPPER, and Sam Washburn sat alone in the locked up bank. Sweat trickled down his forehead, tears were running from red eyes, and the banker sobbed quietly. The shades were drawn and the lamps turned as low as they would go. The gloom of night equaled his own.

A half empty whiskey bottle sat on the desk along with a primed single shot, flint-lock pistol of ancient age. "I'm not going to prison for what Hitchcock has done." He mumbled.

Was it what Hitchcock had done or what the two of them had done? When one does a criminal's bidding, one is a criminal, no? "What's in that vault will send many of us there, though." Simply sitting at the desk as he was and that pistol at hand were more than signs of guilt, Washburn knew he was a party to many of Hitchcock's plots and schemes.

Documents detailing the nefarious dealings of many of Lincoln County's leaders were there along with crooked schemes, highly detailed and carried out. And a full disclosure on how Federal Judge John T. Olsen came to his conclusions on why Lincoln County water rights were a federal matter, not the state of Nevada's.

Washburn was a banker of some note when Hitchcock brought him from Kansas to Pioche. It was the lure of money, lots of money, that turned him from a good banker to a crooked co-conspirator. He was as deep into mining scams, water theft, and land speculation as Hitchcock, Olsen, and that other man. He never knew who Hitchcock's other partner in the operation was. With the amount of money that rolled in, it didn't matter who that might be.

It did matter, though. Washburn always had it buried in his 'things to do if caught' program to tell all and throw himself on the mercy of the court. All he knew about this other person was he was in government service. Where and what kind of service, he did not know.

Washburn had to destroy all the papers locked up in the vault. Fire would be the most effective. Burn the building down, bank and all. Make damn sure it was a major conflagration, and then, pull the trigger.

It was then that he remembered that second vault, the one he put cash and papers from the saloon in. He took a sip of whiskey, looked at the loaded pistol, and smiled, ever so slightly.

"That marshal didn't say a word about Pendergrass's safe." All thoughts of lighting a big fire and blowing his brains out vanished and he walked to the bank's vault and started gathering papers and documents. Cash money from the saloon vault moved to the bank's, and papers from the bank vault moved to the saloon's.

Pendergrass would never let them get into his vault, his safe. On the other hand, if they get a warrant for the bank's safe, it surely would not include Pendergrass's private property. He won't even know this is in there and we'll clean it out when all this blows over. Washburn worked hard to convince himself that with that move he wouldn't have to use that evil little single-shot pistol that seemed to glare at him as he worked. Alcohol and criminal greed spurred the man on.

He didn't try to separate any of the documents and papers. They all went into the considerably smaller safe. Stuffing them into the Silver Crystal safe was slow work and Washburn stopped by his desk from time to time for a drink from the quickly emptying bottle. He left a daily ledger along with several thousand dollars in the big vault, closed it up, grabbed his bottle and left the bank. He was carrying a box filled with personal belongings.

I won't be returning and I won't leave anything of mine for those vultures to go through. The plans, as such they might be called, included finishing another bottle and riding out at first light. *North,* he thought. *North to Salt Lake. Judge Olsen will protect me. We've certainly taken care of that bastard over the years. His turn to take care of me.*

He remembered many manila envelopes filled with money, mine shares, and shares in other businesses being sent north. Mills operating separately from mines were a bonanza for those dealing in fake certificates. *Hitchcock, Olsen, and Mr. X own controlling interest in most of the operations in this district. How many shares of mining stock in mines that don't exist have those two sold?*

Washburn wasn't a partner, more like an operations manager, and was paid well for his knowledge and ability. Most of what the three partners did would look absolutely legal and above board to the average man. That was Washburn's job and he did it well.

Between glasses of whiskey, Sam Washburn packed one valise with necessary clothing and another valise with cash that didn't make its way into the vault. There was a third pack, filled with very legal documents indicating Washburn's shares in legitimate operations. He was paid well. He fell onto his bed, drunk, a few hours before dawn.

GINNY WHIPPLE HAD SLIM CALHOUN'S FOOT PUT BACK TOGETHER quickly and gave him something that allowed him to sleep through the night. She was a bright light in his eyes the next morning. "You are one lucky son of a gun, Slim Calhoun. You gave the wound a couple of days to get the healing started before you tried to destroy things. No infection, nothing I couldn't fix. It won't look pretty when a real doctor sees it, but you won't die either."

"That's always good to know. My Lady." He bowed and limped into the restaurant. Bull and the two judges were already mostly through with their breakfasts.

"Back on your feet, are you?" Bull motioned for Slim to join them. "We have the warrants, my friend, so be quick with your eating. I want to get at those vaults as soon as possible."

"Have we heard back from Judge Baker? Have we heard anything else from Pete Flannigan?"

"Nothing yet but the day's early. Since we weren't able to get the men we're holding before the justice of the peace yesterday, Judge Schaffer will hold court while we're at the bank. Deputy Thompson will be there and Spike Loring will have two men to back him up if any of those fools try something."

"After they're arraigned, I'll hold district court tomorrow," Judge Mallard said. "It will take several days, I'm afraid. You've done a fine job catching these men and doing the paperwork properly. It's a pleasure working with the marshal service."

"I've said for years that you should be on the federal bench, Greg," Schaffer said. "You're a stickler for accuracy."

Ginny came up to the table. "Someone at the back door to see you, Marshal. Won't come in."

"Thank you," Bull said. He nodded to Slim and started for the back door. Slim made his way out the front of the diner and headed around the building. Knowing Slim had his back, Bull walked straight to the door. "I'm Marshal Morrison. Who are you?"

"Name's Murphy, Tony Murphy. Sandy Hitchcock gave me some papers to hold. He said in the event he was killed I should give them to the sheriff, but the sheriff is in jail. I think maybe I should give them to you. Mr. Hitchcock said it was most important that the sheriff get these."

Hitchcock didn't take into account that Tony Murphy was a law-abiding citizen of good character. He told the busted up hard-rocker that the papers should go to the sheriff. That is, to a lawman, thus, he is offering them to a U.S. Marshal. Bull Morrison could not hide his feelings, and nodded, as if to say, 'thank you, good citizen.'

Murphy handed over a large folder filled with various sized envelopes and loose leaf sheets. "Thank you, Mr. Murphy. I think you did the right thing. Were you and Mr. Hitchcock friends?"

"I worked for him until an accident shut me down. He's been helpful and I do small jobs for him."

Bull Morrison motioned for Slim to come on up to where they were standing. "This is my deputy, Mr. Murphy. Slim Calhoun. Slim, Mr. Murphy gave us some important papers he's been holding for Sandy Hitchcock. Maybe you better take a look at them." Slim took the large package, tied off simply with cord, and walked back into the café.

"Thank you, Mr. Murphy. Where would I find you if we have questions about something?"

"Often at the Lucky Lady, sometimes at the Silver Crystal. I don't drink that much but it's better than sitting in my room looking at the walls. Been interesting these past few days." He had a wry smile and Bull had to chuckle.

Bull handed the man a five dollar gold piece and slipped into the diner, showing off the closest thing to a smile he was capable of. *Papers to be given to his criminal sheriff in the event of his death. No, that's not what he said. He said in the event he was killed. There's a big difference there. I'll bet those papers outline how his little empire was to be broken up. And another silver dollar bet we'll be led to Hitchcock's partner.*

Bull rejoined the table. "A change or two, I'm afraid. Slim, I'd say what Murphy just gave us is as important as what we'll find at the bank. Go back to the jail and work your way through that mess. I'm going to find Boots Kindle and get a couple of miners, deputize them, and raid the bank."

Bull looked back and forth at the judges. Neither one indicated anything was wrong with what he said and got up to leave. "Pendergrass is sure to raise hell over this warrant, but that's too bad."

BOOTS KINDLE WAS SITTING AT HIS DESK IN THE MINERS' UNION HALL, reading a newspaper. "Marshal Morrison. A bit early for a social call, eh? What can I do for you?"

"You and two of your members can become my deputies for a few hours for one thing. For another, other than the people I've come in contact with, who was close to Sandy Hitchcock?"

"Your deputies? You been drinking, Marshal?"

Bull chuckled. "I've been known to, but not this time. I've simply run out of people, Boots. All the local lawmen are either dead, wounded, or behind bars."

"So, me and my miners become fodder, eh? Tell me why and maybe we will. As to your other question, have you had the pleasure of meeting the chairman of the Lincoln County Board of Supervisors? One Lawrence Lerude Samples?"

"No I haven't. We believe that Hitchcock had a silent partner, one with a quick mind, and not afraid of breaking the law. He also had his bank filled with papers that I believe will send members of Hitchcock's gang to prison, including a federal judge. I have a search warrant to tear that bank apart and need three deputies with me."

"Samples fits your description, Marshal. So does Pendergrass, Loring, and maybe another one or two in this old camp. I can get two men right now, but you have to know they are going to want to get paid for this."

"Your government will compensate you, gladly, Mr. Kindle. Gather your men. We'll walk down to the bank."

"Won't be open this time of day."

"Oh, yes it will," Morrison chuckled. "Indeed, Mr. Kindle, we will see to it that the bank is open, ripped open, if need be, from roof to cellar." He waited for Boots to gather his men and thought about what the man said. *The chairman of the county commission would be in a good position to deflect interference in Hitchcock's operation. Might be why no one from the courthouse has bothered to contact either Slim or me. I wonder if there's one single soul in this little mining camp who isn't running at least one scam?*

"Boots, I want you to go into the Silver Crystal and just hang out near the saloon entrance to the bank. Don't say anything to anyone. These gentlemen will help me through the front doors and we'll come open the saloon door. If Pendergrass is there, please don't say a word to him. That's my job."

The front doors of the bank were easily pried open. It was

early but even so, a few passersby looked on. "I'm Marshal Morrison," he said to them. "Here on business." Some looked at him suspiciously, others turned away quickly. Only one demanded proof that Bull was a marshal. "You bet," Bull said. He produced his badge and told the man thank you. *One out of a hundred had to be sure. Maybe good odds in Pioche.*

He led his new deputies inside the small bank. There were three areas, no expensive Italian marble or highly oiled fine hardwood. The front area was for the public, the vaults, and Washburn's office were off to the side. "Let's get that other door open and find Pendergrass," Bull said.

Kindle and Pendergrass were standing together when the door opened. "Marshal," Pendergrass said. "What's this about?"

"I have search warrants, Pendergrass." Bull produced two papers. "One for the Pioche bank in its entirety and one for a vault that I believe is for your use. The bank will be closed until further notice."

"You're not going into my safe, Marshal."

"Yes, Mr. Pendergrass, I am going into your safe." Bull turned to his deputies and motioned them into the bank proper. "This door will be locked from the inside. Any attempt by anyone to enter the bank, using force, will be met with force. Understood?"

"Who authorized that warrant?" Pendergrass demanded. "Was it that goat lover Schaffer?"

"No, this warrant is authorized by Nevada District Court," Bull said. He turned and stepped to the door.

"We'll see about that," Pendergrass said. Bull closed the door behind him and locked it and turned to his deputies.

That man's riled, I think. I'm about to learn something here. Will he go straight to Judge Mallard or will he go to commissioner Samples? "Boots, let's you and me take Mr. Washburn's office apart. We are specifically looking for the combinations to the two vaults. Don't destroy anything. And you two, get the stove lit, make some coffee, and see to it that no one comes through either door. No matter how official they say they are, they aren't. I'd rather you not shoot anyone, while on the other hand, do not let yourself be shot."

The miners set themselves to the tasks and made the front lobby area their home place. "Ain't nobody gonna shoot me," Gus Opal said. The other, Shorty Bellows nodded in agreement. "Kindle say how much we be gettin' for putting our lives on the line?"

"More than we were gettin' sittin' in the union hall," Bellows said. Both were laughing getting the fire started.

CHAPTER 25

PENDERGRASS MADE HIS WAY THROUGH THE EARLY MORNING COLD, cussing under his breath, eyes blazing with anger. *How dare that judge give those marshals access to my money and private papers. I'll see to it that he's removed from the bench, disbarred, run out of the county. I should have seen this coming. Damn that Hitchcock.*

The angry saloon owner burst through the doors of the still in progress courthouse and stomped into the county commission offices. "Where's Samples?" He demanded of the clerk.

"It's a little early for the gentleman, Mr. Pendergrass. Can I help with something?"

"I would have asked if I thought you could." Pendergrass stomped out of the office and slammed his way into the jail. "Where's Mallard?"

"The judge hasn't arrived yet," Deputy Thompson said. "Judge Schaffer will be holding court in about half an hour. He's in the back now."

Pendergrass bellowed a string of obscenities and walked back onto the street. He spotted Mallard heading into the Lucky Lady Hotel. "Mallard. I want to talk to you," he yelled.

"Been expecting you, Pendergrass. Let's have a belt, eh?"

Greg Mallard had seen angry men before, knew where his Colt was, knew how strong he was, and smiled at the saloon owner.

"You don't mind drinking at the Lucky Lady, I presume?" The two men made for the end of the bar where Jimmy Lassen was holding court with two lovely ladies just going home from a long night.

"Brandy, Rolf?" Pendergrass just nodded. "Two then, Jimmy. This little show have something to do with a search warrant?"

"You damn right it does," Rolf Pendergrass thundered. "Don't play your games with me, Judge. You know damn good and well it does."

"I don't know what you might have in that vault, Mr. Pendergrass, and I don't really care." Mallard nodded in thanks to Lassen putting the drinks down. The old judge had seen many angry men over the years, had fought with a few, and knew that the only thing Pendergrass could offer was bluster. "You need to listen to me, Mr. Pendergrass. I do believe I know what might have been jammed into that safe of yours at some point in the last day or two. That, sir, is the point of the warrant. You have a vault on the premises of a man under federal criminal investigation. Anything else you'd like to discuss?"

"You can't just arbitrarily give that marshal the right to go through my stuff because Sandy Hitchcock was an outlaw." Pendergrass did not sip his brandy, he took it down in one gulp and nodded for Jimmy to pour another.

"The bank, those who work for it, its owner, and those who store information that the banker had access to, Mr. Pendergrass. Hitchcock and Sam Washburn had access to your vault, therefore, under my warrant, Marshal Morrison now has access to your vault. I'm relatively sure that Morrison will find far more than you think is stored in that vault."

Pendergrass heard and understood what the judge said. *More than I think is stored, he said. That bastard Hitchcock was hiding evidence of his wrongdoing in my safe. Damn.*

Mallard tried to read what he was seeing in the saloon owner's face. *He's trying to put together everything he knows he has there, wondering how much of it might be evidence against him. Now, he's trying to think about what Washburn or Hitchcock might have placed in the vault.*

"Unless you're seriously connected to Hitchcock's criminal activity, Mr. Pendergrass, I don't think you have anything to worry about." Mallard took pleasure in nasty comments like that and smiled at Pendergrass. "There are charges being discussed about water issues, about land speculation, even about mining conspiracies, Pendergrass. Bull Morrison and his deputy will bring it all to the surface and what's in your vault might lead the way."

Mallard didn't wait for Rolf to say anything, turned and walked out of the Lucky Lady Saloon, only to bump into Lawrence Lerude Samples. "Morning, Commissioner. You'll find him at the end of the bar." He had a distinct smile on his face when he entered the jail.

Sure wish one of the marshals could hear what those two will be talking about. Is Pendergrass as deep into this mess as he seems to be? Or is he just worried about money? Morrison is investigating federal issues and no one is investigating state issues. This damn county is one big criminal conspiracy, all of its own.

Mallard motioned to Schaffer when he entered and took a chair near the stove. "Are there any county lawmen that can be trusted, Dewey?"

"There was one, Three-Finger Jack Daws, but he's doing what he can not to die, right now. One of Lighthorse's deputies, Gary Thompson is working with the marshals, but I don't know about trust issues."

Mallard saw Slim Calhoun going through a pile of papers at the sheriff's desk. "Can you join us for a minute, Deputy? Need your thoughts."

It was the break Slim was hoping for and he moved his chair near the stove. "Hitchcock certainly never imagined that a marshal would be going through his works. What can I help with, Judge?"

"I understand the gravity of your investigation into the workings of Hitchcock and Federal Judge Olsen, Calhoun, I do. But we have other issues here and they need just as deep a looking into," Mallard said.

"Local issues, Slim," Dewey Schaffer said. "The county sheriff is behind bars along with a deputy of his. The only other Lincoln County lawman is Gary Thompson. The Pioche City Marshal is out of service."

"I get the picture, Judge," Slim said. "Our investigation has already produced what many sheriff's would consider a heavy burden. A lot of state laws have been broken by a lot of people and there are no lawmen to do their duty. I can say for certain that Bull and I cannot take on that added burden."

"You've got a hell of a burden already," Mallard said. "Judge Olsen has been sitting on the bench a long time, has lots of friends in high places, and will fight back. No, we aren't asking that either of you take on local law enforcement too. No, my question is about Gary Thompson and if you know of any local man or men who might step in to help?"

"Thompson might be the reason that Bull and I are here. He has been working with one of Olsen's clerks to get us here. What the clerk did might be illegal, and the charges would include Mr. Thompson."

"That's not the best news I've heard," Mallard said.

"On the other hand, there is a man I've watched who just might want to step up. Chago Torres never backed down from one of Lighthorse's killer deputies and was on the right side in more than one fracas at the Lucky Lady. Might want to talk to him."

"Do you know him, Dewey?" Mallard asked.

"I do indeed. He has helped me with my goats many times over the last few years. Even showed me a couple of Mexican shortcuts on cheese making. He's a good man and believes in law and justice. I'll have a talk. We need someone like him."

"Neither one of us can simply appoint a sheriff," Mallard said. "It's an elective position, but the county commission can appoint an interim sheriff. That would bring in Larry Samples."

"I'll go back to Hitchcock's surprise," Slim said. "Samples might well be Hitchcock's silent partner. Might want to skirt way around that man right now."

"DAILY RECORDS AND SOME CASH IS ALL," BOOTS KINDLE SAID. HE and Bull brought it out and laid it on Washburn's desk. "Sure no evidence of criminal activity there."

"You're right, Mr. Kindle, which tells me what I'm looking for has either been destroyed or is in that safe right there. Let's get 'er open." Bull was on his knees and held what he hoped was the combination. It took two tries and the handle turned fully, opening the heavy door to the safe.

Jumbled papers, files, and notes fell out onto the floor. "Stuffed in," Bull murmured. He eased the rest of the safe's contents out and moved everything to a table near a window. "We need to separate what we believe is Hitchcock's records from Pendergrass's."

"I need help," Shorty Bellows yelled out from the saloon entrance. Bull raced across the bank and came face to face with Lawrence Lerude Samples trying to push Shorty Bellows aside. Bull grabbed the man, spun him around and planted a right fist in his mouth. Samples, more than two hundred fifty pounds of Samples, fell to the floor, unconscious.

"You know him, Shorty?"

"Sure, Marshal. He's the chairman of the Lincoln County Commission. That's Larry Samples. Hard to believe he was a miner once. Used to be one big strong man. Now he's just a fat old bully. Took to the good life of money and ease, he did."

"How's that?" Bull reached down and took a Remington from the man's waist band.

"Works for Hitchcock, Marshal. Thought you knew that."

"Well, now. Let's get him inside and propped up some. And get that door closed and locked." Bull and the two miners dragged the politician inside the bank and left him on the floor near the open bank vault. *Works for Hitchcock. Lighthorse works for Hitchcock. It seems that much of what passes for Lincoln County government works for Hitchcock.*

A couple of hard slaps across the face and Samples started to come to. "Get off the floor," Bull shouted in his face. "You look like a fat old drunk down there. Get up, man. After all, you represent this county."

Samples had a hard time focusing, saw a heavy, dangerous man hovering over him, and tried to lash out. It was a feeble attempt, quickly swatted away. "Don't be an ass. Get up," Bull said. Samples managed to get on his hands and knees, grabbed at a chair and slowly got his bulk into it.

"Who are you? How dare you raise a hand to me? Do you have any idea who I am?" Samples laid his pride out for the world to see. "What's going on here? Is this a bank robbery? I'll see to it you all will be strung up at high noon in the center of town." His voice rose a bit with each comment and he was yelling by the end.

"Get it all out, Samples," Bull said. The marshal walked around the front office of the bank, made sure the door was closed and locked, and came back to stand in front of Samples. "We're takin' a lot, Mr. Samples, but not robbin' nothin'," Bull chuckled. "Tell me about this comfortable little relationship you have with Sandy Hitchcock? You tell him what to do? Or does he tell you?"

"Who are you?"

"I guess we haven't been properly introduced. I'm U.S. Marshal Bull Morrison, Commissioner. Answer my question."

"Marshal? But Olsen ..." and Samples stopped. He glared at Morrison. *How did Olsen let the marshals in? My God, Sandy Hitchcock is dead, Lighthorse is in jail, and this man says he is a federal marshal? Olsen said there would never be a fear of marshals.* "I have nothing to say to you. Where is your badge? You say you're a marshal? Prove it."

Bull Morrison dipped a hand into his vest and came up with his badge. He slammed it into the side of Samples' head. "Take a good look at this shield, Samples. Look," and he jammed into the man's face. "Again, sir. What is your relationship with Hitchcock?"

"I'm chairman of the county commission and he owns mines in our county. We have a considerable amount of business in common. What is this all about?" Always a bully, always demanding respect even if it shouldn't be forthcoming, Samples had been taken by surprise and was having a hard time getting his feet back under him. He took a long look around.

"You have no right to be in here. This is Mr. Hitchcock's bank." *The vault is open, those papers must be Hitchcock's. How much does this animal know? How has this happened?*

Samples knew about the search warrant from Pendergrass but never dreamed that Hitchcock would have so much paperwork in his vault. *I have to get to Salt Lake. Olsen has always promised he would take care of us. I'll play along with this brute of a marshal and get the hell out of Pioche.*

"Just what are you looking for?" Samples asked. "The county does a considerable amount of business with the mines, with Mr. Hitchcock."

"Do you personally have considerable interest in Hitchcock's businesses?" Bull asked. He pulled a chair over and sat down across from the rotund politician. Bull picked up a file and opened it. "Water," he mumbled and set the papers down. "Water? Hmmm. A consortium of mine owners and county officials own water rights, Commissioner?"

"I want my attorney. You have no right to go through those papers. I want my attorney."

"Very well, Commissioner." Bull pulled his cuffs and had Samples stand up. "Turn around, please." He pulled the man's hands behind him and fastened the cuffs. "Let's take a little walk, shall we?"

"Where to?" Samples demanded.

"The jail, of course. You, sir, are under arrest for conspiracy to obtain water rights by way of fraud. To have monetary influence over a federal judge, and for fraudulent land speculation." Bull turned to Shorty. "Open the front doors, Shorty, and help me escort our prisoner to jail. Mr. Kindle, lock the door behind us and continue sifting through those papers. I'll be back soon."

Bull Morrison took great pleasure escorting Samples to the

jail, seeing numbers of people pointing and talking among themselves at seeing the chairman of the county commission in chains. One or two hollered out nasty comments, and Bull hurried things along. It was one thing putting on a bit of a show, quite another to incite a riot.

JUSTICE OF THE PEACE DEWEY SCHAFFER WAS JUST OPENING COURT when Bull, Shorty, and Samples burst through the jail door. "Court is in session, Marshal. I must ask for quiet."

"No problem, your honor. I just need to book this man in. We can do it in the back, sir."

The two judges, Deputy Sheriff Thompson, and Deputy Marshal Calhoun sat almost open mouthed and watched Bull move his troop in to the cell block. Slim had to testify at the hearing and knew he couldn't follow, but District Judge Mallard could.

"First big fish, Judge," Bull said. He turned to Shorty Bellows. "Find Sam Washburn, Shorty, and bring him here. I expected to find him at the bank. We need him in custody as soon as possible."

Shorty passed Mallard as he left the cell block. "So, Mr. Samples in irons, eh? Give you some trouble, did he?" Mallard asked. He was eyeing bruises, spots of blood, and a well smashed nose, still dripping blood.

"Not much. I'm charging him with assault on a federal officer, Judge. He tried to force his way into the bank, assaulting Shorty Bellows. Holding the other charges until we're farther along in our investigation. He's a major cog in the water and land conspiracies, and I believe him to be Hitchcock's partner, not just a part of the organization. How are things progressing out front?"

"As expected. Be very careful with your evidence, Marshal. Very careful. Judge Olsen has many friends higher up the chain. They may take this as an assault on the judiciary."

Samples was booked and put in a cell, awaiting his first hearing before Schaffer, which would be sometime the next day. "You wanted an attorney, Mr. Samples. Who should we call?"

"His name is Fletcher, Stephen Fletcher. You'll find him at the Silver Crystal." Samples wheezed some and slumped on a cot. Lighthorse sat in an adjoining cell and never said a word.

Bull Morrison indicated that Calhoun should join him at the bank as soon as he could get free and hurried back to the bank. *I need ten more people carrying badges right now. I should have seen this coming and will make sure that Judge Baker knows I was wrong in not asking for help. I should have brought five men with me.* It wasn't a long walk to the bank, but Bull never let his mind slow down, either.

"We're missing something," he murmured."Enforcers!" The comment all but exploded just as he reached the doors to the bank. More than one person more interested in getting inside the Silver Crystal was taken aback by the comment.

Gus Opal let him back into the bank and he joined Kindle at the desk. "How we comin', Kindle? Bring me up to date quickly. I have to get some thoughts down on paper before I forget."

"I've tried to put this into some kind of order, Marshal. Glad you invited me to the party. A lot of questions I've had for some time are getting answered." He couldn't hide a smile.

"I take it there are the kinds of evidence we talked about?" Bull sat down across Washburn's desk from the union boss. There were several distinct piles of papers and files spread across the large desk.

"Indeed there is. This group is related to water, this bunch to land situations, particularly with ranch deeds and mortgages, and this mess has to do with how Hitchcock and Samples have organized the mines, the conspiracies dealing with mines that don't exist, and with how local, state, and federal representatives are involved."

"There is something there that specifically names Samples as Hitchcock's partner?" Bull was more than excited at the possibility.

"Here," Kindle said. "Read these contracts between Hitchcock and Samples. They seem to line it out in detail. Hitchcock must have believed that all of this would be destroyed if he were arrested or got himself killed."

Kindle rustled some more paper. "Hitchcock's various organizations all come under one heading, a consortium of corporations and partnerships. State legislators, political leaders, and other county people are involved. None of this should have been available to you."

"Exactly, Mr. Kindle. That's why I'm surprised to find all this. Also more than surprised not to find Mr. Washburn demanding that we quit our search." Bull Morrison sat back and read what Kindle thought was a contract between Hitchcock and Samples. It was even more than that. "Amazing," Bull muttered several times.

"A document with all the names and their particular positions in the conspiracy, Mr. Kindle. Amazing," Bull said again. It was when he got to the fourth page of the file that he stood straight up. "It's a three way cabal, Kindle, with Hitchcock acting as lead man but all three holding equal shares of responsibility. Hitchcock, Samples, and Olsen. My God in heaven."

Morrison paced around the small banker's office, re-read

the papers again, and sat back down. "Find a flask anywhere?" He asked with the best attempt he had ever made at smiling.

"No," Kindle laughed.

"I have one," Gus Opal said.

"Thank you, kind sir," Bull said. "I'll leave you some." He took two long drinks and settled back in his chair. "Have we separated what Pendergrass would claim as his?" Kindle nodded and pointed to some bundles of cash along with a few papers. "Good. Stuff them back in his safe and let's put the rest of this together so we can get it to the jail. Amazing," he said again.

The papers and files were in three packages, tied off with strong cord, and the three left the bank for the jail. They were about half-way there when Shorty Bellows met up with them. "Where's Washburn?" Bull asked.

"He wasn't home, his personal belongings are gone, and so is his horse and buggy. I could follow the buggy tracks to the main road. Looks like Washburn is traveling north, Marshal. I didn't try to follow."

"No need to. He's heading for Salt Lake where he thinks he'll be safe. Stick with us, now, Shorty." Court was just wrapping up when the three stepped into the jail offices. "Eureka," Bull said, setting the packages down on the sheriff's desk. "High grade and nothing but." The old prospector's yelp at finding gold echoed through the building.

"This is getting complicated, Bull." Slim said. "Having the jail, court, and our offices all in the same rooms. I think we need to set up our marshal operations across the street at Marshal Daws'. Judges, investigators, and criminals all traipsing back and forth ain't working. I already took the keys from Three-Finger Jack. He's fine with it."

"How's he doing? Shouldn't even be alive," Bull said. Slim

started to answer just as Paul Stewart came in, panting.

"For you, Marshal. Marked urgent." He handed the wire to Bull. "Whew. Quite a run for an old man. Got any coffee?"

"Right here, Mr. Stewart. Sit down because I'm sure I'll have an answer for you to send." Bull motioned for Slim to pour the coffee and paced around the office reading the long telegram. Judges Mallard and Schaffer moved around the stove waiting to hear what was sent.

"Gettin' help, Slim. Should be here in a day or two. Judge Baker sending four marshals this-a-way and four more to Salt Lake. Our bowl of goldfish has become a large lake filled with criminals. We have got to work hard now separating the local crimes from the federal. Baker will hold trial in Salt Lake, the scene of most of the federal crimes even though most of the criminals are here in Pioche."

"What did you mean, help separating?" Slim asked.

"Two of the four men he's sending our way are from the Nevada Attorney General's office. They'll work the local and state, and we'll concentrate on federal crimes and criminals."

He handed the wire to Judge Mallard and plopped down in the sheriff's chair and started writing. "Washburn probably fleeing to Salt Lake, have others in custody." He read what he was writing. "Will arrest all that we know of. Will travel as a caravan to Salt Lake after investigation complete. Strong evidence of bribery, complicity, and active involvement by Olsen." *Baker will enjoy this.* "Need heavy security on these piles of evidence. Sure to be attempts on them."

Bull had a small army including Kindle, Opal, Bellows, and Calhoun to move their operation from the jail to Three-Finger Jack Daws's offices. Bull took Opal and Bellows aside. "Are either of you fellows married?"

They both shook their heads. "Good. I'd like to offer you

temporary employment. You've both done a fine job today and our job isn't over by a stretch. I need two guards who can sit in this office and protect with their lives, these piles of paper and files. I have to be honest, there will be attempts to steal or burn every scrap of paper here."

"You can count on me," Shorty Bellows said. "Looks like the mines are gonna close anyway when you boys are through."

"Me, too," Gus Opal said.

"Good." Bull said. "No one in this building except us four. No one. That might mean you will be fighting off people you've known for some time. We don't know everyone who was connected to Sandy Hitchcock. You two set yourselves up. Slim, we have an appointment with Spike Loring."

Calhoun caught the sly wink and slipped out the door with Morrison. "I thought of this earlier and Bellows just answered my question, Slim. We've been missing a big key to Hitchcock's operation."

"I know. We haven't found out how he has gotten away with his maneuvers. Somebody damn strong has to be backing the operation. Every criminal gang like this has to have an enforcer. It wasn't Lighthorse, it wasn't Buster Cranston."

"I think I know who the enforcer is but we need to shake him out soon. There's another problem that is about to explode in our faces. Bellows said it. The mines are surely to close, Slim. All hell will break loose since Hitchcock owned or was heavily invested in most of the others. We need some strong local law enforcement."

"You think Spike Loring is the answer?" Slim asked. "I don't."

"No, I don't either. He's behind what we're doing because it benefits his business. No, I'm thinking the ranchers, Quincy Pierce and Tom Donovan. They have big strong men riding for them."

"With a lot to lose if everything breaks down," Slim said. "Make a visit as soon as our back up rides in?"

"No, my friend and trusty deputy, you're making a ride today. After we visit Loring."

Bull Morrison was still chuckling as he and Slim walked to the end of the bar. "Cold beer, Jimmy Lassen, and a bottle too, if you please. Spike around someplace?"

"Coming up behind you now, Marshal."

Bull turned and was surprised to find Tom Donovan walking with Spike Loring. "Just talking about you, Donovan. Glad to see you. Spike, I have some papers that seem to spell out how the Sandy Hitchcock/Larry Samples operation works, but there are missing pieces. Who saw to it that what the boss wanted the boss got?"

"In a strange way, it was Buster Cranston, his mine boss, but through other lead men at the various mines. There was no one man who saw to it that things were done Hitchcock's way."

"That makes it bad," Slim Calhoun said. "Tom, let's you and I take a table for a short chat. Keep the beer coming, Jimmy. We'll need it."

"Actually, now that I think about it there were two men who just about everyone feared," Spike Loring said. "You did away with Pizon Oakley but the second man is simply a brute. He's called Ephram Boxer and is to be feared. There is not a single redeeming feature about the man."

"Boxer, eh? I'll look forward to our meeting," Bull said. "He would be muscle, Spike. What I'm looking for isn't just muscle. An enforcer sees to it everyone stays in line. This means the troops but also, often maybe, those just below the bosses. Who besides Sandy Hitchcock directs traffic? He has to be smart, efficient, and strong."

"It would not be Boxer. He's just a brute. He would work

for this enforcer," Loring said. "I'll think on it."

While Slim and Tom talked about rebuilding the Pioche law enforcement, Bull and Spike discussed the problem of the mines closing. "Tom, we have to build a town law department. We're going to try to get Chago Torres appointed interim sheriff, but he will need strong deputies. Would any of your men, or Pierce's men be interested? It wouldn't be long term. Just until this mess is cleared up and elections can be held."

"I can think of a couple and I'm sure Quince would be able to as well. I'll spread the word when I get back. I have put two men on the water gates, Slim. That's what I came to tell you. They have orders to keep those gates open and shoot to kill anyone who challenges my order."

"That's good. I'm expecting some serious trouble, Tom. Hitchcock kept a close hold on his operation and without him directing traffic, I'm expecting the mines to close. That could bring chaos and possibly riots from the out-of-work miners. That and those trying to protect themselves from serious criminal complaints, are going to make the next few days damn dangerous around here."

"I'll head back to the ranch now and see what kind of help I can get for you. No new wires coming through, though."

"No, we're using the local office. Got that problem cleared up." Slim rejoined Morrison at the bar. "Donovan has people at the water gates, and he'll be sending a couple of men our way. If word gets out that the mines will be closing because of all this, we'll need every gun in the county on our side."

CHAPTER 26

"FLETCHER, YOU GOT TO GET ME OUT OF HERE, BUT JUST AS IMPORTANT, you got to get with Ephram Boxer. How these marshals come to be here I'll never know, but they know everything and must be done away with." Samples was more nervous than the ancient attorney had ever seen him. He tried to sit on the cot to talk with his attorney but couldn't sit still for a minute and was pacing faster and faster.

"They only have you on trying to force your way into the bank. You shoved a deputy or something. They'll set bail in the morning and you'll be fine." The effects from a breakfast of whiskey had slowed the already weakened mind of the once able attorney and Fletcher only saw the obvious.

"You idiot. They know my position with Hitchcock. Listen to me, Fletcher. You're in this almost as deep as I am. You better understand that. You get with Boxer. The mines are shutting down and he needs to get all the men from all the mines fired up. There needs to be an uprising, the marshals and everyone connected with them need to die, and I need to be out of this jail cell. You got that?"

With each phrase his voice rose until he was all but screaming at the befuddled lawyer. He was punching holes in the air, arms flailing about, even kicking at the cot. *Why did Hitchcock put so much trust in this fool?* Samples continued his pacing, Fletcher fought his way through the alcoholic fog, and the two were not on the same page in their life book.

Samples saw an end coming that was dark and frightening while Fletcher only looked out far enough to see the next bottle. From Hitchcock's point of view, Fletcher was the right man since Hitchcock believed that every decision had to be his and his alone. Fletcher simply followed orders.

Samples' size frightened Fletcher, his anger was getting out of control, and the two were locked in. "Take it easy, Larry. I'll take care of it, but you really don't have to worry that much." Stephen Fletcher called to be let out of the cell amidst some strong cussing from Samples. The attorney headed for Hitchcock's North Pass Mine. Fletcher had lost his edge as an attorney years ago and was just following a trail laid out by Sandy Hitchcock.

Hitchcock has all the doors bolted, he and that federal judge. Larry doesn't really have to do this. Fletcher was a believer in all that Hitchcock did and said. He believed that Judge Olsen would protect the organization. With Fletcher, it was always fair weather and tomorrow would be better yet. *Well, I'm paid well, I'll get with Boxer even if I'd rather shoot the bummer. Foulest man I've ever met, but he is good at what he does best.*

Ephram Boxer stood about five feet and ten inches, slim at the hips and broad at the chest and shoulders. He made as much money fighting on days off as he did underground and had a great dislike of Stephen Fletcher. "What do you want, Shyster?"

Boxer lived in a filthy cabin on mine property. The cabin was just one small room filled with a small cot and equally small table. There were two chairs set amidst overwhelming clutter. The man's clothing was hung on nails pounded all about the walls. A wood stove dominated the center of the room. There was a steaming coffee pot and a food encrusted pan on its top. Fletcher took a deep breath and eased his way into the filth. He was horrified by what he saw on the table.

"I have a message for you from Larry Samples, Ephram. He wants you to get the men upset because the mines will be closing. They need to riot, burn the mine buildings, tear up the town, kill everyone wearing a badge, and free Mr. Samples from jail. He says there's five hundred in it for you."

"What about the others?"

"Mr. Samples said they could have whatever they found, no questions asked." He was watching the killer and wanted to run. The table was covered in blood. "He wants you to start immediately."

"Yeah, yeah," Boxer said. "Tell him I want eight hundred, not a penny less, and I'll start as soon as I eat. Now, get out of here."

Boxer was skinning and cleaning a hare, its guts and blood splattered on the table top. No bucket for the remains, no cold water for liver and heart. Nothing to clean one's hands. Fletcher turned and ran from the cabin. Boxer's laughter joined the sounds of Fletcher's retch in the day's warmth.

I can get the men started but I'll never be able to get 'em stopped. Hope that fool mouthpiece knows that. Once they get to looting, it's all over. This town will burn to the ground before tomorrow ends.

Boxer wrapped the rabbit's offal in its skin and tossed it out the door. He then fried and ate the rabbit before setting out to gather his mob. This wasn't his line of work. He was the enforcer, the one who broke heads, arms, legs, to see to it that something was done. *I'll get these busters movin' but I'd rather be bustin' heads.* From mine to mine he spread the word. "Eat well, me hearties," he cried at each stop. "Drink up, boys, and come dawn burn the mine you used to work for and then move into town. If you see a man with a badge, kill him. I'll see to it that Mr. Samples is set free."

"Who's going to be paying us and when?" One miner had the guts to ask.

"You aren't smart enough to loot the building before you set it ablaze, Matey?" The man's complaint was stifled with laughter. "Loot first, then burn. Not hard to remember," Boxer howled. He found great delight in hurting the others, shaming them before their mates.

At every mine-site, drunken laughter filled the air and as the cobalt of night turned to early gray dawn. Fires began erupting at several mine sites and alarms were rung in Pioche. Only a few of the townsmen responded to the hammering brass bells. Jacob Overby had an anvil chorus singing loud at the stables. Slim and Bull, Gary Thompson and Justice of the Peace Schaffer had spread the word of coming disaster and many in town hid, thinking they were safe in their homes.

They should have known better. Ever since the marshals arrived there hadn't been any local law enforcement. The sheriff was in jail, most of his deputies were dead, and the city marshal was shot up bad. Card sharks weren't busted, thieves ran rampant, and there had been even more men murdered or simply gone missing. Now, the threat of riots.

Was this dangerous and outlaw infested mining camp ready for a drunken mob? Slim and Bull had themselves positioned to hold the jail and Shorty and Gus protected the Daws' building. They had criminals behind bars, they had evidence they were not willing to lose. Most of all, they had people and property to protect.

Rolf Pendergrass had what few employees would stand with him ready to protect the Silver Crystal, and Spike Loring had his people ready to defend the Lucky Lady. Both saloon owners knew their businesses would be prime targets. Looters love whiskey.

Up and down the main street, shop owners and home owners were terrified but ready to make what pitiful stand they could. Chago Torres hadn't been appointed interim sheriff yet but wore the badge in anticipation. He and Gary Thompson, his only deputy, were near the apothecary's.

As the first blush of dawn came on, five riders came in, each armed with rifle, shotgun, and one or two handguns. "Donovan said you might want a little help here. Name's Des Moines. They call me Frenchy." The big man stepped off his horse, towering over Bull Morrison. "Where do you want us and what do you want us to do?"

"Glad you're here, Frenchy. There'll be a mob of drunken miners coming into town at any moment," Bull said. "I want the prisoners in the jail there kept safe, and I want what's in that office kept safe." He pointed at the town marshal's office. "With a little luck, we might even be able to keep the town half-way safe. Just imagine it's your family these men want to kill and hurt."

"I guess in a way, it is," Frenchy said. He moved two men to the jail and he and two others took up positions around Daws' office. "We could see the fires at the mines as we rode in. Donovan said to tell you that Pierce would be sending some men up here, too."

The mob that descended into town was about fifty strong. More than that were involved in the mine fires but whiskey, looting the mine offices, and fighting over what was available took a toll and this was what was left. Many carried torches in one hand and a weapon or bottle in the other as they moved onto Pioche's main thoroughfare.

Ephram Boxer saw the lawmen spread out across the street and pointed them out to the mob but didn't follow along. Instead, he cut up a side street, planning on invading the jail and springing Larry Samples. Samples, after all, had the purse with which to pay Mr. Boxer. Stephan Fletcher stood at the second floor window of his office/home, watching the drunken mob surge forward.

Onward to doom and the glory that was Sandy Hitchcock. He raised a half empty bottle to the men in the street. *All that Hitchcock built will be gone by sunset as will you, the wretched miners he idolized.*

Appleby, the apothecary, had his shotgun and extra rounds in hand as he watched the procession. Even if they didn't throw a torch on his balcony porch, he was going to shoot somebody. A man named Sinclair seemed to take the lead and urged the men to attack various businesses as they came down the street. Doors were kicked in, windows splintered, and within minutes, flames could be seen inside only a few of the shops.

Grabbing valuables became more important than burning the town or killing lawmen and the men came out from the shops carrying what loot they could grab. Gunfire exploded in fights over who got what. The apothecary got his man from the balcony but paid for it with a shot to his mid-section. Appleby died reloading his scattergun.

Slim led his pitiful little group straight at the screaming men and when there was about a twenty-five-foot separation, another group of men stepped out from between two building to join Calhoun. "This is a pleasure, indeed, Mr. Overby," Slim said. Jacob Overby had Terrible Tommy Tucker and Zeke

Trumple with him, all carrying shotguns.

"We're with you, Marshal," Overby said. "Shall we just lay 'em out?"

"No, Jacob, no," Slim called out. Now, along with Gary Thompson, Slim had some firepower. "All right, listen. We will each fire a round at their feet, all together, at the same time. If they don't turn and leave, then pick your man and be accurate. Don't just shoot into the crowd."

Terrible Tommy Tucker laughed. "That's how I shoot ducks and quail, Marshal. I'll pick me the biggest meanest target first."

"All right, now," Slim said. "On three. One, two, three." Five shotguns erupted in flame, white smoke, and heavy lead shot, at the feet of the approaching mob. Some of the men went down with bleeding ankles and legs, others raised their weapons to fire back and were the first targets of Slim's little army.

Those not so drunk that they couldn't think turned and left the scene, some at a high lope. Others took the challenge and prepared to fight the lawmen, taking a terrible loss. Five shotguns were fired and reloaded over and over into the mob until it finally dispersed. Slim saw Spike Loring leading a group of his employees in fighting the fires, some of which were close to being out of control.

Local storekeepers joined the Loring crowd, and at the other end of the main street, Slim could see Pendergrass and his people doing the same thing, getting control of fires quickly. No one saw the lone man slowly approaching the side of the jail building, a knife in one hand, and a Colt in the other.

CHAPTER 27

Frenchy Des Moines was standing just inside the open door of the sheriff's office and heard someone step onto the boardwalk off to his right. *I can see the marshal and those people across the street. There shouldn't be anyone coming this way. Marshal said no one was to come in. Hope I'm right.* He took one step back and leveled his double-barrel shotgun at the doorway.

Ephram Boxer stayed as close to the building as he could get, easing his way through the deep shadows, almost half a step at a time toward that open door. Everyone's eyes were on the melee on the main street and never saw Boxer stoop low and make a fast move into the office. All Boxer could see were the open ends of two massive barrels aimed at his middle. He fired the Colt at the same time Frenchy lit off both barrels.

Frenchy was flung back five feet but Boxed was almost cut in half by the blasts. Frenchy felt the bullet tear through his leg and fell across the desk, rolled off it and onto the floor, pulling his sidearm as he fell. There was no need. Boxer's remains were blown right back through the open door and onto the street outside.

Bull Morrison and Shorty Bellows were at Boxer's side

almost before the man's body stopped. "Ain't much of a fighter now," Morrison said. "Go on back Shorty. Stay with that evidence." Morrison stepped onto the boardwalk. "Hello, inside. This is Marshal Morrison. Don't shoot."

"I'm hit, Marshal. Come on in." Frenchy was tying his neckerchief around the wounded leg when Bull kneeled down. "It ain't that bad," the buckaroo said, his speech already slurred from loss of blood.

Bull tied the rag as tight as he dared and was amazed when Ginny Whipple moved him aside and took over. "Oh, my God, woman. I didn't know you were still here. Are you all right? I'm so sorry, Miss Whipple. You should not have been here."

"I am, so let it go, Marshal. Help me get him onto a bunk back there. He needs my help fast. That bullet severed a main artery in his leg, and he'll be dead in minutes if I don't get him tied off."

Bull picked the large ranch hand up like a sack of grain and Ginny led him back into the cell blocks. Put him there, on Washington's bed. George, get me some water and some strong cord. Hurry."

The jailer was able to move about, fighting off the affects of the blow to his head and got what Ginny needed. "Get his boots and pants off, Bull. Don't be nice about it. Hurry," Ginny said. Bull ripped the boots off and simply cut the man's suspenders before pulling his pants off. Ginny was on her knees at the side of the bunk cleaning the wound and looking for the source of the heavy bleeding.

Bull nodded to Washington and walked out of the cell block all the way to the street. *That woman's full of the right stuff. Got two men back there that should be dead and she don't even see that she shouldn't be there.* He looked out on an ugly scene. Some of the miners were down in the mud and dirt crying out for help, others were fighting each other over the loot they managed to grab before setting the fires.

Bull saw Slim and some ranch hands with Loring and motioned for them to join him. They walked out onto the center of the street. "Let's clean up this mess, Slim." Anger boiled at the surface and the marshal could only see devastation that never should have happened. "Move the wounded over to the walkways, tell the others to go home or ..." He wanted to say kill 'em but he held back.

"Tell 'em to go home or knock their heads a good one and we'll fill the jail. The county is gonna need their fines to rebuild this town."

"What happened at the jail? I heard shots," Slim said.

"Frenchy killed Boxer but got shot bad. Might die. Bleeding hard. Ginny's with him."

"Ginny? My God, Bull. Was she still in there when the riot started? Is she all right?"

"She's fine, Slim. When you get the street cleared you might want to stop in and say hello." He chuckled as he dragged a man with bleeding ankles onto the boardwalk. Slim was already half way back to the jail. "Don't mind him," Bull said to one of the buckaroos. "He gets all jittery around women."

"ANOTHER SUNRISE IN WHAT'S LEFT OF PIOCHE, SLIM. YOU AND THOSE cowboys did a good job of getting things under control. Good job. We've got a mess in front of us now, though." Bull Morrison was pulling his boots on. "I've got a meeting with the county this morning. Get Chago in as sheriff and get all these men run through justice court."

"Judge Baker wants us in Salt Lake next week, Bull. Ain't no way we can make it. The deputies will be here sometime today and we'll spend most of the day separating those mounds of evidence we've collected. There were three county commissioners. Are you sure that only Samples was on the take?"

"Not by a long shot and I hope to find out for sure during the meeting. A leading question or two should open a can or two."

They walked out of the Lucky Lady Hotel, gave the still cluttered street a look and it was Bull that spotted light coming from Ginny Whipple's café. "Is she open?" They hustled the half block and found the diner open with one of Donovan's buckaroos doing the cooking, and another doing the serving.

"That lady has mended all of us more than once," one of them said. "It's the least we can do for her. Breakfast, Marshal Bull, Marshal Slim? Got steaks and spuds. That's about all Slicker knows how to cook."

"Steaks and spuds it is then," Bull said. "And a gallon or two of coffee."

"Took food and coffee to the jail earlier, Marshal. Frenchy is going to live and it looks like Three-Finger Jack will too." The ranch hand called Wade said. "Every man on our crew has asked for that lady's hand at least once. Amazing woman. The worse the wound the more she loves fixin' it."

Slim nodded in complete agreement. *Don't think I've ever met a woman quite like Ginny Whipple. What's worse, I don't know what I'm going to do about it either. If anything. I'm in no position to buy a ranch, get married, and settle down and I don't think I want to, anyway. But that woman is tempting. More than tempting.*

He fought to get his mind back on the business of catching outlaws. "When's your meeting with the county?" Slim asked.

"I told 'em to be at Daws's office at eight. I also suggested they would not like it if I had to come looking for them. I think they got the message. Any idea when our deputies will be riding in?"

"Don't know when they left Elko, Bull. I'm just thinking it should be sometime today. Is court going to be continuing? We already had a half full jail, and sure added to it yesterday."

"Schaffer said he would hold court every day until everyone is processed. Then it's Mallard's turn. That will take longer."

"This thing of not having help at the local level is slowing us down, Bull. We're local law, state law, and federal law and without any help to speak of. Is Gary Thompson holding up his end? He was sloppy yesterday out on the street. Could have been shot two or three times by just walking up on a wounded rioter."

"He wants the prestige of being sheriff and it ain't gonna happen." Bull finished his coffee and wagged his head some. "Man isn't cut out for law work. Thinks about what he looks like doing something instead of doing something. You know what I mean."

"I do. While you're prying the truth out of the commissioners I'll see if I can find a couple of deputies for Chago. He looked like he'd been carrying that badge for years. The man's good, Bull."

They were about half-way through big steaks when Stephan Fletcher walked in. He looked like he'd spent the last twelve hours drinking and then doing his best to sober up. His long hair hung limp, his face was sickly, sallow to the point of gray, and his dull eyes looked mostly at the floor when he advanced on the marshals' table.

"Got something that needs to be done and said." It was just a simple statement and the man plopped down in a chair without being invited. "I've failed the law, Marshal, failed my life, but I won't die as a failure. I won't. I've been an arrogant ass most of my life, believing that life owed me a grand living. That's how I got tangled up with the likes of Sandy Hitchcock."

He took a long drink of the coffee Wade brought, sighed, and continued. "The man was a first-class salesman. I saw miles of blue skies, mountains of gold, and lived the good life defending his lies and fables in a court he already owned. You've heard it said and I've seen it done. The man could sell you a pig's ear and you would believe you bought a silk purse."

"And, you, sir are here because ..." Bull drawled it out. *Ain't a lawyer alive can say "Hello" in less than a thousand words.* "Let's get it on, Mr. Fletcher. I've other people to deal with today."

"Yes, yes. Of course," he said. Fletcher was still half-way under the influence and put on a bit of a show as he straightened up in the chair and pushed some hair back. "I believe you are aware of the partnership of Hitchcock and Larry Samples?"

"Just the two?" Slim asked. Bull tried to smile at the question, hiding it behind a napkin.

"Well," Fletcher said. He looked back and forth at the two marshals, saw the buckaroos hovering around the table and folded his hands in his lap. *Maybe I picked the wrong time to go straight. Do these men know about the judge in Salt Lake? Maybe I've just sent myself to prison.* He coughed, tried to take a drink of coffee.

"A partnership of two, Fletcher, or was the number a bit higher? Say, maybe three?" Slim watched the weasel squirm in his lie and continued the prod. "You came to try to make yourself look good in our eyes, sir. You're not doing a good job of it. Tell us about this partnership, because withholding evidence is against the law. You do understand that, don't you?"

"Tell you what, Mr. Fletcher." Bull Morrison cut in. His voice was calm, soft even, but his eyes bored deep into the man's very soul. "If you become a witness for the prosecution, if you tell us and the others you will soon meet, everything you know about Hitchcock's partnerships and deals, I can make it easier for you, get you into, well, maybe a little nicer prison for a little shorter stay."

Slim nodded his head, gave the man a slight smile, but also drummed his fingers on the table. "Marshal Morrison has meetings scheduled this morning, Fletcher, but I'm free for an hour or so. Will you come with me and tell me everything you know of the Hitchcock operation? It would be to your benefit, sir."

Fletcher hesitated for just a moment. Has Fletcher's romance with the bottle dimmed his view of reality? Does he even understand what's being offered? Is there anyone worth saving? Really, is there? Hitchcock's dead, these marshals seem to know about Judge Olsen.

Slim watched the man look down at the table. What was he thinking? An easier prison in which to spend his old age? Shorter stay there? Or was he conniving, thinking how he could get all that but not sell out his clients? Slim watched Fletcher's face change, a time or two from worry to calm to anxious.

"They'll have me killed, you know. That judge has friends all the way to Washington. I wouldn't be the first man he put out a contract on."

"All the more reason to work with us, Fletcher," Bull growled. "Take him to the jail, Slim. I have to meet those others at Daws' office. Court won't begin for another two hours." Bull looked at Fletcher and scowled. "If you're working to protect someone, I'll see to it that you spend a long time in a nasty federal prison in Texas. Think about that, hard." He stood up and strode from the diner.

"You boys did a fine job with our breakfast. I'll see to it that Ginny knows it. Are you coming along, Mr. Fletcher? Or will it be the hard way?" Slim nodded to the lawyer to get up.

"Yes, Marshal, let's have a long talk. I think I have much that needs saying." He saw chains, ugly prison guards looking to gouge his eyes out, uglier prisoners needing to kill the man who turned on Judge Olsen. "You have to protect me, Marshal. They'll have me tortured before they kill me."

Calhoun simply nodded. What the attorney said was the truth.

CHAPTER 28

"What is that noise? Moody, find out and have it stopped immediately. This is a federal courthouse not some saloon or bawdy house. Get that noise stopped this instant." There were sounds of people moving about outside the judge's chambers, boots scuffing marble floors, and chairs being scraped on the floor. "Most annoying, Moody."

Judge John T. Olsen was in a foul temper on a stormy spring morning in Salt Lake City, Utah. Rumors were circulating about problems in Pioche, about the marshal service sending men to the mining camp, and worse, he hadn't heard from Hitchcock for more than a week. His clerk, K.C. Moody seemed to be slacking in getting paperwork to the judge when it was asked for, and others were seemingly aloof in their reaction to his needs.

His was a sour temperament at best and when things went wrong the people around the long-serving jurist paid a dear price. The courthouse was Olsen's, the people served the judge, and woe be to whomever forgot that.

This business arrangement with Hitchcock had paid the old judge well. He tried to think what would cause these problems he seemed to be facing. Hitchcock liked to think it was his operation, but Judge Olsen corrected him often. Olsen stood about five feet and ten inches and weighed less than one fifty. Hitchcock weighed close to three hundred pounds and Olsen took great pleasure deriding the corpulent partner on his weight.

The fact that the business arrangement was illegal and immoral didn't have any impact on Olsen at all. He seemed immune to the fact that he was subverting federal law to his benefit while serving as a federal judge if he even gave it any consideration at all. Did he consider himself or his position as being above the law? Was he the law? What would he do if he were to be confronted by the law?

I think Mr. Hitchcock is getting a little too independent. Might need to have a long talk with His Heaviness. I won't tolerate this kind of treatment. We pay those county officials well, and it's Hitchcock's responsibility to keep me informed of activities there. This operation of ours only works because of me and they better not forget it.

Was there more? Olsen had paid no attention to the rumors of marshals in Pioche but the thought of Hitchcock not keeping in touch and the rumor of marshals came together on this spring morning. *Why would marshals be there? They work for me. Nonsense.* He tried to let the thought drop but couldn't.

I've got to clear my calendar and make sure any paperwork that might exist is destroyed. I've been careful all these years, but little things are the ones that take you out. Simple bank slips, deeds that shouldn't be known, tax payments. He glanced toward a wall safe but was interrupted by more noise out front. He rarely kept personal papers in his chambers, but he still needed to check.

The noise of people in the outer office was annoying and Olsen yelled again at Moody to stop the noise. Moody left the judge's office and strode into the marble lined outer office. U.S. Marshal Peter Flannigan waited with two others. "Is he alone?"

"Yes," Moody said and stepped aside. Flannigan had two deputies with him, along with an arrest warrant issued by Judge Baker in San Francisco and a warrant to search the offices. The deputies had cleared the outer office and that was the noise the judge was complaining of.

"Damn, I wish Bull was here to do this." He looked at his deputies and nodded. "The man has a fiery temperament, but I don't believe he will fight us. He'll storm and yell, but I believe that's all."

"I hope you're right, Marshal." Deputy Peabody said. "This isn't the time to ignore the possibility of gun-play."

Flannigan was born to work for a government agency of some kind. "He's a federal judge, Peabody." How he ended up in the marshal service would always be a wonder to the man. He believed in every sheet of paper having a reason for being, that the more sheets the better, and that one out of position would be reason enough to discard all of them. A stickler for secondary rules.

How did it come to this? His mind went back to the previous night when two Deputy U.S. Marshals banged on his door. "We're from Judge Baker in San Francisco, Marshal, and we have papers you need to read immediately" The men had spent days on the train, hadn't shaved or bathed, but Flannigan didn't see any of that, only the sheaf of legal papers handed to him.

"My God," he said after paging through them. "Judge Olsen indicted?" He sat down and motioned the deputies to do the same. "I've known this man for years, Milford and never heard even a hint of impropriety. Are you sure of this?"

Deputy Marshal Milford Peabody nodded. "It's a sad day,

Flannigan. Sad." Peabody outlined the case as Judge Baker saw it with everything that was known from Bull Morrison's investigation in Pioche. "Bull and Slim have done an outstanding job of gathering evidence, Peter. Baker wants the trial to be held in San Francisco. Bull of course wants it in Pioche, and I'm sure Olsen will want it here in Salt Lake."

"Baker would have the lead unless someone in Washington over rules him," Peter Flannigan said. "We will need to act with precision and perfection, gentlemen. One mistake on our end and Olsen will walk. How did Baker get these indictments without anyone in Salt Lake knowing?"

"Grand juries really are secret sometimes," Peabody laughed. "Bull and Slim provided enough by way of sworn testimony that the grand jury took little time handing down the indictments. Olsen, though can't be counted out."

"No, he certainly can't," Flannigan said. "We'll meet in the corridor outside his chambers in the morning, arrest him and alert Judge Baker. The man has a terrible temper but I imagine he will not be a threat. Let's have a brandy or two and make this a real plan," Flannigan said.

FLANNIGAN MOTIONED HIS DEPUTIES TO FOLLOW, KNOCKED ONCE AND walked into Olsen's private chambers. "What's this?" Olsen demanded, standing up quickly. "What do you think you're doing, entering without being invited, Marshal?"

"Judge John T. Olsen, it pains me to have to do this. Under the authority of Federal Judge Timothy Baker, Pacific Division, I have been authorized to place you under arrest. The charges are outlined in this grand jury indictment." He handed the paperwork to the judge. "I'm also authorized to place the contents of this office and your home under control of the marshal service until further notice."

"How dare Baker. Out!" Olsen screamed the words. "Get out of my office. Baker doesn't have jurisdiction. This is my jurisdiction. Get out. Send Moody in." The man's face was red, perspiration covered his forehead, and his eyes darted to the safe on the wall. "I'll not tolerate this, Marshal Flannigan." He started to move around his desk but stopped. He didn't step forward or offer any other aggressive move.

"I'm sorry, Judge. This is all legal and you are under arrest." Flannigan motioned Peabody and the other marshal to move around the judge. "Please, sir, come with us now." Flannigan stepped forward to take the judge's arm and the man stepped back suddenly, pulled a revolver from his waist and fired two shots into Flannigan's chest. Deputy Marshal Miles "Tall Man" Sinclair drew his weapon and fired twice, driving Olsen back against the wall. Olsen clawed at the wall, tried to hold on, but slowly fell to the carpeted floor leaving a trail of blood on the rich wallpaper.

"My God," Moody exclaimed rushing into the office. A heavy white cloud of gun smoke hung motionless in the air. The two deputy marshals were just as motionless. Moody found himself looking down the smoking barrel of Sinclair's revolver and stopped immediately. Flannigan moaned, tried to move but couldn't, and Sinclair yelled at Moody to get a doctor.

Moody stood stock still, staring at the dead judge he had worked so hard to get out of office. There should have been good thoughts in his head, but what he had planned and worked for was Olsen out of office, his once good name sullied, not dead, bleeding all over official papers.

"Get a damn doctor, Moody," Tall Man Sinclair yelled again, that pistol waving, menacing, frightening the clerk. The clerk spun and ran from the office. Sinclair tucked the revolver back in its leather and kneeled down by Flannigan's side. "My God, Peabody. Flannigan said he didn't think this would happen." Sinclair pulled Flannigan's coat back and knew the end would be soon.

"Doctor will be here soon, Marshal," he said. He motioned Peabody to bring a robe for the man. The two shots were high in the chest area and Sinclair could see bright pink coming from the marshal's nose and mouth with every troubled breath and knew Flannigan's death was imminent.

The worst job he had ever been ordered to do and it killed him. Sinclair had known Flannigan for years, was familiar with his family back east. *He worked years for this judge and we had to convince him with the strongest evidence to make the arrest. Looking back, it is obvious he should have come in with his gun in hand. It broke his heart to have to arrest the man he worked for and now it's killed him.* Tall Man's thoughts lingered for just moments before the responsibility that accompanies a marshal's badge kicked in.

By the time Moody returned with the doctor, Peter Flannigan was gone, and Sinclair and Peabody were beginning their search of the office and its cabinets full of files. They hadn't searched for the safe's combination yet. "Moody, get the combination to that safe. I want the courthouse security chief here pronto. Move it, Moody." Sinclair's voice carried a threat that Moody caught right away.

"Doctor, you stay with the bodies until the security people get here. I want that door closed and locked when you leave, Moody. No one will be allowed in here, period." Sinclair's size and tone of voice made it clear that he was now the lead marshal.

It didn't take ten minutes for the news of the two deaths to spread through the federal building and just an hour for the news to be covered by reporters and rumor mongers.

"I've got to get wires off to Judge Baker and Marshal Morrison." Sinclair said. "Be slow and thorough with all the paperwork, Peabody. Don't miss anything. We'll start with his home tomorrow."

Tall Man Sinclair walked through a crowd of court workers and didn't answer a single question. *Blood thirsty mongrels.* He fought crowds of the curious all the way to the telegraph office, just across the street from the federal building. He had to produce his badge in order to get the telegraph operator away from a mob of reporters.

"You let out anything I'm about to send, I'll see to it that you rot in prison." One long wire to Judge Baker in San Francisco and one long wire to Marshal Bull Morrison in Pioche. It took a long time to get the phrasing right for the wire to Flannigan's family back in Missouri. "A most terrible day," he muttered, making his way back to Judge Olsen's chambers. To add to the problems of the day, a hard rain driven by furious wind pelted the shining city.

In his report to Baker, filed later, he suggested that in all future arrests of public officials, at least one deputy marshal on the scene will have a drawn weapon, visible to all, particularly the person being arrested. "Marshal Flannigan died because he was arresting a long time friend," Sinclair wrote. "Something else that needs to be discussed. One of us should have had the lead."

CHAPTER 29

BULL WAS SITTING AT THE CITY MARSHAL'S DESK, STARING AT THE wall clock. He had a fire going, coffee boiling and was willing to shoot the two county commissioners if they were even so much as one minute late in arriving. They surprised him by arriving five minutes early.

He let his mind wander through what he and Slim had discovered so far, in particular the possible involvement of a federal judge, the working relationship of a member of the county commission, but still lacking in who it was that Hitchcock used to keep everyone in line. The enforcer.

Murders take place in every community and Pioche has the reputation of being a dangerous and murderous mining camp, but the big crime has been this massive conspiracy to own the mines, the water, the land. Hell, Hitchcock probably thought he owned the minds and souls of everyone in town. Morrison had to hold in a snicker as the commissioners walked in the door.

"Good morning, Marshal. Coffee smells good." Claudius Perkins was tall and thin, his balding head shone in the lamp light when he doffed his hat. The man was raised in Boston, had attended the military academy but was released because of injuries during training, which still caused him to limp some.

Perkins was a 'glad-hander' type politician. Everything was rosy, even while he was picking your pockets. A smile that seemed plastered in place, the man was impeccably dressed and coiffed at all times, and seldom ready to buy someone a drink. Perkins offered that smile to Marshal Bull Morrison who almost shrank back.

The second man was Lemuel Stark, a miner turned politician. He was the kind of man who did what he was told and rarely had a thought of his own. "Morning," is all he said. He poured some whiskey from a flask into his coffee cup but didn't offer any around. Hitchcock paid good money to get Stark elected but got his money's worth at every vote of the council.

"This is not a friendly little meeting, gentlemen. For the record, I'm U.S. Marshal Bull Morrison and I'm investigating allegations of federal law breaking. Pour your coffee and sit down." Brusque and to the point, no welcoming, no social graces offered.

"This man who will sit with us is Lincoln County Deputy Sheriff Gary Thompson who will be acting as witness on the one hand and taking notes on the other."

"It is more than possible that what is said at this table will be read in court. If you have any questions, now is the time."

"Do we need to have an attorney present?" Perkins asked.

"If you feel you need one, by all means, invite one," Bull said.

"I ain't done nothing wrong," Stark said.

Bull looked at Perkins, the question obvious in his face. Perkins shrugged and Bull got right to the point. "Mr. Samples was arrested and charged with conspiracy for some of his dealings with Sandy Hitchcock, his land law abuses, his water law abuses, and his payments to a federal judge. I'll start with you, Mr. Stark."

"Why me? I ain't done nothing."

"I hope that's the truth," Bull said. *This Mr. Stark hasn't a clue, has no idea even on what a conspiracy is, how one becomes involved, and I would bet he doesn't know how he got elected. A jury will ring him up in five minutes or less.*

"You favored a couple of county rules to restrict the water to ranches in the valley in favor of more water to Hitchcock's mines. Is that right?" Morrison asked.

"Of course I did. The mines are more important than a bunch of dumb farmers." Perkins tried to interrupt but Morrison shut him up. "Besides," Stark continued, "Judge Olsen said it was our right. Damn right I backed the resolution. Hell, Marshal, I authored it."

"Just how did that resolution come about, Mr. Stark?"

"Well, we were sitting at the Silver Crystal saloon one night when Sandy told us about what that judge said."

"Who was sitting at that table?" Bull was not about to let this get away from him. He was going to get validation of the names he had been hearing for days. "You and who else?"

"Shut the damn hell up," Perkins yelled and reached for his sidearm. Thompson moved for his but Bull was far the fastest at the table. He whipped that heavy Colt out and smashed Perkins across the side of the head knocking him clear across the room. Bull raced to his side and relieved the man of his weapon.

"Well, so much for a nice friendly little discussion, eh Thompson? Take this ass across the street and book him for attempted murder of a federal marshal. Mr. Stark and I will wait for your return." Stark had not moved an inch during the fracas. His eyes were wide, maybe not so much in fear, but in seeing someone Bull Morrison's size move that fast.

Thompson hustled the wounded man to his feet and across the street. "Now, sir," Bull said, "you were saying who was with you and Mr. Hitchcock at the Silver Crystal? Probably the sheriff, eh?"

Stark hesitated for just a moment, gathering himself, it seemed. "Oh," he said. "Um, yes, Sheriff Lighthorse was always at our meetings. We had formed a corporation, you see, to handle these affairs so that it didn't look like we were conducting county business. Mr. Hitchcock said that what a corporation did was safe from too many people knowing and members of the corporation couldn't be arrested." He sat back with a smug look that told Bull the man had been led down the rosy path by Hitchcock for a long time.

Bull cocked his head, raised his eyebrows, and did his best to hide a terrible attempt at smiling. "He did, eh? He said that." Stark nodded with a look of absolute innocence on his rough face. Bull reached over and grabbed the coffee pot and poured some for both of them. "You figured Mr. Hitchcock was pretty smart? That you could make some extra money and it would be all right? Well, who else besides you, Hitchcock, and the sheriff?"

"Most of our meetings was the three of us commissioners, you know, Perkins, me, and Mr. Samples. Larry and Claude were the really smart ones." He ducked his head a bit, showing some embarrassment. "Mr. Fletcher was always there, too. Our corporation made a lot of money and Mr. Fletcher said it was all legal."

"I don't want to break your heart, Mr. Stark, but Mr. Fletcher and those smart friends of yours are wrong. Do you have any paperwork about this corporation? I'd love to see it." Bull was sure there wouldn't be any. Even a drunken lawyer wouldn't be that stupid.

"I have it all at my cabin, Marshal. I'm sure it's all legal."

"What say we take a little walk, Mr. Stark. I'll tell you for sure if it's legal when you show it to me." *I'm stealing candy from a baby and I don't feel bad about it. This man was put in office for one reason only and that was to see to it that Hitchcock and Samples got their way every time. Is Perkins along for the ride or is he as involved? He sure acted like he was an instigator.*

The long walk, fresh air, and anticipation of possible binding evidence lit Morrison's mind on fire. *I can't get it out of my head that Hitchcock is not the boss. Who else could have put all of these schemes and plots together? Maybe there are more than one boss? Would Olsen be in a leadership position? A federal judge leading a conspiracy of this magnitude?*

The two walked from Daws' office half a mile up the hill to a little shack where Stark had the corporate papers framed and hanging on the wall. Penmanship of the highest order outlining the fact that the corporation owned the waters of Lincoln County and could determine how they were distributed were fully detailed. The document outlined how the various members of the corporation received their shares, and who the officers and members were.

Almost answers the question of leadership. Bull Morrison thought seeing Sandy Hitchcock listed as corporation president and John T. Olsen as vice-president. He knew that if that document was offered up in court, heads would roll and prisons would fill. *I hope Mr. Stark is as stupid and proud as I think he is. I have to have this charter.*

"That's a fine document, Mr. Stark. Let's bring it back with us so it doesn't accidentally get destroyed."

"Yes, Marshal. See? I haven't broken the law." They were on their way out of the door when Stark said, "We formed three corporations, Marshal. This one is for the water, we have one for the land program, replacing these vast ranches with small individual farms of less than forty acres that we sell to easterners. The framed piece is eloquent. I learned what that word means by looking at it. It's in the other room."

Morrison couldn't get to it fast enough and wondered why Stark would have these. Why wouldn't they be at Hitchcock's home or bank? Or even at Samples' place? "Why are you the keeper of these fine documents, Mr. Stark?"

"Mr. Hitchcock said no one would ever look for them if I kept them. That way, they would be safe."

"Safe from whom?" Bull asked.

"I don't know. Mr. Hitchcock said he had enemies."

Poor dumb sumbitch is going to jail for a long time and will never understand why. How many other ignorant fools did Sandy Hitchcock and his judge crony destroy? How many stupid people back east lost every dime because of these frauds? How many other documents like these exist that people swear by? A herd of swindles dealt by a herd-boss who knew how to play people. Who is the boss, Judge Olsen or Sandy Hitchcock? It was a long walk back.

CHAPTER 30

PAUL STEWART ARRIVED AT THE COUNTY JAIL ABOUT THE SAME TIME as Bull and Commissioner Stark. "Got two wires for you, Marshal. I have to read them when I get them, and I want you to know that you won't like either one."

"Thank you, Stewart, thank you." He turned to Thompson. "Put Mr. Stark in a cell at the marshal's office. Don't want him talking to the others." He grabbed some coffee and sat down at the sheriff's desk.

"But, I haven't done anything," Stark said.

"I know you think that, Mr. Stark, but you're in more trouble than you've ever been in your life," Bull said. "You've been lied to and at some point, I really hope you come to understand all of this." He waved Johnson and Stark away. "Where's Calhoun," he bawled out after reading the first wire.

"I'll get him," Thompson said.

"I heard," Slim said, stepping in from the porch. He had Ginny Whipple with him and she ducked back into the cell block to check her patients. "Sounds important." They had been at the café, supposedly to check on his foot.

"More than, I'm afraid. Olsen's dead." Morrison handed Slim the message. "Flannigan too. What a mess."

"My God," Slim said. He read the wire again. "Olsen shot Flannigan? That must have been one horrible scene. I worked with Tall Man a couple of times. He has to feel terrible, killing the judge he was sworn to protect." Slim just stood and shook his head back and forth, looking at the telegram over and over.

Bull sat back in the chair and read the second telegram. "Judge Baker wants us to wrap this up and head back to San Francisco." He handed the second wire to Slim and reached for the framed corporate documents. "Take a look at these." He handed Slim the corporation documents. "Never seen one to look this authentic. Where's that flask."

Judge Mallard handed him his. "Many of these prisoners are both alleged federal and Lincoln County law breakers, Marshal. Are you planning on transporting all of them to California?"

"I surely hope I'm not," Bull snickered. "No, I'm going to let the various judges in California, Utah, and Nevada, you among them, work their way through what Slim and I have found, and let them decide on what to do. It's a long ride to Elko and the railhead, and it would take a large posse to get this whole bunch there."

"With that in mind, I believe it would be best for Judge Schaffer and I to continue hearing as many of the local cases as we can and you then put federal holds on the ones you want for federal court. I'll release any documents you need, as well."

Bull nodded and wrote a couple of long messages, one to Judge Baker and one to Tall Man Sinclair detailing what they learned in just the last few hours. The corporation papers alone, signed by Judge Olsen and Hitchcock would be the final nail, even though both men were dead. He told Sinclair to keep working as if Judge Olsen were still alive and told Baker that he and Slim were close to wrapping up their end.

Spike Loring was coming down the stairs from his office as Bull and Slim came through the saloon doors. "The wrecking crew has arrived, I see," he joshed. "You look like your mother just got killed."

"Our number one crime boss just got killed, Spike. Better bring the bottle, Mr. Lassen. Olsen killed a marshal and was killed in turn. We'll be wrapping up our part of this foul job in the next few days, I think."

"You make it sound like something's missing," Loring said.

"We don't have the enforcer." Slim said the words quietly, almost as a whisper. "Hitchcock was a fat man who couldn't walk fifty steps without stopping to take a breath. The county commissioners seem more dandies than criminals, and none of the miners come off as paid killers, hired to keep everyone in line. There are some mean ones but the enforcer has to be able to think and we're not seeing that in any of them."

"I always believed it was Lighthorse," Loring said. "His deputies did a fine job of keeping everyone in line."

"Maybe, but he isn't the brightest. He hired killers, but was he told to do so? And who gave those orders? No, Harvey Lighthorse is just a bank robber wearing a badge." Slim took a long drink and stared at the bar-top.

There are only two men in Pioche who fill the job description. I'm talking to one. Spike Loring fits except that he was rarely seen with Hitchcock. Rolf Pendergrass is the other. Daily contact, shared a bank, and Pendergrass seemed to have control over Lighthorse and Buster Cranston. Bull and I need to have a long talk with the gentleman.

"Bull, do you remember the reaction of those around when you punched Sheriff Lighthorse that first time? When I took Hitchcock's money at the poker table? It was Pendergrass who simply told Lighthorse to knock it off. Any other sheriff would have gone after you and there wouldn't have been anyone to say no."

Terrible Tommy Tucker, the teamster from Overby's shipping company, sidled in. "Heard part of the conversation, Slim. I remember you talking about that when we were bringing Pizon's body back. Been grinding on it since." He motioned Jimmy Lassen for a beer.

"Mr. Hitchcock never did nothing without Rolf Pendergrass being right with him. They was inseparable. Pendergrass is the one who gave Lighthorse his orders, saw to it who had access to Hitchcock, and who didn't."

"Why do you know all this, Mr. Tucker?" Bull Morrison gave the huge man a long look. "Why would a mule-skinner know about Rolf Pendergrass?"

"Overby's shipping routes go south to Arizona Territory, west to California, and north to Salt Lake City." Tucker looked back and forth at the two marshals. "Hitchcock has a lot of business and other dealings with Salt Lake and Pendergrass often sent rather secret messages in locked boxes to people in Salt Lake, always paid for by Hitchcock."

He drank the first beer down in one gulp and pounded the bar for another. "Use the big glasses, Jimmy," he laughed. "These are for children." The humor ended immediately when he turned back to Slim. "Return packages were to be delivered to Pendergrass and then he would give them to Hitchcock. The boxes were heavy going out, considerably lighter coming back."

Slim saw right away that it would be gold going out and paperwork coming back. "I see the picture, Mr. Tucker. How would Pendergrass control others?" Slim wanted to know how Pendergrass could keep Lighthorse, Buster Cranston, the county commissioners, and the other mine operators in line. "He's not a gunman, not a fighter. How would he maintain control?"

"He was the center of distribution, Slim." Bull Morrison cut in. "I would bet he distributed a lot more than paperwork or orders."

"Gotcha," Slim said. "He distributed the money. Do what you're told and you'll get paid. Don't, and you won't get paid and might lose everything. The ultimate enforcer." He laughed and downed his beer. "So, Terrible Tommy Tucker, would you care to join Bull and I for a cold one in a big glass at the Silver Crystal?"

CHAPTER 31

"JUST FOLLOW MY LEAD WHEN WE GET THERE," BULL SAID. "I'D LIKE
to get him to spill it out, I'd like him in irons without gun-play,
and I'd like one more beer before all of that." Terrible Tommy
Tucker had ridden from Pioche to the hot springs and back
with Slim Calhoun, came to idolize the deputy marshal and
was taken aback by Morrison's glib attitude.

Slim saw the look on Tucker's face and held in his chuckle.
"If we get him talking, we might learn a lot more than if we
just throw questions at him, Mr. Tucker. It's not always hot lead
and splintered furniture in this business."

"I've been going to school from the moment I met you, Slim.
Thank you. Pendergrass is not the dandy that he appears. According to Jacob Overby the man has a mean streak and there
are rumors of men disappearing after visits from him. Along
with his side-arm, he also carries a hefty knife on his belt."

"Good to know, Tucker," Bull said. "Doesn't strike me as a
killer but I've been wrong before." They found the bar about
half filled and ordered beer. The Silver Crystal was almost
quiet as the three looked around the gaudy saloon. Gaming
tables had a few players and about half the drinking tables
were full.

Was it in anticipation of a ruckus? After all, that was Bull Morrison and Terrible Tommy Tucker standing at the same bar. "Pendergrass around?" Bull asked.

"Probably in his office," the barman said. "He said not to serve you."

"Good for him. Where is his office?"

"He doesn't want visitors," the barman said. He started to walk away when strong, hairy fingers latched onto his neck and stopped him. Bull yanked the man back.

"I'm talking to you, mister, and so far, I've been a gentleman. Get rude with me again and I'll plant your face inches deep in this oak bar. Where is Pendergrass's office?" The scar across Bull's face was scarlet, his eyes seemed to be screaming for blood, and he jerked the barman right up to his face. "Please?"

"Upstairs to the right," he said, and Bull lifted him over the bar and threw him onto a table where four miners, off shift, were having their beer. Men, beer, whiskey and chairs went flying.

"Thank you," Bull said. The words carried a dare that the men sprawled about on the floor did not answer. He motioned the others to follow him upstairs. "Just don't much care for rude people," he muttered. Muttering was heard from around the saloon but no one stepped forward or tried to intervene. Did they work for Pendergrass or just drink in his saloon? Would they come to his rescue? Slim didn't see one man make any kind of move.

"What's going on?" Pendergrass came through a doorway down the hall. "Oh, it's you, is it? You're not welcome in this establishment, Marshal. Please leave or I'll have you thrown out."

"You might have a lot of money but you don't have enough to buy as many men as you would need, Pendergrass." Bull actually laughed as he pushed the man back into his office. Pendergrass stumbled across the small office and into his chair behind a highly polished desk.

"You two stay out here and protect me from whatever army might be coming." Bull slammed the door behind him.

Tucker looked at Slim. "Is this how he gets a man involved in a conversation?"

"Bull has his own ways, Tucker. There isn't time to try to explain Bull Morrison right now, just accept the fact that he will come out of that room with the answers he wants."

Bull walked up to Pendergrass's desk. "Judge Olsen is dead." Bull said it right out and watched Pendergrass for reaction, which came quick.

"So?" He tried to be nonchalant, pass it off, but Bull saw through it.

"Just about makes you the head man on the Lincoln County Water Distribution Corporation, doesn't it? Stop me if I'm wrong. President is Sandy Hitchcock, VP is John T. Olsen, Federal District Court Judge, and Treasurer is one Rolf Pendergrass. You're the only one alive here."

How the hell does he know that? My God, those corporation papers Hitchcock insisted we leave with Lem Stark. "I have no idea what you're talking about, Marshal. Again, you're not welcome here. Leave, please."

"I'm going to and I'm taking you with me. Tell me about these fine business ventures of which you seem to hold the money bags. A corporation that owns all the water in Lincoln County? Come now, Pendergrass, that's a bit absurd, isn't it? Another corporation designed to acquire, not necessarily buy, existing ranches and knock them down in size to sell to poor dumb bastards back east as a remedy for poor health?"

I begged Hitchcock not to have those papers ever drawn

up more or less given to Stark. He had to play the part, make a show out of them. How the hell did this brute come by them? "You're talking in riddles, Marshal." Bull didn't see Pendergrass pull hard on a cord tucked under his desk. The bell behind the poker table rang and the dealer signaled several men drinking at tables near the rear of the saloon. The dealer gave a quick glance up the stairs and the men jumped to their feet.

Slim heard the bell and dashed into the office. "He just sent out an alarm." Slim knocked Pendergrass aside and found the cord. "Rings a bell downstairs. Got company coming, girls. Better hunker down."

Terrible Tommy Tucker ran to the top of stairs and found five men charging his way. His shotgun nailed two of them and they fell back on the followers. Tucker ran back to the office. "Ain't much of an army now," he said.

Downstairs, the barman motioned at others scattered around the saloon and they joined the survivors at the staircase. Pendergrass had his army and they were prepared for battle. "I ain't going against that scatter piece," one said.

"You will if you want to get paid," The poker dealer said. "Let's go, men. Pendergrass don't ring that bell unless he's about to die." The dealer took the stairs two at a time with a mob behind him. When they reached the landing and turned down the hallway they came face-to-face with three men holding three shotguns blasting their hot death.

Five men lay bleeding and dead, most of the others turned and either leaped off the staircase or ran down and out the saloon door. In just moments, Bull and Slim, their scatter guns reloaded, led Tucker and Pendergrass slowly down the stairs. Tucker had his shotgun shoved under Pendergrass's chin.

"One wrong move, many of you die, Pendergrass dies," Bull

said to the few left in the saloon. "Open us a path through this miserable place and I mean right now."

Tables were shoved out of the way, chairs thrown about, and Bull slowly moved toward the batwing doors. Slim covered the right side, along the bar, and Bull the left. Terrible Tommy's eyes darted all over the saloon and gambling hall, never letting that shotgun move from Pendergrass's throat.

Not a soul offered resistance but every eye followed the group out. Outside, people were gathering following the heavy gunfire. Pioche was a mining camp filled with men working every scheme known, filled with thieves, murderers, and extortionists, and Bull wondered which of those fine citizens he could see would be the first to fire on him.

"Walk behind me, Tucker. Slim, cover our butts." Bull led them down the street expecting to be shot at each step. They were less than a hundred feet when he saw several storekeepers come out on the boardwalk, holding guns.

"Look at this, Pendergrass. Seems as though we have an army too." Bull tried hard to smile as he watched the storekeepers and other members of Pioche high-society come out on the street to guard the marshal's walk to the jail. "This old camp has possibilities, Slim."

As they neared the Lucky Lady Hotel and Saloon, Spike Loring led five members of his staff, all armed, to join the parade, and within ten yards, Tom Donovan and three buckaroos joined in. "I love a parade." Bull yelled at the throng and moved Pendergrass into the sheriff's office.

"I THINK THAT'S ABOUT IT FOR US, JUDGE." BULL AND SLIM WERE sitting at a table in Ginny Whipple's café, steaks and potatoes heaped on their platters. At a near-by table there were three other men wearing badges from the marshal service. "We'll put our prisoners in a wagon in the morning and with our escort, ride north to Wells and the railhead." Bull wanted out of Pioche.

The three deputy marshals from San Francisco weren't pleased with the plan since they just finished a five day ride south from Wells. Ginny Whipple wasn't pleased with the plan, either.

"Ain't right, Slim. You need more doctoring."

If I got any more doctoring, I'd never leave this old camp. Slim gave her a big smile. "I've never had better doctoring in my life, Ginny, but orders are orders. This old badge I wear carries a heavy responsibility tacked to it. *My heart tells me to stay. I want to stay except that I wouldn't be able to. I can't think of a single deputy marshal who is married and has children. Ain't in the program.* "I'm a deputy marshal, my lady, and I'm afraid I'll always be one."

"I'll always remember you, Slim Calhoun." She kissed him on the cheek, turned and ran into the kitchen before anyone could see the tears rolling down her bright red face. *Damn you, Slim Calhoun. And damn me for falling for you. Just damn the whole world.* She ran all the way to her room and flopped onto the bed, blubbering like a baby.

CHAPTER 32

DEWEY SCHAFFER, GREG MALLARD, AND SPIKE LORING WERE AT THE stables along with Chago Torres and his deputies to get the prisoners loaded for the long ride to Wells and the railhead. "Again, Marshal Morrison," Judge Mallard said, "you've done a fine job here. To think how many people's lives Hitchcock and his federal judge partner have destroyed, well, you stopped them from ruining more lives."

"Thank you, Judge, but Slim and I had a lot of help. You, Dewey Schaffer, and the good citizens of Pioche, the ranchers. Everyone helped at every turn." Morrison caught the smile from Slim, knew he was blushing at his little speech, and coughed slightly to hide it some. He wanted to say more but couldn't. Mallard did.

"As far as Pioche goes, you cleaned up the sheriff's office, cleaned up the board of county commissioners, and cleaned up the water problems between the mines and ranches. Not bad for a couple of drifters come to town to make trouble." That brought laughter from everyone, including Jacob Overby who was supplying the wagon and teams for the ride north. Terrible Tommy Tucker demanded he be the teamster.

"Elections have been called to fill all the empty seats on

the commission, fill the sheriff's position, and that of town marshal," Mallard continued. "Pioche will have to live with the reputation it's built but it will be a far better community because of you, Bull, and you, Slim. Wish you could stay and watch the changes."

"Better get this show on the road, Slim," Bull said. "Can't be standing around jawin' all day. Thank you, Judge." Bull had to cut it off. *Give a judge an opening like that and he'll talk all day. We got a long ride with a wagon full of desperate criminals and Mallard wants to talk some more.*

Boots Kindle walked up and whacked Bull across his shoulders. "Didn't think anyone would ever bring Hitchcock to his knees, but you did a job of it, Marshal. I'm proud to have done a small part of it. Good luck."

"Thank you, Kindle. Tell those two men of yours thank you, too. Think you can save the mines?"

"There's gold and silver down there, Bull. High grade and lots of it." He was laughing hard as he walked away and Bull knew at least some of the mines would re-open. He looked over at Slim. "There are a few good people in this old camp, Slim. A few."

Overby had a large freight wagon with six up for the long haul north. Half the cargo was supplies for the trip and the other half was filled with prisoners. There were five marshals riding horses and five prisoners in the wagon with Tucker and Zeke Trumple as teamsters. "It's a good road north, Bull. We'll make twenty miles a day or more if the weather holds." Tucker was up on the seat and ready to roll. "Just give the word."

"Let's move 'em, Tucker," Bull hollered and Tucker cracked a long whip, smartly moving the six mules out. As they rode past the courthouse and jail facility, town marshal Three-Finger Daws sat in a wheelchair pumping his fist and smiling. Everyone gave him a high sign and wave.

"Wouldn't even be here if it weren't for him and that jerk clerk in Salt Lake," Slim said. "Ironic, eh?" Bull didn't try to answer, just urged his horse forward, on the road out of Pioche.

Before the parade reached the Lucky Lady Saloon, Tucker pulled the team to a halt. "Marshal, you better get up here," he hollered out. Bull and Slim rode back quick to find a fight going on in the back of the wagon.

Slim jumped into the middle of Lighthorse and Pendergrass trying to fight even though they were chained and manacled. Pendergrass had slammed the sheriff across the head with his manacled hands, opening a bloody gash. Lighthorse had his arms locked around the saloon owner's neck, choking him.

Slim fired one shot into the air and slammed both men to the floor of the wagon, smashing Pendergrass in the nose with a fist, and jerking Lighthorse's arms free of the man's neck. "Gonna be a long and mean ride if this is the start," he muttered. "We gotta have one of the deputies riding back here with these fools, Bull."

Before Bull could get one of the deputies up into the wagon, Samples went after Lem Stark, trying to kick the man in the face. The chains slowed the kick but the heavy chains did some damage to Stark's face. "Damn it," Slim said, smashing Samples with his revolver, knocking the heavy man out. "Send two of them, Bull."

The three tired deputy marshals, Jake Jordan, Slim Hoskins, and Augie Peters rode up to the wagon and tied their horses off. "We'll take care of things, Bull," Slim Hoskins said. Hoskins was far from Slim. Coming in well over two hundred pounds and towering over Slim Calhoun. "You gentlemen will sit quietly and if you don't I will tie you to a wheel. Understand?"

He was looking at Pendergrass in particular. "I'll tie you to a wheel and ask that huge gentleman with the whip to run them mules as fast as they'll go." He was screaming in Pendergrass's face and Slim was trying to hide a smile.

Before Tucker could get things moving again, Paul Stewart came running up. "Wire, Marshal. From Frisco."

"Ain't gonna get out of town, are we, Slim?" Bull said taking the wire. Slim watched the marshal's face cloud over some and then brighten. "Well, it ain't all bad, anyway. Let's get this show moving, Tucker." He handed the wire to Slim. "Sometimes I think there are just too many people making too many decisions in our lives, Slim."

The wire was from Judge Baker and said that trial would be held in federal court in Carson City, not San Francisco since the crimes were committed in Nevada and Utah and involved the Utah Division and Nevada Division. The few members of the outlaw conspiracy that were still alive in Salt Lake, the banker Washburn and the clerk Moody, would join those being brought in by Bull and Slim when they reached Wells.

"You're right, Bull, but nobody can take what we've managed to do here away from us." Slim started laughing and Bull rode up alongside him. "Think about it." Slim said. "Hitchcock and most outlaws and criminals would want a town without law and order and without lawmakers. We shut down the marshal's office, jailed the sheriff, and arrested most of the county commissioners. We created a criminal's haven."

"Ain't gonna write that in my report," Bull snarled and then the humor caught up with him. "Well, hell's bells, Calhoun, maybe I will."

"One more nice thing about having the trial in Carson City?" Slim said. "We'll be stuck in one of the prettiest little towns in the west for more than a year, Bull. Not in fog-bound San Francisco."

"You know better than that, Slim. Baker will find some horrible crime ridden hell to send us off to even while the trial is going on. Nope, old friend, we ain't riding toward a vacation. You just wait and see. That trial is going to last a long time, I'm thinking."

"Why? There's enough evidence to convict twice over." Slim said.

"Olsen is why. He's dead, but his is a stain on the judiciary, and his friends in the courts and in Washington will do everything in their power not to let his actions be known to the general public. Baker has his work cut out for sure. There will months of filings, months of underhanded dealings before the trial ever gets underway."

"You sound like you hope so," Slim said.

"I do, Slim. I do. This will give Baker the chance he needs to send us off to some other hell and that would be better than just sitting around waiting."

IT WAS A TOUGH RIDE TO WELLS WITH CONTINUAL FIGHTS BREAKING out between the prisoners and short tempers flaring among everyone. On the second night Bull saw to it that the prisoners were chained, individually, to wagon wheels, with one to a tree. "One more fight and none of you will make trial." He called a meeting at the fire ring.

"Enough, gentlemen, enough. We have at least three more days to the railhead and then more days on the train. At the way things are going, some are sure to die before we reach Carson City. It's my mistake and I'm taking responsibility for the problem."

"Don't know why the prisoner's actions are your responsibility, Bull," Slim said.

"Thought the idea of the wagon was a good one, but it ain't. Prisoners should be horseback and we should have pack mules." He looked around the gathering and saw several agreeing with him. "It sounded good, the idea of the wagon, but not with these fools we have as prisoners."

"You got a plan to make things work for the next several days?" Hoskins, the largest of the deputies had been the busiest breaking up fights and knocking heads. "Pendergrass and Lighthorse have a great hate for each other."

"Samples, too," Peters said.

"Here's my plan and if someone has a better one, speak up. The prisoners are to have their hands behind them in manacles, and their feet tied tightly and secured to the wagon floor. With any luck they won't be able to fight or create problems."

The rest of the ride was far easier on the marshals and the teamsters, and they arrived in Wells without a loss of life. "We can't put these animals in with other passengers, Slim. We'll have to ask for a car of our own. Baker won't like paying for that, but safety first," Bull joshed.

They lodged their prisoners with the Elko County resident deputy and found Tall-Man Sinclair and Milford Peabody waiting for them. "You just have the two, Tall-Man?" Bull asked.

"Washburn and Moody, Bull. The action was centered in Pioche, not Salt Lake. Looks like you spent some time whuppin' on those boys."

"Nope, they whupped on each other as often as they could. Worst ride I've been on in a long time, Tall-Man." Bull said. "We need to arrange for a separate car and then chain these muckers to their seats. One to a seat."

"I already took care of that. With fourteen of us, I figured it would be the safest. Didn't know about the fighting problems."

Tall-Man said. "Train leaves at five tomorrow morning, so let's get a drink, a steak, and a good night's sleep. We've got one car for our horses and one for the prisoners and us. Hotel's across the street and waiting for us."

"Wire for you, Marshal Morrison," the hotel clerk said.

Bull read the wire and handed it to Slim. "See? I told you. I told you."

"Bank robbers at Angels Camp, eh? You wrecked a saloon the last time we were there," Slim laughed.

THERE WERE TWO RAIL CARS, ONE WITH THE MARSHAL'S HORSES AND one with the marshals and their prisoners on the long train that pulled into the rail yards in Carson City. Judge Baker left word for Bull and Slim to report to his office on arrival. "Good to see you, Bull. Slim, you look good. Sit down, please." He poured brandy for the three and sat at his desk.

"Good job. Well done." He toasted them. "Most awkward, at the least. The power boys in Washington have ignored the entire situation so far, and I think they will all the way. They're going to let the cards fall where they land. If Olsen had lived, had stood trial, it would have been different I'm sure."

"It is a black eye but not fatal," Bull said.

"Yes," Baker said. "They'll pass it off as an individual's failure, not a court failure. I want full reports from you two, and then go bring that bank gang in. You'll be called of course, to testify, more than once, I'm sure, but get those reports and I'll cut you free."

"Thank you," Bull said. The two walked out of the office with smiles on their faces. "I told you, didn't I?" Bull smirked.

"You did. Writing the reports while on the train was brilliant, Bull Morrison. Brilliant."

TWO MEN ON HORSEBACK, LEADING A PACK MULE, HEADED OVER THE
Carson Pass the next morning. "You still angry, Slim?"

"No, Bull, not angry. I just wish when you pick a fight you
see to it that the man doesn't have large heavy objects to throw
at you. I know at least one rib is bent if not broke, and my leg
will have a bruise for a week."

"Be all fine by the time we hit Angels Camp, Slim. Thank
you for the fine job of backing my play."

"Any time, Bull. It's in my contract, you know."

A LOOK AT: NAME'S CORCORAN
TERRENCE CORCORAN
(TERRENCE CORCORAN WESTERN)

TERRENCE CORCORAN CARRIED A BADGE IN VIRGINIA CITY, NEVADA until one day, in a drunken stupor, he shot the sheriff. Now he's returning to the Comstock looking to get his badge back and stumbles into a conspiracy that might put the sheriff, district attorney, and others in jail for a long time. A lovely working girl is brutally murdered, a Hungarian duke wants a Wells Fargo gold shipment, and the sheriff rehires him after first kicking him in a most tender spot. Corcoran was born on the ship bringing his family to this country, ran away to the frontier at an early age and brings his ideas of the old country and knowledge learned of the west to whatever mess he finds himself in. He's carried a badge, found himself in jail, and stands four-square for right, honor, and truth. You gotta love the guy.

AVAILABLE NOW

ABOUT THE AUTHOR

RENO, NEVADA NOVELIST, JOHNNY GUNN, IS RETIRED FROM A LONG career in journalism. He has worked in print, broadcast, and Internet, including a stint as publisher and editor of the Virginia City Legend. These days, Gunn spends most of his time writing novel length fiction, concentrating on the western genre. Or, you can find him down by the Truckee River with a fly rod in hand.

Gunn and his wife, Patty, live on a small hobby farm about twenty miles north of Reno, sharing space with a couple of horses, some meat rabbits, a flock of chickens, and one crazy goat.

9781647347536